"They didn't with relief. **"Can we go now?"**

"Not yet." Jack cupped her chin with his left hand. "You've been really brave, Mia. Just hang in there a little longer because it's going to get easier. We just got out of a very difficult situation, and we did it together. Take courage from that."

Without thinking, Mia lifted her hand and placed it over Jack's. His skin felt reassuringly warm and comforting. But no sooner had she felt slightly better than another vehicle sped past them in the same direction as the first. Her hand dropped away, and she gasped.

"Do you think they'll figure out what we're doing and follow us?"

"If I had to guess, they'd presume we'd make a run for Little Rock. That's where all my resources would be for the area. What they won't know is my family lives in Oklahoma, and it makes more sense for me to head there instead."

"Who needs the Lone Ranger when they've got Jack Brannon," said Mia.

Dear Reader,

I am thrilled to join the Harlequin family with *Witness Protector*.

As a writer, I base my stories in locations I visit and create characters that resonate deeply with me.

I love a strong female lead. In *Witness Protector*, I wanted to convey it is not a sign of weakness to be afraid. The real strength is knowing how to conquer the fear.

I set the book in the Ozarks because of its pristine beauty, and my deep respect for the National Parks Service. I put my main character, Mia, a tourist from England, into a beautiful, foreign place in the USA, then turned her life upside down.

I'm a sucker for unrequited love. Mia is the victim of a lost love affair. In life, any misunderstanding can alter the trajectory of your future.

Writing this was a joy, and I'm not ready to say goodbye to the National Park Law Enforcement Rangers. I hope you stay the course with me as time passes and I introduce new characters from Northern Arkansas.

Thank you for going on this journey. I hope you enjoy Jack and Mia's story.

Jude Bayton

WITNESS PROTECTOR

JUDE BAYTON

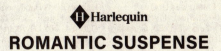

Harlequin

ROMANTIC SUSPENSE

MIX
Paper | Supporting responsible forestry
FSC® C021394

Harlequin®
ROMANTIC SUSPENSE™

Recycling programs for this product may not exist in your area.

ISBN-13: 978-1-335-47178-9

Witness Protector

Copyright © 2026 by Deborah Bayton-FitzSimons

For questions and comments about the quality of this book, please contact us at CustomerService@Harlequin.com.

TM and ® are trademarks of Harlequin Enterprises ULC.

Harlequin Enterprises ULC
22 Adelaide St. West, 41st Floor
Toronto, Ontario M5H 4E3, Canada
www.Harlequin.com

HarperCollins Publishers
Macken House, 39/40 Mayor Street Upper,
Dublin 1, D01 C9W8, Ireland
www.HarperCollins.com

Printed in Lithuania

Residing in Oklahoma, a far cry from her native London, **Jude Bayton** still travels the world through the settings of her books. Having lived on four continents, writing gives Jude an opportunity to draw from the amazing places she's seen and wonderful people she has met. Though she loves a good romantic mystery, Jude's greatest joy is hearing from her readers. Contact Jude at judebayton.com.

Books by Jude Bayton

Harlequin Romantic Suspense

Witness Protector

Visit the Author Profile page at Harlequin.com.

For John 'Jonny' Frost, West Point Graduate,
class of 1947

My favourite Centennial and a true gentleman.

With love.

Chapter 1

Jasper, Arkansas
October 11

Her reflection was still a shock. It was her, yet she looked nothing like herself.

Mia ran fingers through cropped, bleached hair. Blonde wasn't her color, and she'd never worn her hair this short before. She yearned for her long, curly locks. Brutal as it had been to cut them off that awful night in a Tampa gas station's grimy bathroom, she'd had no choice but to do it if she wanted to get away. The curls would eventually grow back—but not if she was dead.

She rubbed her hair with a paper towel after arriving at Billy-Jo's Diner in a downpour. Riding a bike to work sucked, but it beat walking. She shrugged off her wet T-shirt and grabbed a clean one from her locker, shoving thoughts out of her head as they forced their way in. Enough with worrying. She'd made it this far, hadn't she?

Yet where was the woman who months ago had radiated with happiness at the adventure before her? A fantastic trip to the USA—exploring destinations on a well-honed bucket list, before settling back down to get on with an empty life. Another glance in the mirror showed voluminous eyes in a gaunt face etched in worry.

The locker room door swung open, and she jumped. A chubby redhead filled the space. "Mia. Get a move on, hon, I'm getting slammed out here!"

"Be right there, Nancy," Mia replied, lengthening the vowel in Nancy's name to maintain the fake American accent she'd adopted since running away from her real life.

She threw the bag in her locker and headed into the kitchen. With a quick wave to Cody, the short-order cook, she headed straight for the dining room.

Thirty-seven dollars and change in tips wasn't bad for a lunchtime rush, but a drop in the ocean for the money needed to buy a forged passport and a ticket home to England.

Kelly Murphy, Mia's only friend and resource in the US, had already been her savior. Kelly had rustled up a couple of dodgy leads on how to go about getting the passport under the radar, but it would take cold hard cash, which neither woman had. A kindergarten teacher and a waitress weren't exactly flush.

She'd never be able to repay Kelly, not monetarily nor by deed. Dear Kelly had gone above and beyond, supported her destitute British friend by helping her get back to Arkansas and a semblance of safety. Mia would be eternally grateful for the temporary loan of the rickety old RV that belonged to Kelly's grandpa, who no longer used it. It was her current home, situated at a campsite near the Buffalo River, a far cry from her small but comfortable flat in England. It had seen better days, but a campground was the perfect hiding place for a woman who dared not be found.

Mia finished cleaning off her tables, rolled a tub of silverware ready for the evening rush, and went into the kitchen. One perk of waitressing was she could eat for free. With a plate of chicken-fried-steak, green beans and a dollop of potatoes, she headed back to the dining room and took a seat in a corner booth. It was her last break before Nancy left for the day, leaving Mia as the only waitress until the place closed at nine.

Cody's chicken fry melted in her mouth. Mia was no fan of Southern food, but Cody had almost changed her mind. She liked Cody. A nice guy who spent his days frying at Billy-Jo's, and his nights doing stand-up in Harrison, the nearest large town, fifteen miles away. Cody had been friendly since they'd met, but Mia kept her distance. She couldn't get close to anyone.

Nearly three months had passed since her arrival in Jasper. She ate her food, ruminating over her wretched predicament as she did every day, every hour. How had life turned into such a rotten, frightening TV movie? One minute she'd run off on a great vacation, and the next, was running for her life. Stuck without a way to get back into her own country... How had it come to this?

The answer was easy.

Carlos Rodriguez.

His devastatingly handsome face filled her thoughts. Dark, smoldering, Spanish features and a heartbreaking smile. Good looks and plenty of charisma were a deadly combination. He was eligible, a well-respected doctor, and every woman's perfect guy.

Only he wasn't.

He was a monster.

Mia swallowed the last bite of food, struggling to get it down. She mustn't think about the past—not now. She must focus on the immediate future, making money and getting home to England alive.

She took her plate back into the kitchen. Just thinking about Carlos made Mia nauseous, and got her heart thumping against her ribs. Dangerous as a tiger, deadly as a cobra…could he still be a threat?

Mia placed her dishes into the sink and gripped the side of the draining board. Life had changed forever that awful night in July, when she'd run away. Yet almost three months had passed and no one had come after her.

For all she knew, Carlos Rodriguez was dead.

Jack Brannon was ravenous. He hadn't eaten a bite all day and the sounds emanating from his stomach were audible over the voice on the radio. He'd better get something pretty quick. But where to go? He cruised down the main street in Jasper and spotted a small building with a bright pink neon sign he'd passed a couple of times before. Billy-Jo's. There weren't many cars in the parking lot, but at two in the afternoon it was hardly lunchtime. Jack parked the Bronco, put on his hat and stepped out of the vehicle.

Even outside, the aroma of good food grabbed his senses, taking him right back to his gran's kitchen in Tulsa, before she died. Jack's mouth salivated with a sudden craving for something fried and a plate of biscuits and gravy. He was still enjoying the novelty of eating Southern cooking again, after years of living with a health food junkie. Jack never wanted to see tofu again in his lifetime.

Inside the restaurant his eyes adjusted to the change in light. Only a couple of tables were taken, and he couldn't see anyone who worked there. Should he seat himself? He chose a corner booth facing the door, nodding to the other customers as he passed.

Generally, people were friendly to National Park Rangers. In his years serving, Jack had only encountered a handful of belligerent jerks. Usually sunburnt, drunk, and not happy being told they couldn't fish, or camp, or engage in unlawful activities. One look at the weapon Jack was required to carry usually gave them better manners.

He sat down and took off his hat, laying it on the seat next to him, then picked up the menu and scanned it quickly. He was not disappointed.

"Hi. What can I get you to drink?"

She'd come up behind him while he was engrossed in the menu, and he hadn't heard her approach. Jack glanced up to give the waitress his order. She was slightly built, wearing jeans, and a dark green shirt with the words Billy-Jo's Diner—Your Belly's Best Friend. He looked up at her face and did a double take. The breath caught in his throat. It couldn't be...

"Emilia?" He stared into moody eyes at the familiar yet unfamiliar woman, absorbing all that was wrong, the hard planes of her face, the short spiky hair. Yet it looked just like her. But that was impossible.

She shook her head. "Sorry, sir." She glared at him. "You're mistaken."

Jack's glance dropped to the plastic name strip pinned to her shirt. *Mia.* He frowned and stared at her once again, his mind reaching into the past for a comparison. Damn, she was a total ringer for Emilia. Sure, it might have been ten years, but he'd never forget those soulful gray eyes, the cute, upturned nose with a dash of freckles, that full mouth which had brought him such pleasure.

"What are you gonna have to drink, sir?"

The voice was all wrong. Emilia was English, her accent impeccably a Brit's. This woman sounded like a local.

"I'll take iced tea," he said quickly, aware he'd sounded like a weirdo. Jack didn't want to freak her out saying anything else.

She moved away from the table and went into the back. Jack rubbed his eyes as though he'd seen something he still couldn't believe. Okay, he was tired, but not blind. Uncanny how much the waitress resembled the one woman he'd tried so hard to forget. And until now, he'd done well keeping Emilia in the hidden recess of his mind. After all, it had only been a fast holiday romance in a foreign country. But did a man ever forget his first love?

Bizarre. Strange that he was seeing her double, right here, slap-bang in Arkansas. What were the odds?

Allowing her memory to surface, he now found it hard to put her image away. *What was Emilia doing these days?* More than a decade had passed since the incredible month they'd spent together. Jack sighed. No doubt she was married with three kids, living in a quaint village in the British countryside.

Mia ran into the bathroom, heart pounding like a jackhammer, and quickly splashed her face with cold water. *No no no, this could not be happening.* It was crazy. Ridiculous. Like some alternate reality, because there was absolutely, positively no way Jack Brannon could be sitting in Billy-Jo's dining room this very minute, large as life.

But he was.

Her hands shook, her head a pinball machine with thoughts pinging inside as she searched frantically for some kind of explanation. *Take some slow breaths, Mia. You need to think!*

Memories raced through her mind. Jack was from Tulsa, Oklahoma, a neighboring state, but holy cow, that still *wasn't* Jasper, Arkansas. What about the uniform Jack was wearing? The badge read Ranger. Her stomach flip-flopped. *Dear God, it was Jack all right.*

Ten years ago, Jack had said his trip to England was a last vacation before he began his training to be a National Park Service Law Enforcement Ranger. He'd just finished regular college and planned to get certified as a ranger. He'd told Mia that once qualified, he could work anywhere in the USA where there was a national park.

Surely that meant Yellowstone, or the Grand Canyon, somewhere huge and impressive. But Arkansas?

Mia dried her hands and rubbed the damp paper towel against her face. America had to be forty times bigger than the UK, so how had fate crossed their paths? It was like a bad joke. And as much as she didn't want it to be Jack Brannon, didn't need it to be Jack, her gut told her it was him.

Mia left the restroom, went to the kitchen door and peeked through the porthole window. She studied the ranger's profile. Remembering the line of his nose, the squareness of his chin, the way his black hair grew straight and thick—a reminder of his Cherokee heritage.

Ten years had made his features a little sharper, but there was no mistaking it was Jack.

Now what?

Mia's heart did a little skip. She remonstrated with herself not to think about the times life had been far less complicated, when a handsome, young American had walked into her world bringing the sunshine with him, and taking it away when he left.

That was then.

Now everything couldn't be more different. She was in trouble...serious trouble. And no one, especially Jack, could know about her situation.

Mia wasn't the same person on the inside anymore and had taken great pains to look different on the outside too. Thank goodness. With a fake American accent, bleached blond hair cut short and spiky, and skinnier from a diet of no money and living on fear, she could convince Jack Brannon she was *not* Emilia Jones. She just had to make it through this shift.

She poured a glass of tea and went back out to the dining room, wishing Nancy had still been here so she could dodge this bullet. The ice rattled as she set down the plastic tumbler. She pulled out a pad and pen from her back pocket.

"What would you like to order?"

Jack asked for the fried chicken special, and Mia turned on her heel without comment. She dared not say any more than she had to.

Other patrons arrived. Tending to new customers kept Mia from focusing on the ranger sitting in the corner booth. Though she didn't glance in his direction, his eyes burned holes in her back as she moved about the dining room.

When his order was ready, Mia approached Jack's table and set the plate of hot food in front of him.

"Here you go," she said. "Anything else I can get you?"

His dark eyes fastened on her face. She steeled herself. He'd aged slightly, but it was the same Jack Brannon she remembered, and she struggled to keep her expression neutral.

It worked.

He said, "No thanks, this is great." And Mia walked away.

She kept busy while Jack ate his food. She was wiping off empty tables, when from the corner of her eye she spotted the ranger get up and step out of the booth. He put a few bills on the table next to his tab, then picked up his hat and put it on.

Mia snatched a quick look at the handsome figure he cut in uniform. He looked good in khaki and beige. But the irony of his being here stung. Right before her stood one of only two people she knew in the entirety of America, yet she couldn't tell Jack who she was—or more importantly, the trouble she was in and how very frightened she was.

Jack strode to the door and Mia's heart weighed heavier with every step he took. She tried to look away, but it was impossible. Would he stop and turn back to see her staring?

He didn't.

As the door closed, Mia hurried over to the front window and watched Jack Brannon climb into a big National Park Service SUV, start the engine and back out of his parking spot. Helpless, she stood frozen to the spot, her mind telling her to run after him, while her legs refused to move.

Jack drove away from the diner, still rattled by seeing Emilia's doppelgänger. His second day on the new assignment was proving interesting, he thought, turning onto Highway 74, toward the small town of Ponca, and the Buffalo River.

His mind threatened to take a trip down memory lane to visit images of a summer love affair, but he knew he must stay focused on the current investigation. After all, that was what he'd been sent to Jasper to do.

Forcing his thoughts away from that bruise in his history, he drank in the scenery around him. The Buffalo River sure was a lovely area, and a far cry from Arizona and the previous parks where he'd served. Here, the trees were thick as the bristles on a hairbrush, and every color of autumn: green, brown, rust and yellow. There wasn't a cactus in sight.

Parallel to the road, the pristine river widened and narrowed. It snaked through lush green pastures, and cut between solid walls of limestone cliffs, some as high as four hundred feet. The land was rich and fertile, with minimal residency, being a protected area. It was as pretty as he remembered.

Jack had been nine, and his brother, Neil, ten, when both Junior Rangers visited America's first national river. Their grandfather had helped the boys apply to the National Park Service program, which encouraged kids to both appreciate and protect the beauty of their land.

Junior Ranger to becoming a full-fledged National

Park Service Law Enforcement Ranger had been a long stretch. But Jack had made a pact with Neil, and it had been worth all the hard work, even though his brother hadn't been there to see him graduate.

The familiar weight of the past pressed down on his shoulders. Jack couldn't bear thinking about it too much because he knew it would devour him. A sixteenth birthday marking his coming of age, and the untimely death of his brother. He'd been living for them both since then, or at least trying to. Wasn't that what you did when you walked away from a car wreck without a scratch, but your brother wasn't so lucky?

Jack gave a long sigh and pulled his mind back from the all-too-familiar thought path. He reminded himself that it was a new chapter now. He was unconvinced his current change had been the right career move to make, but his grandfather's recent diagnosis of prostate cancer made the decision an easy one. Sure, it was still a four-hour drive from his family's place in Tulsa, but far easier to jump in a car instead of catching a commercial flight from Phoenix. Jack wanted to be on hand should they need anything from him—it was the least he could do.

He was the only grandson left, after all.

With the recent move to Arkansas, he'd rented a small cabin. It was adequate, situated just outside of Jasper, a small community with a population of less than five hundred. Jack's boss, Ed Mills, had sent him a packet of information so he'd have an idea of what to expect.

He knew Ed was native to the state. His career had begun in this area, so it was dear to his heart. He'd given Jack the scoop on how it was there. Told him you could buy staples locally, but everything else required a drive into the nearest city, Harrison, about fifteen miles away. Fayetteville was the closest large city, also home to the University of Arkansas.

Jack spotted a group of parked cars at one of the popular pull-ins off the main road and slowed down the Bronco. He'd stopped there on his first day back, remembering it was the best place to look for elk, as a herd had been introduced into the area years before.

He slowly drove past people with camera equipment aimed at the majestic beasts in the distance, when his phone rang. He took a nearby turnoff and parked in one of the public areas by the river to take the call.

"Brannon."

"Jack." It was Ed Mills. "How you settling in?"

Jack leaned back in the seat. "Okay, thanks. I'm still getting my bearings. It's changed a lot in the past few years. But you weren't wrong, Ed. It's still pretty out here."

Ed gave a sigh on the end of the line, and Jack pictured his boss in a swanky DC office, sitting in a chair with size twelve cowboy boots on top of a fancy desk. Director Mills would always be tied to the Buffalo. No city boy, he often talked about retiring in Arkansas.

"Did you get unpacked?" he asked.

"Kind of," Jack replied. He'd brought nine small boxes of personal belongings, most of them books, and seven were still unopened. "Got any updates for me, Ed?" The case Jack was on was tricky. He'd volunteered for the Arkansas post knowing exactly what he was getting into.

"Yes," said Ed. "Been a little activity headed toward your neck of the woods. Not sure which outfit is behind this particular shipment, but the DEA's watching it closely." He mentioned the name of a well-known Floridian crime family.

"Agent O'Malley's tailing the shipment, Jack. But I promised we'd help where we could, so I need you talking to people. Someone around there knows something. Usual routine—see if anyone local gives your gut a tug." Ed rambled on a while longer and then signed off.

Jack set the phone down, mulling over his boss's comment. He'd already met one of the locals, and she'd had more than a tugging effect on his gut. She'd thrown him completely back into the past.

Ten years ago, he'd strolled along a Cornish beach at the height of an English summer, when Emilia Jones had walked down the shore and straight into his heart. Jack hadn't seen it coming. Not the girl, or the way she made him feel.

The phone rang again.

This time it was Tex Callahan, a guy from Austin who'd come to Arkansas only a few months earlier. Tex was new to the Park Service after a stint in the military, and Jack liked him already.

"Hey, Jack," Tex said. "Got a problem down at Steel Creek Campgrounds and I sure could use your assistance."

"Sure. Let me check my bearings." Jack punched in the destination on the Bronco's navigation system. "I'm five minutes away, Tex."

He hung up the phone then took off with his lights flashing, but no siren.

Jack had interpreted the message correctly. Tex needed backup from a ranger who carried a gun.

Chapter 2

Jasper

She couldn't sleep.

Mia had returned to the RV, a drowned rat from all the rain. She took a quick hot shower, pulled on Kelly's comfy pajamas, finished a piping hot cup of tea, then huddled underneath her warm blanket. But no matter how hard she tried to settle down, it was useless. She'd seen Jack Brannon again.

He'd casually stepped back inside her world and blown her mind after a ten-year hiatus of being gone. The gamut of emotions it brought surprised her. A kick in the stomach when she'd first recognized him, a racing heart while he ate lunch, and then the unbearable sense of loss when he left the diner and walked out of her life. Again.

Thank God he hadn't realized it was really her—the dramatic change in appearance and fake accent had worked. And if Jack didn't recognize her, then Carlos, the cops, or anyone else hunting her wouldn't either. That was reassuring.

But what was Jack doing in Jasper? Stupid question. The man had on a uniform, so he was obviously working—this was a national river after all. Did he live here? Was there a wife and kids?

Maybe it was a fluke? Jack might be passing through, on his way to another city, another state even. But Mia knew it was unlikely. Jasper was a small town in the middle of the Ozarks, and not a shortcut to anywhere. Jack had become a ranger, just like he always said he would, and probably worked here.

A twinge of sadness plucked at her chest. Seeing Jack's badge today was the only clue to his career, because after he'd left England a decade ago, she'd never heard from Jack Brannon again.

Mia closed her eyes, traveling back to sun-drenched days on a beautiful sandy beach. Memories danced down streets of time with snapshots of her and Jack together. A visit to Tintagel Castle to explore Arthurian history. Hikes in cool, shadowy forests, riding on the train to Scotland, and so many wonderful adventures they'd shared.

A perfect summer, until the last night when she'd finally got up the nerve to ask Jack what would happen next between them.

A noise from outside the RV made Mia's thoughts instantly evaporate. Alert, she jumped out of bed and rushed to the window. Carefully, she pulled the curtain back a smidge, and looked out into the darkness.

The old plastic window was cloudy, making it difficult to see anything in the dark, but the rain looked heavier and the wind was up. Trees swayed and shook their branches. Perhaps one of them had snapped and that was where the noise came from? She hoped to God that was the case.

Mia huddled in the corner of the kitchen area, ears pricked like a frightened rabbit hiding from a hawk. It had been like this since she'd run away. Constantly scared someone was coming for her. Her body wilted and her mind, though sharp, was exhausted. Fear did that to you. But how could she feel anything but terror after what she'd seen that unforgettable night at the clinic in Miami.

Now Mia had more enemies than friends. She was the prey running from known and unknown predators. What, or who, lurked around the corner of her immediate future was impossible to foretell. Be it Carlos, the Marino family, or even the police?

She trusted no one, except the dearest friend she had. The only person on her side. A kindergarten teacher named Kelly.

Mia listened intently. All quiet once again, other than the rain tapping like sharp fingernails against the windows. It was okay. It had just been the wind. Letting out a breath of relief, she made her way back to bed and lay down to sleep, listening to the raindrops chink on the metal roof of the RV.

She lay quietly for a moment, and then closed her eyes and waited for Jack's face to appear once again. Mia studied it intently, and the burn of unrequited love washed across her heart.

What would her world look like today if she and Jack hadn't parted? She'd never known, as Jack had made it blatantly obvious he did not want to be in her life once he returned to the US. Mia would never forget how her simple question about their future had escalated into an argument on Jack's last night in England. She'd pressed for a commitment that he refused to agree to, claiming he had to focus on his career first.

She hadn't seen him off at the airport, and later felt

guilty about it. He'd ignored her calls and her texts, until pride stopped her from trying beyond that point. If Jack ever wanted to speak to her again, he would have to make the next move.

But he never had.

Mia's eyes welled with tears of regret. She cried for the past, but her sorrow was combined with the present. It was grueling living in perpetual fear of being discovered by people who terrified her. Angrily she wiped her eyes.

Why couldn't she have a normal life? A home, a job. Everything was such a mess, a horrifying, horrendous mess.

One she might not survive.

With a moan of despair, Mia rolled over and buried her face in the pillow.

Run!

Blood pumped through her veins, her heart a piston while her muscles responded, fueled by high-octane fear.

Still, he drew closer with every moment… Dear God, she could hear him breathing.

Suddenly, excruciating pain seared through her head as he violently grabbed a fistful of her long hair.

A strangled scream left Mia's lips and she woke up gasping. She shot upright in the narrow bed, heart pounding, and gulped air like a landed fish. Her eyes registered the faded interior of the trailer, and gradually, confusion cleared.

Relief flooded her senses.

Another dream, like all the others she'd been having. Mia trembled. It was hard enough shaking off shadows when her dreams were of the too recent past. Yet it was the nightmares she had while awake, which were not so easily forgotten.

Staccato voices reached her ears. Wayne and Georgia, the retired couple in the RV next to hers, were already up and bickering. Their strong Arkansas accents reminded Mia how far she was from her real home. Thousands of miles and an ocean separated her from England. Sometimes she wondered if she'd ever get back there.

She stretched her arms toward the ceiling, then turned her neck from side to side, straightening out the kinks from sleeping on a wafer-thin mattress. A glance at her watch told her it was time to get going.

Saturday, her least favorite day of the week, meant a double shift at Billy-Jo's. For a small, run-down restaurant, the diner had a slew of regular customers each of the six days they were open. Mia's aching feet were a testament to that fact.

She climbed out of bed, tidied the sheets and blankets, then took two short steps into the minuscule kitchen and flicked the switch on the kettle to boil water for tea. She peered out of the window. Through the murky plastic and the mist of a cool October morning, the Buffalo shimmered. The wind was still up, judging by the water lapping against the shoreline like a cat at a milk bowl.

Years ago, after graduating university, Mia had visited the Buffalo area with Kelly. She'd been enchanted by the crystal clear water running like a ribbon cutting through gigantic walls of limestone.

Well, things were different this time around. This was no vacation; it was a sanctuary. A place to hide and never be found.

But for how much longer?

Almost three months had passed, and Mia had made little progress toward leaving the United States to go home. Saving for an airline ticket and an unauthorized passport was tough when you were on the run and trying to be incognito. If only she'd still had her documents and money, she could have instantly left Miami and danger behind. But Carlos had made sure she had no access to anything. And with the police involved, even contacting the British Embassy wasn't an option.

Mia understood how an animal in a trap must feel. Chewing off your own leg to escape was always a better option than being killed.

Damn Carlos. Damn her own blind stupidity.

And now Jack Brannon.

Thinking about him made her reel. Just the sight of him not only brought back the past, but if she were honest, a snapshot of security. Okay, he had broken her heart, yet in this current situation, Jack's solid, stoic presence could make her feel safe. In uniform, he exuded a sense of strength she lacked but desperately needed, especially now.

Mia hated feeling so weak, so vulnerable.

She pushed away her thoughts and got ready for work. Her stomach growled, but she ignored it. She'd eat something at the diner.

At least it had stopped raining.

When Mia locked the RV door, she spotted Wayne leaning against the side of his camper, smoking his first cigarette of the day.

"Hey, Mia," he greeted her. A plume of smoke accompanied his words, thick in the chilly morning.

"Hi, Wayne. How's it going?"

His brows raised in a "how do you think?" expression, and Mia grinned at the older man. Wayne practically lived in the doghouse.

"You should bring Georgia for breakfast at the diner. Maybe you'd score some points?" She liked Wayne. He was always friendly, even when he'd taken a scorching from his wife. Wayne was a short man, whose nose, mouth and eyes looked as though they'd been put on the wrong face. They were too large. He boasted a wardrobe of floral, gaudy-patterned shirts, khaki shorts and sandals, and was overly liberal with Old Spice. He'd pull it off in Hawaii, but in Arkansas he stuck out like the proverbial sore thumb.

Wayne took a long pull of tobacco, blew it out, then nodded. "Mebbe. But it'll take more'n that today. She's mad 'cause our son ain't coming to us fer Thanksgiving. She'd bin looking forward to it a while."

"I'm sorry," Mia said sincerely. "I know she must be disappointed." She gave Wayne a weak smile of encouragement and moved away. She had no desire to get into a long conversation about family issues. She'd enough of her own problems to think about today.

Every table in the diner stayed full, from the time the restaurant opened, until ten thirty. They'd run out of silverware twice, and Harvey, the new dishwasher, had gotten behind. Even Billy-Jo had come in to help, and between the owner, Nancy and Mia, they'd kept up with all the orders.

Now, with only one table left to wait on, the waitresses

made the most of the chance to sit and rest their aching feet before the lunchtime rush. Billy-Jo had already left.

Nancy examined chipped blue polish on her finger-nails and sighed. "Dammit. I just had these done last week. I swear, Mia, I cain't keep doin' this for a livin'." She reached up and tapped the back of her bright red hair, currently held up with pins so it added a couple of inches to her height.

"Maybe wearing nail polish isn't a good idea when you wait tables," Mia said with a glance at the woman who re-minded her of Lucille Ball. Nancy's cinnamon hair color and penciled-on brows matched exactly. With thick black eyeliner and bright green eye-shadow, the older woman looked like she'd either stepped right out of the fifties, or was trying to emulate Amy Winehouse and failing—Mia couldn't make up her mind which.

"Hon, I ain't about to change my life because I work in this dump." Nancy surveyed the diner. "I mean, I work to live, not live to work. 'Sides, I gotta look good for my Randy."

The diner door opened, and Nancy automatically glanced up.

"Well, now," she drawled, apparently forgetting about Randy. "Will ya look what just came in for dessert."

Mia, used to Nancy's appreciation for the male form, peered over at the door and her heart skipped.

Jack Brannon.

Nancy got to her feet quickly and practically ran over to him.

"Hi there, hon. Are ya in for a late breakfast or an early lunch?"

Mia couldn't hear Jack's response. She watched him

take a seat in the same booth as yesterday, while Nancy fetched him a cup of coffee. The waitress chatted for a moment, and then took his food order and disappeared into the kitchen.

Mia carried on rolling silverware into napkins. After a minute she became aware of his scrutiny. His stare, a laser boring into the side of her face. She turned her head and their eyes met and held. Mia was the first to look away.

Why had he come back to Billy-Jo's? Mia was suddenly filled with dread. Had he seen through her disguise once he'd had a chance to think about it?

Worry sparked and flickered. The flame of fear ignited while common sense tried to douse it. *Calm down.* She was overreacting. There could be tons of reasons Jack was back at the diner. It wasn't as though Jasper had many restaurants to pick from.

The door opened once again, this time admitting two men Mia had never seen before. That wasn't unusual. The Buffalo River drew people from many other states, especially in the Midwest.

She got up and carried the silverware tub into the kitchen where Nancy and Cody were chatting as he cooked pancakes, then returned to the dining room and approached the two new customers sitting diagonally across the restaurant from Jack.

"Hi," she glanced from one to the other. "What can I get you to drink?"

She guessed both guys were in their thirties. One, clean-shaven, with groomed black hair, a fake tan, an expensive shirt and a manicure. The other, a big man sporting a bushy red moustache and trimmed beard. He took off his ball cap to reveal a shiny, shaved head. He looked like a biker.

"You got a Bloody Mary?" the bald one said, and Mia detected an East Coast twang.

"No, sorry," she replied. "We don't serve alcohol."

"Shame," he said, staring hard at her face. His pock-marked skin made him look rough. His eyes were black. "Guess I'll take a Coke."

"Yeah, me too," said the other. They picked up their menus.

Mia walked off to get their drinks. Jack threw a glance her way as she passed but said nothing. Once inside the kitchen, she peeked through the door window and looked at the two men reading their menus. What was it she found unsettling about them? All types stopped in the diner on any given day, bikers, hikers, kayakers, most of them passing through to look at the scenery and spend time on the Buffalo.

But these guys had city written all over them. And something she couldn't quite pin down.

"Watch out, hon. Order up." Nancy warned as she made to get by Mia and out of the door. She carried a large breakfast platter and a stack of pancakes, which she took over to Jack.

Mia followed her out and delivered the Cokes to her new customers. She took their food order, and as she did, noticed the tidy guy glance over at Jack's table, where the ranger was currently devouring his meal. Mia caught the quick shift of the man's look as he made eye contact with his partner and gestured with a nod of his head toward Jack.

Her gut clenched. She understood they'd just clocked

Jack was in uniform, though it was easy to see he was no cop. Mia hurried back into the kitchen and gave their order to Cody, then went back to stare through the door to the dining room.

Something was off. The men sat talking and sipping their drinks, while Jack, seemingly oblivious to them, focused on eating his breakfast. Yet Mia sensed they were aware of one another, just as a cat knows when a bird lands close by.

She watched as Nancy cleared off the table of the customers who had just left, and then Mia switched her attention back to Jack, and the two men on the other side of the room.

"Order up," called Cody.

Mia placed hot plates of breakfast in front of her customers, and they sighed simultaneously with pleasure.

"Smell that bacon," said the bald-headed man. "And look at them biscuits. Gotta love the South, right?"

"Damn straight," his partner agreed.

Mia left them to it. But as she made to pass Jack's booth he gestured for her to stop.

"Need a refill?" She pointed to his coffee mug.

Jack shook his head. He spoke quietly. "Those guys you're waiting on, do you know them?"

Mia frowned. "No. Why?" A shudder of apprehension rippled through her.

"No reason. They didn't look local. I'm just being nosy." He picked up his cup. "Maybe I'll take that refill after all."

Mia retrieved the coffeepot and filled Jack's cup, all the while aware the two men were watching.

"Thanks," Jack said. He returned to his food.

Puzzled, Mia went back to rolling silverware. Before long, Nancy joined her and began chatting about a dress she wanted to buy at Target. Mia pretended to listen, but her attention was still stuck on Jack and her two customers. The atmosphere in the diner felt tense. Or was she imagining it?

Jack left first. He thanked them both on his way out the door.

The strangers weren't far behind him. The slick guy left Mia a crisp $10 bill as a tip. That was unexpected, but she was pleased.

She placed their dirty dishes in the bus-tub, then went over to wipe down the booth. As she dusted biscuit crumbs to the floor, Mia noticed a small piece of yellow paper stuck in the crevice of the seat. It must have slipped out the smooth guy's back pocket.

It was a folded Post-it note. Mia opened it up and gasped. The name on the paper burned into her eyes.

Emilia Jones.

"One guy looked like a pimp, the other a thug. Could they be the guys you said O'Malley was trailing?" Jack asked Ed, phone to his ear.

"Yeah. Sounds like them. Fresh up from Miami, but out of Jersey. Nasty pieces of work, but small potatoes. Don't hassle them, Jack, we want bigger fish, okay?"

"Sure." Jack put on his blinker and turned down a dirt road. "Hey, boss. This is off-subject, but I need a favor."

"Shoot."

"I want to look up the whereabouts of a person." He gave him Emilia's full name and told him she lived in the UK.

"Brannon, if it's an old girlfriend you're looking for, I don't think it's for the National Park Service to find her. The Brits don't like people in their business."

"Yeah, I get that, boss." Jack's tone was serious. "It's probably nothing, but something's bugging me and I want to make sure she's okay." He daren't mention he thought he'd seen Emilia in Jasper. That was too far-fetched to believe. Still, this would put the nagging feeling to rest. "You owe me for last year." He played his trump card.

A groan sounded at the end of the line. "It isn't gentlemanlike to remind another man of his obligation," growled Ed.

Jack had driven through a nasty snowstorm, so bad that roadside assistance crews had refused to venture out when Ed's grandson's car had broken down in Flagstaff, while he'd been on his way home from college.

"Okay, I've got a contact with the FBI. I'll see what I can do," Ed Mills said before hanging up.

Jack grinned.

He got out of the SUV and headed inside the office, a prefab building that had seen better days. Was he losing the plot? A chance encounter with a woman resembling Emilia was not that far-fetched. Did it warrant digging deeper?

On some level, Jack knew he was being a little crazy. There was no way the waitress could be an old girlfriend from another country. But seeing her had brought back a lot of memories. He'd even spent part of the previous evening searching for Emilia Jones on the internet. Without much luck.

That struck him as odd. There was nothing. No wedding announcement, no links to social media. Strange.

He scoured Facebook, Twitter, Instagram, and any other platform he could think of. Nothing. No presence.

That sealed the deal. His gut told him something was weird about that scenario, and so he'd asked the favor. Maybe he was nuts. So what? He didn't really care. He just wanted to know Emilia was okay. What was wrong with that?

Everything. Was he a hypocrite to care now after walking away from her all those years ago? But back then he'd had no choice. He'd made a promise to his brother, and nothing would have stopped him from fulfilling that promise.

Mia's shift was passing in slow motion. She fought the impulse to bolt out the door and get to the safety of her RV. But would it be smart going back there? What if those awful men were already on to her?

No. She was stuck at work for the remainder of the day, which might actually be safer. At least here she wasn't alone.

Mia stood near the front window, staring out at the street ahead. The small piece of paper burned like an evil amulet in her pocket. She tugged it out and looked at the two words written there. *Emilia Jones.* Those guys had to be working for Carlos, or the Marinos. But how had they tracked her here?

Her pulse quickened and a sudden wave of nausea rippled through her stomach. She must not panic. It was imperative she keep her head on straight. Mia felt fairly certain the men who'd come into the diner didn't know who she was. Even if they'd got her photo, they'd be looking for a woman with long dark hair. She'd done a good job transforming her appearance, and even her fake accent was decent.

Yet here they were, right where she was hiding out. If they found the RV they wouldn't learn anything else about her. She'd made sure not to keep anything personal; even her pay stubs were trashed at the restaurant.

Stunned, as her true predicament finally took hold, Mia told Nancy she'd be right back, and stepped outside the rear of the building. She gulped in the cool autumn air and fought the urge to be sick.

This was bad...really bad. She'd have to move on, get away from here fast before those thugs put everything together. But where could she go? Kelly was the only person she knew in the entire country, and she'd already helped so much. Mia couldn't show up on her doorstep again and put Kelly directly in harm's way.

Engulfed with fear, Mia breathed quickly. Her chest tightened. Panic rose through her body like a gigantic wave building in the ocean. Just when she thought things couldn't get any worse, they had taken an ominous turn.

She leaned back against the building as her legs turned to jelly. Her heart pounded in her ears and suddenly Mia felt very strange.

She blinked, dug her nails into her palms and willed herself to get a grip. Being terrified wasn't helping anything. This was what it felt like to be truly alone. She was vulnerable, scared and in mortal danger of being killed. The hunter was closing in on his prey, and Mia had nowhere to turn.

Except she did.

And his name was Jack Brannon.

* * *

He'd thought it was Tex coming into his office. Jack glanced up from the file he was reading and frowned. It was the waitress from the diner, Mia, standing in the doorway.

Puzzled, he got to his feet. "Come on in," he said, gesturing to a chair across from his own. "Mia, isn't it?"

She nodded.

"Have a seat."

When they were both sitting, Jack took a good look at her. The familiar tug of recognition returned. Bizarre how much she looked like Emilia. But wait. Something was wrong. The woman was pale as a vanilla milkshake, her dark gray eyes like saucers and brimming with fear.

"So, Mia. How can I help you? Have you come to report something?"

She chewed her bottom lip as though conflicted about speaking. Jack remained quiet and studied her. The likeness was uncanny. Everyone supposedly had a double. If he was honest, there had been times over the years when he thought he'd seen Emilia. And here he was, doing it again.

The woman took a deep breath, and her eyes fastened upon his. "You were right, Jack." Her voice was completely different now, her accent no longer American, but clipped and British.

Jack gasped as his brain valiantly tried to catch up with his eyes and ears. "Emilia?" His voice was a whisper.

"Unfortunately," she said with a half smile.

He shook his head in disbelief. "Wait. That's not possible. Yesterday…"

"Yes, I know. I didn't tell you the truth, but I had good reason."

Jack stared, dumbstruck and still unable to process it was really her. Emilia Jones. His first love, sitting in the ranger's office in rural Arkansas, thousands of miles away from where they'd met.

Abruptly he got to his feet. "I'm gonna need another cup of coffee." He strode out of the room.

He returned a few minutes later carrying two mugs, one of which he handed to Mia.

"I added cream and sugar, like you used to drink it."

She accepted the coffee, and a strange expression rippled across her face. She probably thought he was a lovesick idiot remembering how an ex-girlfriend drank her coffee a decade ago.

Irritated, Jack sat back down. "Right. Now that I'm barely over the shock of that admission, how about you tell me what the hell's going on? What are you doing in the middle of the US, looking and acting like somebody else, *and* lying about your identity?"

She took a sip of her coffee.

He could tell she was stalling. "I'm all ears, Emilia."

Mia set the mug on the desk. "Look, Jack. I'm sorry for springing this on you, but honestly, I had no idea you were here until you came into Billy-Jo's yesterday. I couldn't tell you who I was for valid reasons at the time."

"Oh, really? Then what changed?" He could not disguise his annoyance. *Why did he feel so angry?*

She took a deep breath. "Those two men you saw in the diner earlier."

"What about them?"

"They're here to kill me."

Chapter 3

Jasper

Saying the words out loud somehow made the situation more real and utterly terrifying. Yet as soon as she told Jack, some of the tension immediately dissipated.

His face was incredulous. Mia could tell he found her statement dramatic and possibly ridiculous.

"Okay," she said quickly. "I know how crazy this sounds, but I promise I'm not making it up. I'm in deep trouble, Jack. That's why I'm in Jasper. I've been here several weeks, trying to get back home to England, but I don't have my passport and…"

"Whoa." He raised a hand to stop her. "Wait a sec. I'm having trouble getting my head around any of this. Let me get this straight. The last time we met, you were living in the UK, where the most dangerous thing you did was ride a double-decker bus. Now, a decade later, you're sitting in my office, looking like you've been abducted by a punk rock band, while working as a waitress in a small town most Americans have never heard of." He shook his head, in what appeared to be disbelief. "To cap it all," he added, "you show up at precisely the same time I'm sent here to start a new assignment."

She was aghast. "What are you implying?" Her voice went up a notch. She stared at him, trying to process the inference. "You think I'm making this up because I wanted to see you again?" Mia laughed. "Wow. Not too short on your supply of arrogance, Jack. Are you?" She rose to her feet. "You couldn't be more wrong. Trust me, if I'd wanted anything to do with you again, I'd have just picked up the damned phone." She walked toward the door.

His chair scraped the floor as he got to his feet. "Wait," he said. "I'm sorry. I shouldn't have spoken to you like that. Come back and sit down. Tell me what's going on and I'll try and help you."

Mia turned, her hand poised on the doorknob. "Can we go somewhere else?" she asked. "I don't want anyone to hear what I've got to say."

Jack grabbed his hat from the desk. "Sure." He put it on and got out his keys. "I'll take you to my cabin."

They barely spoke on the drive. Mia sat back in the passenger seat and didn't move a muscle. Her mind spun in a web of confusion. How could she tell Jack everything? What would he think of her? If their roles were reversed, what would she think of him? Nothing but bad. She shuddered. How had her life devolved into this rotten mess?

Jack turned off the highway onto a dirt road covered in a spotty layer of gravel. Although Mia thought his place would be nearer town, it was hardly surprising to find he was staying somewhere more remote.

He drove for what seemed like a while, past several

houses, some styled like log cabins, others that looked horribly dilapidated.

The driveway they pulled into was loose gravel and down a hilly drive that wound around a clump of trees, revealing a small, neat cabin with a wide wraparound porch. Jack drew the SUV to a halt, and they both stepped out.

Mia followed him up a few steps and into the cabin, which, she noticed, was unlocked. The place was small, but plenty big for one person. It was a large, open-plan room, kitchen, living and dining, with a staircase off to one side leading up to a loft.

"Have a seat," Jack instructed as he shucked off his Ranger jacket and placed it on the back of a dining room chair. Mia grabbed the nearest spot at the table, while Jack took a chair opposite her.

"You want something to drink?" he asked.

"No, thanks. I'd rather get this over with if that's okay?" It was nice speaking in her normal voice, Mia thought. It had been a while.

"I'm all ears," Jack said and folded his arms.

"My parents died just over two years ago," she began.

"I'm so sorry."

"Me too," Mia said wistfully. It still felt raw. "It was awful. Faulty wiring in the house, a horrible fire. Smoke inhalation killed them." She swallowed before carrying on. "All my things were there as I was still traveling as an au pair. If only I'd been home…" She trailed off.

Jack didn't speak.

"The house was a total loss, and everything in it. It was such a mess. The year that followed is still a blur. There was nothing left. No furniture, photographs, clothes, nothing. I kept on working until eventually Mum and Dad's insurance company settled, and everything went through probate. Their estate went to me. It wasn't a fortune, but a great nest egg. By then, I was mentally and emotionally exhausted. One day I woke up and decided to make a fresh start. I resigned from my job and got a wild hair to do something crazy. I had no responsibilities, no possessions other than clothes. Why not take a bucket list trip before settling down? I'd been to the States once to visit Kelly—"

She broke off suddenly to ask, "Do you remember Kelly, my old roommate?"

Jack nodded. "Sure. She was the American girl I met, right?"

"Yes. Kelly and I stayed in touch after we graduated from university. She's from Harrison, not far from here."

He nodded. "I'd forgotten she was from Arkansas."

"Anyway," she continued, "I'd visited her once before and we'd had a wonderful time. So, I came over to see her, and then went off on my own adventure."

Mia paused, remembering her excitement back then. If only she'd known… She recovered her thoughts.

. "I spent a couple of weeks in Harrison with Kelly. Then flew out to Miami for a cruise to the Bahamas. The cruise was a blast. I got to see beautiful places and made some fun new friends. When the ship docked back in Miami, one of my new friends, Jeannie, invited me to stay on. I had no reason to rush back to Kelly's, so I agreed.

"Jeannie had been a nurse, but recently quit the hospital and started working as an administrator for a Dr. Carlos Rodriguez—to all intents, a real pillar of the community. Carlos ran a clinic for women going through hard times, and Jeannie thought he hung the moon. He sounded too good to be true, but eventually, she introduced me to him, and I could see what she was talking about. He was handsome, charming…and decided he wanted me in his life." Mia stopped. "Maybe I will have that drink. Could I get a glass of water?"

Jack got up without a word. Mia felt awkward. She wasn't trying to elicit any feelings from Jack, but it was important he understood why she was in such a terrible fix.

He handed Mia the glass before sitting back down.

She guzzled half of it down. "I honestly wasn't looking for a relationship. I'd been burned enough."

Jack shifted in his chair and she knew he was embarrassed because he had been the culprit.

"After losing Mum and Dad, I still felt emotionally beaten up and not in a place to have any kind of relationship whatsoever. I told Carlos I wasn't interested and made my plans to leave. But then I had an accident."

Jack sat forward. "What happened?"

"Crossed the street and got hit by a car. I didn't break anything, but got some cuts and bruises, enough to need stitches and a night or two in the hospital."

"And the good doctor wanted to help you recover?" Jack's voice dripped with sarcasm.

Mia glared at him. "Something like that, yes. One thing led to another, and you can guess the rest."

"I'd rather not."

"Really?" She shook her head. "Were you living the life of a monk, Jack? I doubt it. I'll bet you were shacked up with someone. Probably a nice all-American girl with long legs and a Barbie-doll figure." No sooner had the words left her mouth than Mia felt her cheeks warm. That had been uncalled for. She could be mad at the man for leaving her abruptly, but that was all.

"Sorry," Mia said. "That's not relevant." She stared into his face. "Can we just have a truce on the past, Jack? I really need to tell you this without omitting stuff."

He nodded. "Sure. I'm sorry. Carry on."

"I let everyone in England know I was staying on in the US. All my friends said they were jealous, but they thought it was a great idea. It was the perfect time to do something exciting. I had no job, no home to go back to, and everything I needed to do could be handled online.

"I dated Carlos for a few months, and then when he asked me to move in with him, I said yes, with Jeannie's blessing, of course. I thought I'd made the right choice. For the first time in years, I was having fun. We had a busy social life, I loved living in Miami, and I was happier than I'd been in a long while. Everything was going great, until the night Jeannie found out about the women and confronted him."

"Women?" Jack looked confused.

Mia's eyes filled with tears. "The clinic was a front. Carlos was working for a very powerful Cuban family called the Marinos. He used the clinic to bring women in, clean them up and send them on."

"On to where?"

"Wherever the highest bidder chose." A fat tear rolled down her cheek, she brushed it away.

"Human traffickers." Jack said flatly. "Damn."

Emilia looked like a frightened child as she sat across the table, trying not to cry, and Jack wanted to take her into his arms and make her feel safe. It was difficult computing what she was saying, because it wasn't what people like Emilia talked about. Sure, he heard conversations like this in his line of work, but from the guys he knew in law enforcement, or the DEA, not good, decent Emilia. This was crazy.

"Carry on," he said softly.

"One evening back in August, I decided to go to the clinic and surprise Carlos with dinner as he was working late. I knew Jeannie was still there too—we'd texted, but I didn't tell her I was coming by.

"The clinic was closed when I arrived, but I knew the code to the door. There were voices coming from Carlos's office down the hall, and I went into the kitchen with the food.

"Then I heard shouting, and I realized Carlos and Jeannie were arguing. She was yelling at him, calling him awful names. She said he was a monster. She called him a fraud and a crook and a slave trader.

"I rushed down the corridor, and ran into the room, right as Carlos lunged toward Jeannie. He grabbed her by the hair, trapped her in the crook of his arm, and slit her neck open with a knife." Emilia chewed her bottom lip—her anxiety palpable.

"I screamed when I saw all the blood…so much blood. I couldn't help it. And that's when Carlos dropped Jeannie to the floor and came at me with the blade in his hand. I bolted away and got out into the corridor. Just as I did, the door at the end of the building opened, and I saw a cop standing there. He was in uniform, so I shouted for help. He ran in my direction, but when he reached me, instead of helping me, he grabbed my arms behind me and dragged me back into Carlos's office."

"A crooked cop," Jack snarled. They were the lowest of the low.

"Yes. He told me to stay put, then walked over to Jeannie, who was lying unmoving on the floor. He bent over her, and then everything went crazy."

Jack was up on his feet, pacing. His fingers balled and clenched. "What happened?"

"Jeannie wasn't dead, though you would have thought she was, with all that blood. When the cop bent down, somehow she managed to pull his gun from the holster, point it at Carlos and fire. The policeman snatched it from her and punched her in the face, while Carlos started screaming with pain. I took my chance and ran from the office, out of the building, and I didn't stop until I couldn't breathe anymore."

"Dear God." He stopped pacing and pulled out the chair beside hers. He itched to take her hands in his and comfort her, but it wasn't what she needed. "And you didn't call the cops?"

She shook her head, and another tear fell. "How could I? I'd just turned to one for help and look what happened. If Carlos had that cop in his pocket, how was I to know who I should trust? I was too scared to go back to the house, so instead I went to Jeannie's. I knew she kept a little cash there. I took it, grabbed some clothes and her bike. I needed to get away from the area and change my appearance before anyone came looking for me."

Jack stared at her pretty face, remembering her lovely long brown hair. "You cut off your own hair?"

"Yes, at a gas station in Tampa."

"And made your way to Arkansas?"

"With Kelly's help, yes. She wired money to a Walmart, and I rode Greyhound buses all the way to Little Rock. Kelly met me there. At first I went to her place in Harrison, but I worried Carlos would come looking for me, assuming he hadn't died from being shot. Kelly's grandpa has an RV by the Buffalo, and it was the perfect solution to get me away from a city. So, I've been hiding out there, working at the diner to earn enough money to buy a fake passport and go home."

Jack couldn't get his head around all the facts. Everything Emilia said sounded completely far-fetched, yet by the look of her, the shadows underneath her eyes, her face etched with worry and exhaustion, he knew she was telling the truth. Besides, you couldn't make this stuff up. It was all so crazy.

He gave a heavy sigh. "Okay. First things first. You think those guys at the diner are looking for you?"

"They left this behind." Emilia handed him the piece of paper. Jack read it and nodded in agreement. "Looks like they were. But they didn't recognize you, so that's good."

She agreed. "I'm really worried they'll go to Kelly's. If they found me then…"

"You'd better give me her information." He pulled out a small notebook from his shirt pocket and handed it to her. Mia quickly scribbled down Kelly's phone number and address. She'd had to memorize it to find her way from Florida.

"Make yourself a hot drink," said Jack before getting to his feet and going toward the door. "I'm going outside to call this in."

"No!" she shouted, jumping up from the table. She held on to his arm. "You can't. They'll think I shot Carlos and I'll be arrested. If that happens, I'm a dead woman."

Jack covered her hand with his. It felt tiny in his palm, and his chest tightened. She was like a scared little bird, one that had been brave in the midst of true evil. But now Emilia had told him, cracks were appearing in the wall around her emotions. He hastened to reassure her.

"Don't worry. All I'm going to do is have a couple of people I know get Kelly and take her somewhere safe for the time being. They don't need to know why. They'll follow my orders, no questions asked. Let me do that now while we're a step ahead of the guys you saw this morning."

Emilia reluctantly pulled away her hand. "Okay," she said meekly.

Jack called the FBI office in Little Rock. Within two minutes, his contact issued orders for a field officer to go and see Kelly at the school where she worked. Jack intentionally kept the local police out of the conversation. At this juncture, he didn't know how deep the Miami scumbags had infiltrated the police. It was unlikely they had this long a reach from Florida.

The DEA could look into it far better than his department. But it was a start. He'd got the ball rolling, which was imperative. With Emilia's life at stake, he wasn't about to take any chances.

The next call was to Ed Mills.

The older man was on the golf course but took the call anyway.

Jack gave him the names Emilia had shared, the Marino family being the most disturbing. He held back on the details, especially where Emilia was concerned. He needed to understand the whole story before discussing her with his boss any further. After all, statements couldn't be unmade. They scheduled another call for the following day, and Jack pocketed his phone.

He took the porch stairs two at a time, but when he saw Emilia's silhouette through the window, he stopped himself from going back inside. The irony of everything hit him like a baseball bat. A lost love, a decade of regret. A chance encounter just the night before. The coincidence of his being in Arkansas at the very same time as Emilia.

What about all she'd told him? Emilia had fallen right smack in the middle of an extremely dangerous situation. *What if I hadn't been here?* He couldn't imagine what she would have done, a lone foreigner with a bounty on her head? They'd have caught up with her eventually. Jack shuddered at the thought.

But she was here, with him. And in the space of a few hours, being with Emilia had brought back a host of conflicted emotions. How could that be? At her rejection years ago, he'd walked away and chosen his own path. Yet she'd lingered there through time, just beneath the surface of his feelings. Somehow, Emilia had never completely slipped away, even throughout the duration of his long relationship with Aspen.

Now she was within arm's reach, in a heap of trouble, and it was up to him to help dig her out. Though Emilia bore some blame for their parting, Jack had a chance to repay her for his share of responsibility—for the hurt he'd caused by walking away and giving up. Allowing Neil to come between his desire for happiness, and letting guilt steal that chance away.

But not this time. No, this time he'd do the right thing. Even if it meant wading into a mire not of his own making.

Chapter 4

Jasper

He'd been outside on the phone for several minutes. Mia peeked out the window, but all she could see was Jack's broad back, the pull of his khaki shirt across wide shoulders. He had his ear to the phone while the other hand rubbed at the base of his neck. He was obviously agitated, and who could blame the man?

She moved back from the window and walked around the room, the weight of her predicament unbearable. What she wouldn't give to go back in time and never buy that blasted airline ticket to America.

But she'd had to get away after being buried beneath the emotional loss of her parents and the subsequent mess, sorting out their entire lives after the fire.

Charlie and Karen Jones were in their fifties and had made no preparations ahead of their demise. They should have had decades left to live. But an old house and ancient wiring had put paid to that. What had followed was a nightmare.

A trip to see Kelly seemed the right medicine, especially with a side order of a Caribbean cruise. Mia had needed the sunshine, the lack of responsibility and the freedom to rest. How had it gone from an innocent vacation to this terrifying mess?

It always came back to that man, that swine. Carlos.

The door opened and Jack came inside the cabin.

"I've taken care of your friend Kelly. She might get a bit rattled when an FBI agent shows up at her school, but at least she'll be safe should those creeps start nosing around. I've asked him not to question her until I've had time to brief him and my boss."

Mia's pulse raced with alarm. "FBI?" This sounded way too serious, too real.

He stepped toward her. "Don't panic, Emilia. Look, I'm a law enforcement ranger with the National Park Service. I have some authority when it comes to pursuing criminals and making arrests, but only on a low level. You're dealing with a crime family of potential murderers and people traffickers. This is not a job for a ranger, but the FBI, the CIA and the DEA."

With every word, Mia felt on shakier ground. This was way bigger than she knew how to process.

"Am I going to jail, Jack?" She bit her lip when it trembled. "I haven't done anything wrong, but I did run away from a crime scene, and I've been using a fake ID and social security number." Her bottom lip trembled. She bit down on it. Never had she felt so alone, isolated in a world completely out of her depth.

Jack stood a few feet away and Mia longed to rush into his arms. She stared at his face, finding it hard to read.

"Come here," he said softly.

Her feet moved and in a moment she was pressed against him. Her body automatically molded to the contours of his. The fight in her spent, she drew strength from him. Mia buried her face into his shoulder, allowing a second of weakness to surge, to win. Without making a sound, she cried softly.

The moment passed. Quickly, she regained control. Yet Mia stayed put, reluctant to step away from the comforting shelter of his safe arms.

Jack's head rested on top of hers. "You okay?"

She nodded and reluctantly stepped back, out of his embrace and vulnerable once again. Mia turned away and wiped her eyes. "Cheers for that, Jack," she said with forced enthusiasm. "I needed a shot of your courage. It's been a rough couple of months. I got in way over my head living in Florida. And I can't stop thinking about poor Jeannie. I'll always feel guilty because I ran away and left her behind." Her voice trembled. "But I thought I was next."

"Hey, when you're in trouble, always follow your instincts. I've no doubt you wouldn't have gotten out of there alive. So don't punish yourself. You reacted the correct way and listened to your gut." Jack walked into the kitchen and filled up an electric kettle. He flipped the switch on. "Look, we're going to have to talk in more detail. Officially, I must take a formal statement from you. That way, my boss can act on it, find out what has happened to your friend Jeannie. He has to look for Carlos Rodriguez, maybe discover the extent of his injuries. You and I need to figure out how this should be presented, because I don't want any negative attention put on you."

Relief flooded Mia. "Thank you for believing me, Jack. After all this time, you have every right not to. I feel like I stepped into the middle of a TV show. Even now, when I think about what I saw, it's so surreal." She felt her face grow warm. "I'm an idiot for believing everything at face value. Carlos was a complete fraud, and I didn't see it. My head was turned by flattery and a lifestyle that blew my mind. I'm ashamed of myself." She walked over to the window and stared out.

Jack came to stand next to her. Together, they quietly contemplated the line of trees and the sweep of low hills in the distance.

"You did the right thing coming to me. Coping with this alone was never going to end well. You and your friend Kelly are mixed up in something you're ill-equipped to deal with. It's going to be a mess, and it's going to be unpleasant, but it will get sorted out. I'll help you every step of the way so you don't have to do this on your own."

Tears welled once again. Mia had not been this weepy since her parents died. She didn't like it. But the sense of overwhelming gratitude toward Jack was immense. She turned and looked at him.

"Thank you, Jack. Thank you for saving me."

He shrugged his shoulders, and his expression grew serious "Don't thank me," he said softly. "It's the least I could do after…"

The click of the electric kettle interrupted.

Jack made them both a mug of strong tea and gestured to the table.

"Okay. Have a seat and I'll grab my laptop. We'll go over everything once again for the record. I know you don't want to do this, but let's get it over with. Then we can get traction and talk to the other departments who need to be involved. The quicker we do that, the quicker we can get you back to the UK. Sound good?"

She managed a weak smile.

* * *

He knew the following couple of hours were brutal for Emilia. Reliving the night from hell and the subsequent days that followed took every ounce of her energy. By the time Jack hit the final save button on his file, Mia looked like a wilted flower.

With his training and background, Jack understood the emotional toll it was taking on her. Not only living through what she had, but now having to explain it to another person.

He glanced at his watch. "You're exhausted. I want you to go upstairs and get some sleep. I need to read through these notes and get a good handle on what you said, and figure out my game plan. I can do all of that while you rest."

"But…"

"I mean it, Emilia, or do I call you Mia, now?"

"Call me Mia. That's who I've been since I got out of university. But only to my close friends, Carlos never knew it."

"That's why you picked it once you got to Jasper?"

"Yes. It was hard enough pretending to be an American. I had to have a name that resonated with me. It's worked for a while."

His eyes were warm. "You've done a great job staying under the radar. It's admirable you've kept Kelly out of it too. I know this has got to be terrifying, especially when you aren't even in your home country. Listen, you've had a grueling day. The next part is up to me. Go and get some rest. I promise I won't leave the cabin, so you're safe. In a few hours, we'll have some food, and I'll tell you what our next step will be. This is all going to happen tomorrow, so your head needs to be clear."

Reluctantly, she agreed. "You're right. I'm shattered."

Jack walked her up the stairs into the loft and went over to his unmade bed. Looking a little embarrassed, he straightened up the sheets and fluffed up the pillows.

"Sorry," he mumbled apologetically.

She grinned. "All I see is a large bed with fat pillows. I've been sleeping on a mattress no thicker than a slice of bread, and not much wider either. I don't care if your sheets have been on there a year. It's just going to be wonderful sleeping on a real bed."

"Then I'll leave you to it." He walked back toward the stairs.

"Jack," she said softly.

He stopped and turned to look at her. "Yeah?"

"Thanks for everything, today. I'm really glad you came to the diner. I can't thank you enough."

It was his turn to smile.

"Get some rest. You can be nice to me later."

Jack sat at the table with his laptop, trying not to think about the woman lying upstairs in his bed. He logged into the National Park Service's mainframe and began working. Through the park's resources, he could connect to other federal databases, including select FBI data. Before long, he was completely focused, digging through files, trying to acquaint himself with Carlos Rodriguez.

As a law enforcement officer with the Parks, Jack had contacts within the FBI, CIA and local police force. From past cases, he had access to a great deal of information, not to mention people he could ask when he didn't have permission to look at data.

But Rodriguez was not hard to find. A pillar of his local community in a Miami suburb, he cut quite the heroic figure according to newspaper reports. The man was a doctor, specifically an ob-gyn who had opened a women's clinic where he took in not only paying customers, but also underprivileged women without access to birth control and health care.

Judging by the articles online, the man had many benefactors, mostly middle-aged rich women who were likely besotted with the dapper, handsome Cuban.

With a start Jack realized he was grinding his teeth. As he stared at Rodriguez and his smarmy smile, Jack's fingers itched to punch the guy.

He continued searching, reading and periodically making notes. He'd have a good sense of who the slimeball was before he spoke to Ed in the morning.

One of the pictures he found took his breath away. It was the Cuban, dressed impeccably in a white tux, with a stunning brunette on his arm... Emilia. They were at a swanky function, judging by the background and their clothing. Emilia looked like a movie star. Jack saved the image for later. He told himself it was so he could recognize Carlos. But in his heart he knew it was her face he wanted to look at.

It was difficult to process—Emilia being with a man like Rodriguez. The guy was so slick, so all over himself. Even the photographs of him showed his vanity. Emilia didn't like fake people. He remembered her saying that so clearly. But she'd been an Englishwoman alone in the States, and it wouldn't have been hard for Rodriguez to take advantage of her. Emilia would have still been depressed after the death of her parents, been quite vulnerable to a jerk like the Cuban.

Jack got up and poured himself another cup of coffee. He stood for a moment staring out of the kitchen window at the dark grass. The severity of Emilia's situation worried him. It didn't matter who was in your corner when it came to murder. If Jeannie, Emilia's friend, was in fact dead, then this was going to be very tricky.

Though he'd searched, Jack had not discovered anything about Rodriguez being hurt, or even wounded. That hadn't surprised him. If the man was deeply connected to a crime family with cops on their payroll, they'd have the wherewithal to see he got medical attention and made sure it was kept out of the papers.

Another thought came to him.

Jack sat back down at the table and typed in a search for recent murders in the Miami area over the previous two months. He did not find anyone with the name of Jeannie, but there were several other murders of women reported. It would require further investigation. Jack suspected the woman must be dead. If he had to guess, she was probably at the bottom of the ocean by now.

And what about the two thugs sniffing around the Ozarks? They would have to be dealt with. Once he'd spoken to Ed, his boss would brief Agent O'Malley about the situation, so everyone was on the same page. Ed said they were working for the Marinos, which gave them ties to Rodriguez. This was the Feds' game. Who knew what the plan was?

It could all wait until the morning. For now, and the remainder of the day, Jack wanted to focus on keeping

Emilia safe, and determine the best course of action he should take once Ed Mills was properly in the loop. They would need to contact the British Embassy at some point in time, so that Emilia would have their protection and also get the paperwork going for a replacement passport so she could return home.

At three o'clock Jack quietly made his way upstairs to the loft. He needn't have worried about waking his guest. Emilia was sound asleep, curled up with one arm wrapped around his pillow. Jack couldn't resist the temptation to move closer.

In slumber, Emilia looked more like the woman he remembered from years ago, even with changes to her hair. Her face was relaxed and peaceful, unlike the taut, worried expression she'd had while awake. Her breathing was slow and steady, and Jack guessed she'd likely been sleep-deprived since running away from Miami.

The side of her head rested on her right arm. Her hand hung limply. Without thinking, Jack reached out and touched it.

In a flash, Emilia jerked away her hand, sat up, then scrambled off the bed.

"Wait, stop. It's only me," Jack tried to reassure her, but Emilia backed away from him toward the stairs. Her eyes were wild, her breath fast, and he wanted to kick himself for being so stupid.

He held out a hand. "I'm sorry. I didn't mean to wake you up. You're safe, you're at the cabin. Everything's okay."

Slowly the tension eased away, and awareness set in.

Her large gray eyes lost their fear as she recognized where she was and who she was with.

"You scared me," she said accusingly. "I must have been in a dead sleep, because I forgot I was here and thought someone had broken into the RV." Slowly she moved back to the bed and sat down in the middle of it, crossing her legs like she was in yoga class.

"This is all on me," Jack said, feeling like a complete heel. "I came up to check on you and you looked uncomfortable, so I wanted to move your hand. I'm an idiot. Of course you were going to wake up. I'm really sorry. Can you go back to sleep?"

She shook her head. "I don't think so, but I've had a good rest. What's the time?"

"Just after three. But there's no reason for you to get up if you don't want to. I'm just going to cook something here for dinner and stay put. First thing tomorrow I'll be talking to my boss, and we'll figure out what happens next. I think you need this evening to rest. The next few days will be intense, and you'll have to be up for it."

She nodded. "I'm in a lot of trouble, aren't I, Jack?"

"Not in the real sense of the word you aren't. But yes, you are in a very troubling situation. The upside is you've got me, and my department to help you now. As long as everything you've told me is true, we'll get to the bottom of this and get you home. It's going to be a bumpy ride." He gave her a reassuring grin. "Are you hungry? Why don't we have some food and stop thinking about this for a couple of hours?"

Mia yawned. "Okay. Sounds like a good plan. Would you mind if I took a shower?"

"Sure, need to borrow a fresh T-shirt?"

"That would be great. This one still smells of the diner."

Jack showed her down to the bathroom. He couldn't tell her where anything was because he'd only just moved in there himself. But the cabin must be rented out frequently, because in one of the bathroom drawers they discovered a variety of travel-size items. Much to her delight there was even a new travel toothbrush albeit a couple of inches in length.

It would do.

When Mia finished drying off, she pulled on Jack's loaner T-shirt, which swamped her but felt comfortable. She borrowed his comb to tidy her hair and hung up her wet towels. Things went a lot quicker when your hair wasn't very long. She studied her reflection in the mirror. In a way, the new look was growing on her. She looked edgier, even younger, not like an au pair at all.

Mia's mind went to the man in the other room. He'd gotten better-looking with age. Jack was half Cherokee and had inherited the tribes' striking features. Chiseled cheekbones, dark eyes and beautiful, straight black hair.

What had his life been like since they parted? Had he been in love? Married? Goodness, was he married now? The thought hadn't even occurred to Mia since she'd shown up in his office needing help. That he had not hesitated but immediately taken charge of the situation was a huge relief to her. Being alone and on the run had exhausted every fiber of her being.

Jack was in the kitchen, digging about in the fridge. "It's slim pickings for dinner, I'm afraid," he said. "I've only got a few things as I just moved in. But there's bacon and eggs. Would an omelet do?"

Mia joined him. "That would be wonderful, thank you. Can I help?"

"You can put on the kettle. Why don't you make some toast? The toaster's over there." His dark eyes looked her over. "Feeling any better?"

"Much," she said. "I didn't realize how tired I was."

"Sorry I woke you." Their eyes met.

She quickly glanced away, placing her attention on filling the kettle. "Don't apologize, Jack. I'm jumpy as a frog right now. What you're doing to help me is huge. I feel bad dragging you into my problems, but when I saw my name on that paper, it freaked me out." She set the kettle down and turned the switch on.

Jack placed the carton of eggs on the countertop and moved to stand beside her. He reached over and took one of Mia's hands in his.

"Despite what you think about yourself, you've been very brave. Even a seasoned cop would feel out of their depth in your situation. Stop being so hard on yourself, you've done really well."

Mia smiled as Jack gave her hand a squeeze before stepping back to continue with his tasks. She watched him for a minute.

"So, Ranger Brannon, what brought you to Arkansas? Last I knew, you were headed off to school in Minnesota. Now you're a grown-up ranger, rescuing damsels in distress."

He cracked open several eggs and whisked them in a bowl. "When I became certified, my first assignment was a post in Arizona. I liked it there so much I stayed for nine years. Not at the same park, of course. Then I moved here."

"Why Arkansas?"

He added salt and pepper to the bowl and gave a shrug. "I needed a change. Besides, my grandfather recently got diagnosed with prostate cancer. He's in Tulsa, which isn't so far. I want to be around in case the family need any help. Here, I can at least go and see him. Arizona was too far away."

"I'm sorry about your grandfather being sick," Mia said sincerely. "I hope his prognosis is a good one. I know there's been a lot of research with prostate cancer."

"They caught it early. He's seventy-six, and a tough guy, so he's got a good shot at fighting it."

Jack put a frying pan on the stove and peeled off rashers of bacon, laying them in the pan.

"So, is there no Mrs. Brannon?" Mia couldn't help wanting to know.

He glanced up sharply. "There is not. I've had a couple of relationships, but my focus has been on my job, and it's pretty demanding."

"Well, that's not changed, then." It was out of her mouth before she could stop it. Instantly, the atmosphere shifted.

Jack stopped what he was doing, his eyes narrowed. "Do you want to talk about this right now? Do you want to rehash the past when your life is in danger? If it would make you feel better to berate me and tell me all the reasons why I was such a bastard ten years ago, knock yourself out, Emilia. Just remember, it takes two." With that, he turned back to face the stove.

Instantly deflated, Mia reached out and touched his elbow.

"I'm sorry. I didn't know I was going to say that. It came out of nowhere."

He did not shrug off her arm but looked at her. She thought she could see a trace of something there. Regret?

"Mia. We both made some serious errors of judgment in the past. All I can say is I'm sorry I hurt you. Okay? I put my career before everything, and my twenty-two-year-old self thought that was the right decision. It had nothing to do with you as a person. I'd have made the same choice no matter what. It was where my head thought I had to go." *And because I couldn't betray my promise to Neil.*

She dropped her hand. He was right. She could be mad at Jack forever because of how he'd ended it. But what was the point? "I'm sorry. I need to let it go. I haven't been dwelling on our past." She let out a breath. "But seeing you again just brought back old memories and hurts. I suppose with everything going on at the moment, it's easy for me to get maudlin. Let's call the past the past and forget what happened. Deal?"

She held out a hand and he took it. They shook. Mia went back to making the toast.

Chapter 5

Jasper

The omelet was delicious. They ate quickly, with little conversation.

"You're a pretty good cook," Mia commented after her last bite. "If this ranger gig doesn't work out, I can put in a good word for you at Billy-Jo's."

He laughed, and Mia delighted in the way his eyes sparkled and how his face softened for a moment.

Jack got up and gathered their dishes. He waved away her offer of help and rinsed off the plates to put in the dishwasher. He glanced out of the window. Dusk had silently rolled in.

"I'm going to step outside and make sure everything's locked up for the night. Want to come with me, or stay in here?"

"I'll come with you." She did not want to be alone. Mia hated that she felt so scared. She needed to get a grip.

Jack shrugged on his jacket, then went to a coatrack by the door where one item hung. It was a huge gray hoodie. He handed it to her.

"Here, wear this. It'll be chilly out there now the sun's gone down."

She thanked him and put it on. It was so long it almost reached her knees, but it would be nice and warm.

Jack led the way outside. He told Mia he was moving the Bronco and reversed it until it aligned with the back of the cabin, then made sure it was locked.

Mia followed him over to a small shed that was padlocked. Jack checked it was secure and then headed toward several stalls that had been used for horses back in the day, but now were just growing healthy weeds.

"Let's walk around the perimeter of the cabin," he said. "I just got here the day before yesterday, and I haven't examined the windows and doors to see if they look secure. I only brought a few things with me, and I wasn't too worried about anyone breaking in. From what I can tell, the area seems to be decent, and people respect one another."

With that, he set off around the building. Jack checked windows from the outside and the rear door to the cabin, which was locked. He spent a moment studying a smaller area that looked slightly different to the rest of the exterior.

Mia followed but found her eyes straying to their surroundings. What if they were being observed? "Do you think anyone's watching us right now?"

Jack rejoined her. "I doubt it. If they were near the cabin, we would have heard them come down the driveway with all that loose gravel, even if they were on foot. It's always possible they are a distance away and looking at us through some kind of scope." He gestured to the landscape. "But as you can see, we're surrounded by lots of trees and dense bushes with very little open space. That is great camouflage and would impede anyone having a clear look at the cabin. Fortunately, these homes are built with privacy in mind, so it is an ideal place to hole up, if you have what you need to get by."

He was a few steps ahead of her and they rounded the corner reaching the front of the cabin. He stopped abruptly and turned. She walked into him. Mia wobbled and Jack instantly grabbed her elbows until she got her balance.

His touch penetrated the fabric of the sweatshirt and she imagined she felt his skin on hers. It was strange how he evoked feelings that were almost an echo of the past. Was it unfinished business that kept her on edge when she was around him? Did he feel it too?

Mia was aware of her conflicted feelings toward this man. Had she ever forgiven him for the past? No. Not if she was being honest with herself. He had cast her away to focus on his career and never looked back. She'd thought him better than that, but she'd been wrong.

But although Jack had the capacity to hurt her and had, he also had the power to make her feel safe. At this moment in her life, the rest of it didn't matter. If Mia wanted to stay alive, she needed to depend on Jack Brannon. He held her life in his hands.

Mia sat on the couch looking as fragile as a leaf ready to fall from a tree. Jack worried about her, even knowing deep down she was strong and had already proved how brave she was. Anyone whose life was in danger had every right to be scared.

Jack was seldom frightened of anything. The things that made him vulnerable were situations he couldn't control, like it had been with his brother Neil. Relationships were his kryptonite.

His recent breakup with Aspen had been difficult. She'd hated his job; he'd hated her friends.

Aspen was a yoga instructor from Los Angeles, with a healthy body and an even healthier diet. In their years living together, Jack's fitness level had responded to her organic way of eating and penchant for exercise. But his mind had vegetated. He did not care about keto diets; he hated green tea and kombucha. He was a typical guy, who craved the odd cherry limeade and cheeseburger, but uttering those words in front of Aspen was the equivalent of blasphemy.

They had not been unhappy, yet neither had their relationship progressed. When Jack discovered her in bed with one of her yoga students, he wasn't that upset. Just pissed that the guy had used his bodywash in the shower.

The timing had been perfect. Only a couple of weeks after their breakup, Jack's dad had called to tell him about his grandfather. Jack had called his boss, Ed Mills, initially to request some time off to go to Tulsa. By the end of the conversation, he'd been given the new assignment in Arkansas, and would move there after taking two weeks off to spend with his family.

How ironic it was that all these changes should be capped by his running into Mia, after so many years. Timing was sometimes fortuitous. For no matter their past, he was sincerely glad he could help her in this time of need. Jack would hate to see anything happen to the woman who'd once captured his heart on a beautiful beach in Cornwall.

Thoughts tumbled through his mind while Jack led her back inside the cabin and locked the door securely.

He took off his jacket but noticed she kept the sweatshirt on, and realized she was still cold.

There was wood in the stove. He wadded up newspaper, twisted it under the logs and lit a match. The wood was dry, and the fire kicked in quickly. He closed the hatch.

Mia watched from the sofa. "Anyone can tell you're a ranger, Jack."

He chuckled, taking a seat in an armchair. "It's one of my few skills. But I learned how to start a fire in the Boy Scouts. If you can't make a fire, you don't eat. Then I went on to be a Junior Ranger."

"Of course you did."

He frowned. "You look like you're cold. Want me to make a warm drink, or would you prefer something stronger?"

He watched as she considered her options. "After today, I think something stronger might be the better choice. What do you have?"

"Whiskey."

"That will work."

Jack went into the kitchen, poured two small drinks and brought them back into the living room.

For a few minutes it was just quiet while they sipped their drinks.

"This really is a lovely place," Mia said. "The cabin is comfortable, and so cozy. I wish I was here just hanging out for the weekend, not hiding out."

"Me too. Perhaps if we get this all resolved, you can stay a couple of nights and go on a hike, or take out a kayak on the Buffalo. It really is a beautiful part of the country, and more so because not everyone knows about it."

She stared at him. "Do you believe we'll be able to get this sorted out? I don't even know where to start, do you?"

Jack leaned back in his chair. He slowly moved his glass in circles and watched as the amber liquid swilled. "I did some research while you were asleep. I found no reports on your friend Jeannie, and nothing about Carlos, except for cheesy PR stuff."

Mia sat forward. "Does that mean Jeannie could have survived?" Her voice was full of hope.

He shrugged. "I don't want to worry you, but if she sustained the injuries you saw, it's doubtful." He watched her closely to gauge her reaction. The last thing he wanted to do was upset her. Mia had dealt with too much already.

He saw she caught his hesitation.

"Please be honest with me," she said.

"All right. My guess is the Marino family have camouflaged what happened at the clinic, using their many resources. Tomorrow, when I call my boss, he'll have the authority to delve far deeper than I can. He'll contact the top FBI guy in Florida, and then we'll know the real status. I'm sorry, Mia, but if I had to guess, I would suspect your friend has been disposed of. Carlos has probably been attended to and is recuperating from his wounds, if they weren't fatal. But whether he's dead or alive, it does not alter the fact that you were a witness to something they want kept quiet. The fact you haven't spoken to the authorities tells them you're not running to the cops. If you had made it back to the UK they may not have even followed up." He took a sip of his whiskey.

"But those guys…"

"Yes, the two men who came to the diner. I can't disclose everything to you because it's confidential, but those thugs were already on our radar, though unrelated to your situation. The Marino family has been under surveillance for some time. It wouldn't surprise me if their men had been tasked with checking to see if you are around here, because they were already in the vicinity. For example, if they were on one of the interstates, it would not take much to veer off and check out a possible sighting of you. I know you've been very careful, but if they have members of the police or sheriff's departments in their pocket, they might have access to information. It could be something as simple as your friend living in Harrison. With no other leads, they'll know you're in no position to leave the country and that you would have to rely on someone's help to get out of the States. If I was in their shoes, that would be where I'd start."

"Thank goodness you've warned Kelly," said Mia. "I'd never forgive myself if anything happened to her. Other than you, she's the only person I can trust."

He liked the fact she trusted him. "Well, don't worry about Kelly anymore. She's been taken to a safe house, and no one will be able to get near her. It's probably inconvenient as hell but I'm sure she understands that it's necessary. Once I've spoken with Ed and we've initiated our next step, I'll try to arrange a phone call between you and her."

"I would really appreciate that, Jack. Thank you." Mia could imagine Kelly's reaction to the FBI showing up. She would not have gone quietly.

He finished the rest of his drink in one swallow. "Would you like another?"

"Are you going to?"

"Not if I plan on staying alert. But maybe you need

one to help you get some more sleep tonight. I'll be down here, so you won't have to be scared. And don't worry about anyone getting in the cabin. I'm a light sleeper, and you know I'm armed."

"Guns are such an American concept. I'm uncomfortable around something that dangerous, but I'm relieved you have the means to protect us."

Jack got up and poured Mia another drink. He handed the glass back to her. "The best thing for you is to get a good night's rest and let your brain chill. You have been on high alert since you ran away and that is mentally, emotionally and physically exhausting."

Mia sipped her drink. "What's going to happen tomorrow? Will I have to go somewhere else?"

Jack didn't like to answer questions he was unsure of. "That really depends on what Ed has to say. He's based in Washington, DC. But the crime took place in Miami. It wouldn't surprise me if that's where we have to go."

Her eyes widened in alarm and at once Jack felt guilty for causing it. Quickly he sought to reassure her. "Look, I'm going to request that wherever they want you to go, I'll escort you. The guys I work with are good. They'll make sure no one can get to you. Look at what you've accomplished on your own. Now you'll have a whole team of people who can stop anyone from harming you."

Her stare leveled on his face. "They're going to want me to testify, aren't they?"

He nodded. There was no point in lying. "I know that sounds pretty daunting, but it's the only way to sort this mess out. As long as the Marinos have power, you won't be safe in America. Once you go back to England, who's going to look out for you there? Our jurisdiction doesn't reach that far, and unless Interpol have an interest, you would be very vulnerable."

"So, what you're saying is I don't actually have any choice?"

"Unfortunately, I don't think you do. It's just really bad luck you got introduced to the wrong guy."

She gave a derisive laugh. "I seem to make a habit of doing that."

Jack flinched from the remark. It stung. Any other time he would have immediately been annoyed and zinged her right back. But he couldn't. Mia was in an awful place, stuck in a nightmare that was not of her making. He chose not to respond—but it wasn't easy.

Mia spoke again. "I'm sorry, that was unnecessary. You couldn't be more unlike Carlos. I'm just fed up and feeling sorry for myself. I want to turn the clock back a year and make different choices."

"Hey, things could always be worse. Sure, this is horrible, and you feel like you're in over your head. You've every right to feel scared and worried. But you were smart and brave. You got away from that scumbag and his men. You made it across the country, with one contact and no resources, and got yourself safe. If everyone was as resilient as you, there'd be no need for so many cops."

He stared at her face. Her eyes were teary again.

"You've come this far. You're up for this, trust me. Get some rest, get your mental armor on in the morning. We'll go to war tomorrow and fight one battle at a time."

Mia drained the last of her whiskey. She got up, rinsed the glass off and put it in the dishwasher. Going to the bottom of the stairs, she paused before going up.

"Are you sure about giving up your bed? You need your rest too. I feel terrible…"

"I want to be down here. The loft is inaccessible from outside. Up there, I know you're safe."

"Okay," she agreed. "Thanks, Jack. For everything you've done. For dinner, for the bed, and for being my guardian angel."

He grinned. He'd never been accused of being angelic before.

Chapter 6

Jasper

The lull of sleep beckoned, no doubt the result of drinking two glasses of whiskey. But so far, Mia had not fallen into a peaceful abyss, because whenever she closed her eyes, things she did not want to see came into her head.

She was two different people. Most of the time, Mia was frightened, and simultaneously annoyed with herself for being timid. Her defenses remained on full alert. Yet when Jack was with her, she couldn't help thinking about the past.

Though many years had passed, they had not dimmed the memory of his kiss, his embrace, and of being lost in his dark eyes. When she looked at him, she imagined her fingers tangled in his smooth black hair, the firmness of muscle in his shoulders, in his arms. She remembered what it was to be a woman…a woman in love.

Guilt pushed those thoughts and feelings away. How could she daydream like some romantic ninny, when monsters traced her every move? Faced with her own mortality, why did her feeble mind wander through starry nights and along golden beaches, when Jeannie had lain before her in a pool of blood?

Mia disliked herself intensely. She rolled over once again and shoved her hands under the pillows. What would happen in the morning? Would Jack take her away from Arkansas to Miami? Wouldn't that be like stepping into the lion's den?

Though Mia knew little about the law, especially in America, she had a feeling they'd go to Florida. Whatever happened with Carlos or the Marinos, she would have to face them in their own territory with Florida lawmakers.

An owl hooted outside. There were no windows up here, but it was so quiet, you could hear a pin drop.

Mia closed her eyes.

A hand pressed firmly on her mouth, and she woke up, arms flailing. Mia beat her palms violently against something, someone…and then felt warm breath in her ear.

"It's Jack. Stay quiet. I heard someone outside and you need to wake up. Get out of bed without making any noise and put on your sweatshirt. Get your shoes, but don't put them on," he whispered.

Trembling, Mia moved slowly from the bed and did exactly what he'd said. He gestured for her to follow him, and made his way down the stairs, his back against the wall.

When they were downstairs, Jack reached out and grabbed her hand. He stepped slowly down the hallway, to a door Mia presumed to be a cupboard. But when Jack opened it, he stepped completely inside, and tugged her in there as well.

It was pitch-black, and then a pinprick of light appeared.

"This is a hidden way out," he whispered in her ear.

He pointed the key fob flashlight to a panel behind them. "Keep a hold of me."

Mia nodded in the dark. She had no intention of ever letting go of this man until they were safe.

Jack touched the panel, and it popped open. Then he stiffened as a creaking sound broke the silence inside the house. Mia thought it must be the front door being opened. Her blood ran cold. She felt sick. *Keep calm, stay quiet!*

Jack gave her hand a reassuring squeeze, and Mia swallowed. She went through the small gap and then moved so that Jack could close it again.

They were at the back of the cabin somehow, in a small space that could only be there to hide things. Jack flashed the light and Mia saw there was another door, bolted shut, which would lead directly outside.

Jack drew close as he bent to whisper. "Here's what we're going to do. We're going to go out to the Bronco. But once I touch the key, it will beep and the engine will start. When it does, you have to throw open the driver's back door and climb in. Then I need you to lie down on the floor. You got it?"

She nodded dumbly. Her entire body convulsed with fear and her hands shook. She couldn't breathe.

"Be brave, Mia. You can do this. We're getting out of here and away from the danger. Slip on your shoes."

She did.

He grabbed her hand tightly, then moved to the door, unbolted it and opened it to the night. Mia saw now why he'd parked his car on this side of the cabin. Had Jack known someone might come for her tonight?

The chill of night greeted them. Jack pushed the door back in place. He'd turned off the little flashlight, but Mia could see his face under the wash of one of the porchlights that dusted the ground.

The driver's side faced the cabin, and the SUV was pointed the right way to get out of the driveway. Jack really had thought of everything. They had a few feet of ground to cover, though. Mia tensed. Her heart hammered against her breastbone and her breath came in fast pants. Jack gave her hand a sharp tug. He was telling her to get ready. She gulped in the air and then they were off.

Jack sprinted to the Bronco without loosening his hold. When they got to the vehicle, a light suddenly came on inside the cabin. Jack thrust Mia to the back door. A loud beep sounded as he hit the key fob and the engine ignited.

Mia didn't need coaching. She flung open the door, climbed in and slammed it shut, then lay down on the floor of the car. Jack hit the accelerator.

Mia thought she heard someone shout, but it was drowned out by the roar of the engine and the crunch of gravel as Jack raced up the drive.

"Stay down until I tell you," he yelled. "There may be more of them waiting by the road."

She didn't argue.

Mia closed her eyes and tried not to cry or panic. Adrenaline pumped through her veins as her heart pounded. Her stomach clenched.

Jack took the turn at the top of the driveway so fast the back wheels spun in the gravel. Mia sucked in her breath. *Were they going to crash?*

But Jack held the Bronco steady, and they shot from the driveway onto the dirt-and-gravel road. They sped up even faster, roaring down the rural lane, while Mia's body bumped against the floorboards.

"Get up onto the seat Mia," Jack shouted over the engine. "Put on your seat belt and then hunker down as low as you can."

She followed his instructions. Mia had seen enough movies to know what he was saying. He wanted her strapped in if they were chased, but low enough so she couldn't be a target.

Jack hit a button on his dashboard. His phone was Bluetoothed to his radio. He rattled out a bunch of numbers to whoever was on the other line. There was a quick exchange and then he disconnected.

"Listen up, Mia. We're going to book it for a mile or two, and then I'm going to pull in someplace where there's cover and wait it out until backup arrives. Stay still and quiet, okay."

"Okay," she blurted out. She half lay, half sat, strapped into the seat as he turned onto the paved roads. He was going so fast. But she knew he had to if he didn't want them to end up dead.

A few more minutes passed. Jack said, "I'm pulling over now. Stay down until I tell you different. You can take off the seat belt and lie on the seat. But try to be quiet." He pulled off the tarmac and turned the truck around so that it faced the road in front of them. Then he carefully reversed back into the scrub so they would not be detected by passers-by.

He killed the engine, and everything went dark. "You okay, Mia?"

"Yes. A bit scared, but I'll be fine. What about you?" It sounded daft, as Jack had been responsible for them getting away. But he was only human, and his life had been in peril just as much as hers, if not more.

"I'm all right," he said. "Thanks for asking."

"Do you think they're following us?"

"No question," he replied, and her heart sank.

"But," he continued, "we got lucky tonight because the two morons from the diner probably aren't who they normally send to take someone out. My guess is those guys handle other aspects of the business. If it had been a real professional, they would have got in the cabin before I heard a sound. We have a very good chance of getting away tonight. But I don't feel so confident keeping you safe when the real heavies show up. It's imperative we get out of here and into a safe house."

"What will we do until morning?" Mia asked.

"I'm going to drive to Tulsa and recon with another FBI contact. There aren't enough resources here."

"But I thought you called for backup?"

"I did. But they'll send one vehicle to the cabin, and make enough noise to scare anybody off. It's mainly a diversionary tactic. We just need to put some miles between us and this area."

Jack's voice trailed off as the sound of a vehicle echoed in the silence. Mia couldn't help herself and she slipped to the floor, raising her head between the two front seats so she could see out the windshield.

A wash of yellow spread on the road ahead, growing stronger and brighter by the second. Then a flash as a vehicle sped past at high speed, much faster than a tourist would drive, not that there were any of them about at four o'clock in the morning.

Neither one of them spoke, staying alert as the sound of the vehicle faded slowly into the distance.

"They didn't see us, did they?" Mia said with relief. "Can we go now?"

"Not yet," he stated. "We'll hang back for a few minutes and make sure there's not another car, or that they don't double back. Those guys don't really pose a threat other than the weapons I'm sure they're carrying. I don't want to take any chances, nor do I want to call the local cops as I don't have a clear picture about what's going on and who's involved."

Jack turned and looked at her face pressed between the two front seats. He cupped her chin with his left hand. "You've been really brave, Mia. Just hang in there a little longer because it's going to get easier. We just got out of a very difficult situation, and we did it together. Take courage from that."

Without thinking, Mia lifted her hand and placed it over Jack's. His skin felt reassuringly warm and comforting. But no sooner had she felt slightly better than another vehicle sped past them in the same direction as the first. Her hand dropped away, and she gasped.

"There's more of them?"

"Looks that way." She could sense he had a scowl on his face.

"What will we do?"

"Wait a couple of minutes until they are out of earshot and then go back the way we came. We'll head west through Kingston and pick up 412, which will get us all the way to Oklahoma. It should take about four hours, but there won't be any traffic at this ungodly time."

"Do you think they'll figure out what we're doing and follow us?"

"I can't answer that. If I had to guess, they'd presume

we'd make a run for Little Rock. That's where all my resources would be for the area. What they won't know is
my family lives in Oklahoma, and it makes more sense
for me to head there instead. I think we'll buy time doing
that. Once we get to Tulsa, I have more choices of where
to go until I speak with Ed. The advantage we have is
those guys think you're with a regular park ranger, the
kind they've seen on *Yogi Bear*. They don't realize I'm
actually law enforcement, that I'm armed and have had
training on evading pursuers."

"How do you know so much about the highways if you
just moved here?"

"I came here a lot when I was a teenager. But I studied
the area before moving from Arizona. When you went
to bed last night, I looked at the maps online and figured
what our choices would be if we had to make a run for it."

"Wow," Mia said. "You really have thought of everything."

Jack turned his head and smiled.

She saw the white of his teeth in the dark and couldn't
help but smile back. "Who needs the Lone Ranger and
Tonto when they've got Jack Brannon," said Mia.

Jack was worried. Without knowing what was going
on with the Carlos creep from Miami, and with no intel
on the Marino family, he understood how vulnerable their
position was. He'd debated what direction to take when
they'd left Jasper, and though he didn't want to bring
trouble to his family's door, it was the best choice for the
immediate issue.

Once he got to Tulsa, he would go to his parents',
where they could clean up, eat, call Ed Mills, brief him

on what had transpired, and decide on a plan of action. Mia would need clothes and supplies, and his mom would help with that.

Getting away from the cabin had been a lucky break. Thank goodness the guy who'd rented him the house had shown Jack a hidden way out. He'd explained the cabin was built by marijuana growers, who wanted an escape hatch in case the cops ever raided the place.

Jack glanced over his shoulder. Mia was sound asleep on the back seat. That was something, at least. He blinked heavily, fighting against his own weariness and deprivation of rest.

He cracked the window, letting in a stream of crisp autumn air. It was almost daylight, and they'd just crossed the state line into Oklahoma. On familiar territory now, he allowed himself to relax, but only a little.

He was eager to dig into Mia's story. Not having a clear picture of what was, to all intents and purposes, the enemy, made him nervous. Jack had to know exactly what he was up against, and Ed would be able to clarify that. His reach was broad, and Jack had absolute confidence his mentor would know the best course of action to take.

He glanced in the rearview mirror as the red sun bled light into the darkness. This was the best time of the day, he thought. Darkness chased away by the light of the sun was like evil chased away by good. Jack grinned. He was getting poetic in his old age.

Two miles away from the exit to his parents' house, Jack roused Mia. "Hey, it's time to wake up."

He didn't have to say it twice. He watched in the mirror as she sat straight up and blinked a few times. "Where are we?" She looked out of the window at all the infra-structure. "Are we in Tulsa?"

"Yep," he said. "And we'll arrive at my folks' place in a few minutes. How do you feel?"

She rubbed her eyes. "Never mind that," she said quickly. "Are you okay, and have we been followed?"

"I'm fine. And no. I think we fooled them, and they went south. But once we get to the house, we'll put the Bronco in Dad's garage and hide it."

"Do they expect us?"

Jack shook his head. "No. It was too early to call. But they'll be up by now, drinking coffee."

"I'm a frightful mess," she muttered in the back. "They'll think you picked up a scarecrow along the way."

Jack looked at her reflection. Her spiky hair was stick-ing out a bit, but in his mind, she'd never looked lovelier. Her face was flushed from sleep, her gray eyes looked almost turquoise, and her lips were full and kissable.

What was he doing? Jack berated himself and turned his attention back to the road ahead. Was he some kind of weirdo? They were running for their lives and all he could do was think about kissing his ex-girlfriend.

He turned on the blinker and exited the interstate, heading toward Peoria Avenue and his old house. He needed some sleep.

Joe and Shirley Brannon owned a modest-sized house in an established neighborhood in midtown Tulsa. As they drew closer, Jack told Mia it was called the Maple Ridge area, popular because of its proximity to downtown, the Gathering Place and the Arkansas River.

She had not seen the river but saw the Tulsa skyline

in the near distance. Mia had never been to Oklahoma, nor did she know much about it other than the history of Indian heritage that Jack had shared when they first met.

"Oklahoma is a relatively new state," Jack said as they drove down an already busy street lined with restaurants and small boutique stores. "One of the first things we learn in school is we're the forty-sixth state in the union and barely more than a century old. You'll be able to tell that when you look at the buildings, as everything is new, especially in comparison to where you're from."

"Is Tulsa a big city?" Mia asked. "The downtown part looks quite important."

"About half a million, I think. But don't quote me. The capital, Oklahoma City, is the largest town. The state grew significantly over time because of the oil and gas industry being so successful."

Jack slowed down and then pulled into the wide driveway of a two-story house. In the center of the front yard stood a huge maple tree surrounded by chrysanthemums of yellow, orange and dusky pink. Flower beds pressed up against the house, filled with purple pansies. The grass was cut short.

Jack switched off the engine and turned in his seat to look at Mia.

"Can you wait here just for a moment so I can let Mom and Dad know why I'm here? They won't mind us coming but I don't want to shock them by standing on the doorstep with you beside me."

"That's fine" she said.

Jack got out, shut the door and clicked the auto lock. With a quick glance at Mia, he headed toward the front door.

Mia's eyes were riveted on his back, and she craned

her neck to see better when the door opened to reveal an older man standing in the threshold. A minute passed, and then Jack waved a hand for her to join him.

Gingerly, Mia got out of the Bronco and walked where Jack waited for her. The stranger in the doorway looked like an older version of Jack, except his eyes were a lighter color and his hair gray and wavy.

"Come in, both of you," he insisted, and they went inside.

Once the door was closed, Jack spoke up. "Dad, this is my friend Mia. Mia, Joe Brannon."

"Hello, Mia." Joe put out a hand and Mia shook it.

"Is that Jack's voice I heard?" A woman joined them in the hallway, and it didn't take Mia but a moment to know it was Jack's mother.

It was apparent where his Cherokee blood came from, for the woman was stunning. Her straight black hair, laced with threads of silver and white, tumbled down her back. Her eyes were dark, and her lovely face could have been carved by a sculptured hand.

"We weren't expecting you back so soon, Jack," she said pleasantly. "Who is this?"

Mia felt the dark eyes take her in, assessing and curious.

"Hi, Mom. This is Mia, a good friend of mine. Look, can we get some coffee and a bite to eat in the kitchen? I'll explain it all to you in a moment."

Joe Brannon glanced at his wife. "Come on, Shirley, let's get these kids some breakfast."

An hour later, the Bronco was hidden away in the garage, and the four of them sat around the kitchen table having just eaten pancakes and bacon. While his parents cooked, Jack filled them in on their situation, without naming names or giving away anything confidential. He made it clear they were stopping briefly so that no one could trace them in Tulsa. He did not want to jeopardize his parents' safety either.

It would be a fast visit. He intentionally omitted telling them where they were headed, and only used Mia's nickname. She wondered if that was due to their situation, or maybe he had told them about their relationship all those years ago. Not that it mattered.

Joe and Shirley said little until their son was finished. They both had questions. Not about what had transpired, but about what they needed for their trip, and what they could do to help. Mia was genuinely moved by their generosity.

"Mia," Shirley said. "Why don't you come upstairs with me? I'll show you the shower and maybe find something fresh you can wear. I think I'm a little larger than you, but I've some things that might fit you."

The two women left the kitchen, leaving the men to clean up.

Shirley led Mia up the stairs and into a spare bedroom. "You can dress in here," she said before taking her into the main bathroom. She pointed out where everything was. "Have your shower, dear. I'll leave a few things in the guest room, and you can use whatever you feel comfortable in. Jack said you will need some other items. I'll run out to the store and grab them." Shirley pulled out her phone.

"What size are you? I'll get some underthings, a few toiletries and anything else you might need?"

Mia thanked her and together they came up with a list.

* * *

The shower was bliss, and Mia took her time. She still felt tired, but not from lack of sleep, more from worry. She finished up, rubbed her hair with a towel, borrowed the lotion Shirley had shown her, and pulled on the bathrobe hanging on the back of the door.

Mia hurried down the hall to the room she'd been shown. Going inside, she discovered Jack lying on the bed, sound asleep. She smiled. He'd likely been waiting for her to finish cleaning up and passed out from exhaustion, poor guy.

One of Jack's legs was on top of a small pile of clothes Shirley had left for Mia to look at. Carefully, Mia moved his leg slightly so she could grab the hangers. Having successfully maneuvered them away from him, she lay them on an armchair in the corner of the room. One by one, she held the item in front of her to decide which to pick.

Ultimately, she selected a baby blue sweater with a soft, cowl neck, and a pair of thick black leggings. With a cursory glance over her shoulder to make sure Jack was still asleep, she pulled on the pants before shrugging off the bathrobe. She then put on the sweater, relishing the warmth of the wool against her skin.

She tiptoed back down the hall and hung the robe back up where she'd found it. There were several photographs on the hall walls, and now she was fully dressed, Mia stopped to look at them. They were family photos of people she did not recognize. But there were several of Joe and Shirley, with two young babies, and then later, babies grown into children, who she presumed were Jack and a brother? Another picture made her smile. It was the same two boys dressed in identical uniforms, complete with what looked like ranger hats. Jack, back when he was a Junior Ranger. But who was the other boy? She had no idea he even had a sibling. How odd. Why hadn't he mentioned it?

Mia peeked into the spare room, but Jack slept on. She slipped back downstairs and went into the kitchen. Joe Brannon was still at the table reading the newspaper.

"O-oh," she stammered, not wanting to intrude.

"Come on in," Joe said with a welcoming smile and folded up his paper. "I could use the company."

She joined him at the table. Mia looked at the kitchen clock. It was barely nine in the morning and it had already been a long day.

"Shirley should be home soon," said Joe. "The store isn't far away."

"She's nice to do this for me." Mia looked at Jack's dad. "Mr. Brannon, I'm so sorry Jack's having to help me. He's a really good person, and I don't know what I'd do if he hadn't brought me away from Arkansas."

Joe Brannon's eyes fastened on her face. She could see Jack there.

"We learned long ago Jack would make his own way in the world. He's no fool and his job means everything to him. If he's helping you with whatever you have going on, then you can be sure he'll do his very best. We're pleased he could come here and glad to assist where we can." He got up. "Would you like another coffee?"

Mia smiled. "Do you have any tea?"

Jack awoke to the dull murmur of voices. He glanced at his watch, then shot off the bed like a bullet. Ten o'clock. He'd passed out for more than two hours.

He shook off sleepiness and headed downstairs, where

the hum of conversation grew louder as he reached the living room. Inside he found his parents and Mia relaxing, looking as though they'd all been friends for years.

"Feeling better, hon?" asked Shirley.

"Yeah, Mom. But I didn't need to sleep so long." He glanced at Mia. She looked so much better than she had earlier. His eyes lingered on her longer than he meant them to. He couldn't help it—she looked so damn appealing in that blue sweater, with her spiky blond hair.

"I need to make that call to my boss," Jack said. "Afterward, we might have to leave pretty quick. We'll probably be driving."

With that, Shirley was on her feet. "Mia, let's go make some sandwiches. Joe, can you get an ice chest out? We don't want the kids having to stop for food."

Jack looked over at Mia. "I'm going outside to call Ed."

Chapter 7

Tulsa, Oklahoma & Lafayette, Louisiana

"Stay away from airports," said Ed. "Too dangerous and I can't get the protection you'd need." He'd just finished telling Jack what else he'd learned about Carlos Rodriguez and his connection with the Marino family. The man was an absolute barbarian. Thank God Mia had gotten away from him before it was too late.

"Although it adds time, I still think you're safer by vehicle. No one knows where you are, and you can vary your route as necessary. But you have to go to Miami."

Jack figured as much. "It'll take a couple of days, even if we rush."

"That's okay. I'm flying down myself. I'm meeting with the Feds tomorrow evening to hand this off to them and give them an update. By the time you get there, I'll fill you in on what I know and how we're gonna deal with it. You sure you don't need backup?"

"The fewer people involved, the better," Jack said. "We don't know how deep the corruption goes. This Marino family sounds powerful. Mia has no idea of the magnitude of her situation. She understands she's in danger, but not how evil these players are."

"Perhaps that's for the best?"

Jack pictured the pretty woman wearing the blue sweater that changed the color of her eyes. This was all so crazy. "For now, at least."

"Leave your vehicle hidden at your parents. I'll make a call and text you where to go so you can have another ride. It'll take about ten minutes."

Joe and Shirley dropped the two of them off at a car rental place where a smaller SUV was booked and waiting. It was big enough for their purpose and very indistinguishable.

Their goodbyes were brief but sincere. Mia thanked Jack's parents more than once, which he saw and greatly appreciated. It was strange not telling them who she really was, or how they'd met years ago. Jack had never spoken about his European holiday romance. Why bother? Mia had already dumped him.

Jack was pleased with their progress. They were just through McAlester and headed south toward the Oklahoma-Texas state line. He'd picked the southern route, deciding it was safer, and driving through Louisiana gave him options to stay with people he knew and trusted.

But there was no getting away from the fact it was going to be a long journey. All in all, a twenty-hour drive from Oklahoma to their destination. He did not plan to do it in one day. They'd set out so late and were already sleep-deprived.

They would stay with friends tonight, and in the morning, get an early start. Ed Mills had said he'd arrive in

Florida before them, and he'd give Jack instructions where to go once they neared Miami.

Mia borrowed Jack's phone, called Billy-Jo's and left a message that Cody or Nancy would get first thing in the morning. She hated leaving them at short notice, but Nancy had a niece she could call who always liked part-time work and a little extra money.

Mia hung up the phone and handed it back to Jack.

"If you need help driving, I can take a turn at the wheel," she offered from the passenger seat. The car was not particularly roomy, but comfortable enough. She had a small bag in the back with clothes and other items Shirley had picked up for her.

"Do you have a US license?"

"No. But I don't think it would be so difficult. Especially on a highway like this."

"Until we got pulled over. Don't forget, we're trying to keep a low profile." He glanced her way. "But I appreciate the offer."

"How far will we go today?"

Jack figured she had no real sense of distance, coming from such a small country. Though she had made her way from Florida back to Arkansas, it had been on several Greyhound buses. "We're headed to Lafayette, Louisiana, tonight. That's a good six hours from here. Tomorrow, we'll go farther, all the way through to Miami. It'll be more like thirteen hours. We'll probably leave early in the morning. If it gets too much on the drive, we'll stop after about eight or nine hours. But I'd rather get there tomorrow night."

He sensed her discomfort. Without taking his eyes off the road, Jack slid a hand across and took hold of hers.

She did not protest. Feeling the race of her pulse against his wrist, he could only imagine how scared she felt going back to the place where she'd witnessed such carnage.

"It'll be okay, Mia," he said. "Our going to Miami. I'm not going to leave your side. Once you meet my boss, Ed, you'll feel a lot better about everything."

"I hope you're right," she whispered.

His hand on hers was strangely comforting. Having Jack Brannon by her side had given Mia hope for the first time since she'd run out of Carlos's clinic weeks earlier. Sure, she didn't know what was going to happen, only that she would have to give a formal statement against Rodriguez about the night Jeannie had been killed. There was no getting around that. Mia wanted nothing more than justice for the death of her kind friend but didn't want it to be at the cost of her own life.

"What did you find out when you talked to your boss?" She pulled her hand out from Jack's, suddenly at odds with herself. She knew her capacity to remain calm was wafer-thin. Her emotions bounced around her chest like someone playing ping-pong with her heart.

"We'll get to Miami and be directed to a safe house," Jack said. "There'll be armed guards watching over the place. Then, whoever is leading the case will come and interview you to get all the details. He'll talk to me too, and I'll share my notes. If there is sufficient cause, which there will be, a warrant will be issued for Carlos's arrest, and if he's still alive they'll pick him up."

She suppressed a shudder at the thought the evil man was still breathing. "What about the people he works for?"

"Dealing with the Marinos will be a different situation.

Your testimony is not against them, but Carlos. So, other than your pointing them in the right direction, they will already have a search warran t lined up to comb over the clinic. There's a lot of evidence building on that family. I don't think you'll be brought into that mess."

"Are they the ones after me?"

"Yes. Your threat to them is what you know about Rodriguez. But once the Feds step in, you're a small fish. They will be far more interested in how to dodge the legal bullets that will fly in all directions."

Mia hoped Jack was right. Being scared of one man was bad enough. But a whole crime family? She shuddered. "If he's still alive, once Carlos is locked up for good, can I go home?"

"As long as you're legally in the clear. If your passport isn't recovered, the British Embassy will be contacted by our authorities, and they will reissue a new one."

"It all sounds so straightforward when you're talking about it," Mia said. "Yet it's like something off a mafia movie."

His phone rang.

Jack put it to his ear. "Boss?"

Mia could hear little of the muffled voice on the end of the line, only Jack's part of the conversation. She turned her head and looked out of the window. They were approaching a bridge with a huge sign that read Red River, followed by an even larger sign welcoming them to Texas.

Jack got off the phone. "Ed's texting me an address in Miami. He'll see us there tomorrow night. There's been a change of plans, though. The FBI wants to meet us in Louisiana in the morning and bring us in with their protection. They aren't happy about our being on the road for two straight days."

Mia frowned. "Do you agree?"

He shrugged. "Now they've been briefed, you're technically their responsibility if you're going to cooperate and answer their questions. Their jurisdiction overrules ours. I'm okay with it. Ed has made sure I get to go along with you, so maybe we'll be better off letting someone else take us in the rest of the way. We'll stick with our plan for today and rest up at my buddy's place in Lafayette. The FBI want to meet in the morning at eight."

Mia wasn't sure she liked the idea of being taken to the FBI. While she was alone with Jack, she felt her opinions and needs were being considered. But what would federal agents be like?

"I hate this," she said quietly. "I feel like someone else is running my life and I have no say in what happens next."

"That's understandable," Jack agreed. "You can thank your Cuban friend for that. That man is a piece of work. How much do you really know about him?"

"Just what he told me. That he moved here as a boy and was fostered by another family."

"The Marinos raised him. He's like a son to them, apparently."

"I never met them all," Mia said. "Which is strange if they were close to Carlos. I only met one of them."

"Who?" Jack sounded interested.

"Carlos called him a cousin, but I think he was one of Marino's sons. His name was Juan."

Jack didn't know the name, but then he'd just joined

this assignment and needed to be briefed. "What did Juan do for a living?"

"Something in shipping, I think. I thought he and Carlos didn't like one another. But they met often and discussed business. Juan brought new clients to the clinic—at least that's what Carlos told me."

"Somehow I doubt they were the kind of clients you thought they were," Jack said bitterly. "More likely they were the next shipment of people being trafficked."

"It's despicable," Mia said with disgust. "How one human can treat another so badly is just beyond me."

"Power and money," stated Jack. "It makes the world go round. To the victor the spoils, and only the strong survive."

"Until they run out of luck," Mia said. "Carlos didn't realize how unlucky for him I would end up being."

Their journey seemed long. Mia found herself comparing it to being on the road back home in England. In America, people thought nothing of driving a few hours to get somewhere and driving back on the same day. This route they took today would be considered an extremely long drive in Europe. Mia remembered a three-hour trip back home would necessitate a packed lunch and a couple of stops for a break.

That said, the interstates connecting this country were impressive. Sometimes, when she looked out of the window she saw a ribbon of road stretching as far as the eye could see. This land was so vast, so massive, it defied understanding.

There was such beauty in the landscape wherever one looked. But Mia would have paid a king's ransom to gaze upon green fields, and stone walls dividing patchworks of farmland. To see a small village nestled in the crooks of hillsides, and church spires reaching above the trees. Oh, to be home again.

They chatted amiably as they drove along. Their conversation was safe. Jack talked about his time in Arizona and how he had fallen in love with Sedona. Mia enjoyed his descriptions of the scenery there and thought Jack could be more poetic than he realized.

There were a few occasions when she was tempted to ask him who the other boy was in the photographs at his parents' house. But something stopped her, though she couldn't explain what. Jack had never brought up the subject of siblings. Knowing him, there would be a reason for that.

Now wasn't the time to cause friction between them. They'd found common ground and needed to remain within those boundaries if they were to stay together during the immediate future.

Mia needed Jack's help far more than she needed his displeasure. There would be time later to speak about other subjects. Still, she couldn't help but be curious.

An hour after they crossed the state line into Louisiana, Mia looked around with interest. Off to the side of the interstate she stared at huge areas of swampland, nothing like she'd seen in England.

"I think when I caught the Greyhound bus it must have taken a different route," she said to Jack. "I don't recall seeing this kind of scenery on my way to Arkansas. You can really imagine alligators and all kinds of creepy-crawlies down there. This country is quite exotic."

"I guess it would look that way to you. It's funny how different cultures regard one another. I don't think anything about the swamps down there, but I would be flipped out if you wanted me to eat kidneys."

Mia laughed. "You Americans and your fixation on kidneys. You act like British people sit there and eat them by the ton. We don't. They used to put a tiny amount of diced kidneys in with steak pies to add flavor. I don't know why Americans are so obsessed with that. After all, you eat livers, and other offal."

"You've got a point. In some parts of the States, people eat calf fries as a delicacy."

She had never heard of them. "Is that some sort of fried beef?"

"Yes. From the underside of a bull calf."

He took his eyes off the road for a moment to look at her face. She looked puzzled.

"I don't get it. What do you mean, the underside of a bull calf? There isn't anything underneath a bull, except its…" Her face scrunched up and Jack laughed out loud.

"Never." She didn't believe a word of it. "That's disgusting."

"Sometimes they are called Rocky Mountain oysters and they're considered quite the delicacy."

"I'd rather starve," Mia said, which only made him laugh even harder.

They spent the next hour comparing notes on different foods they had tried and where they had sampled them. Mia won, having experienced the greater variety due to traveling all over Europe, and other interesting destinations.

"I can't believe you were a nanny." He sounded incredulous.

"We were referred to as au pairs," she corrected him quickly. "But yes, that was my job, caring for the children of the family who hired me. Most people who can afford an au pair generally are quite wealthy. They travel, especially in the holidays when the children are out of school. The au pair goes along so that the parents can enjoy their time abroad and not be tied down with their kids. It's quite a good job when you're young and have no roots anywhere. I saw wonderful places I would never have visited on my budget."

"And here I thought you'd gotten married, had a few kids, and were living the good life in some pretty country cottage."

"That sounds ghastly," Mia said. "Why on earth would you think that? When you met me in England did you think I was looking for a husband? I wasn't. I was focused on my education. In that way, you and I weren't so different."

He had to agree. "I wonder what we'd make of each other if we were meeting for the first time now? Do you think we'd have hit it off in our thirties?"

She glanced at him. "We're getting along okay now, aren't we?" Mia said. "We haven't had any huge disagreements."

"Only because you're allowing me to be in charge. If you weren't so out of your depth, you'd be locking horns with me at every turn. You never did like being told what to do. I was only with you a short time, but I can still remember that."

"That's what happens when you're an only child," she stated.

He did not respond, but his jaw clenched. Mia realized she was in uncharted territory. It was better to change the subject.

"So, tell me about the people we're staying with. Do you know them through work, or are they personal friends?"

"Both, actually. I worked with Beth many years ago. When Beth met Angie, she quit the Rangers and moved to Louisiana to be with her. She works for the state now, an office job, but in the Department of Wildlife."

"What does Angie do?"

"She's a hairdresser."

"Oh." Mia gave a groan.

Jack glanced over at her. "What's wrong with that?"

"Wait until she sees my hair."

Chapter 8

Lafayette & Florida

Beth and Angie greeted Jack like a long-lost brother. For a moment, feeling like she was in the way, Mia hung back. But then the two women pulled her into a hug and ushered their guests inside.

Mia had been surprised by their appearances. They were the reverse of what she'd expected.

Beth, the ex-ranger, was a petite blonde with large blue eyes, dark lashes and a knock-out figure. While Angie, the hairdresser, stood close to six feet, with the features of a Scot. Red hair, pale skin and freckles. Both women were delightful.

The house was as pretty on the inside as it was on the out. Wood floors, cast-iron fireplace, a kitchen with an old-fashioned, six-burner, box stove. Pans hung from the ceiling, and the room was anchored by a huge table.

"We were so pleased to hear Jack was passing through," Beth said, leading Mia to the guest room while Angie showed Jack the backyard. "It's rare we see the guy anymore, and I do miss him." She led Mia into a small bedroom dominated by a queen-size bed.

"You have a lovely home," said Mia, admiring the peri-winkle bedspread, which she guessed was Laura Ashley.

"Thank you. I don't take credit for it, that's all Angie. Set your bag down, and let's go and get something to drink."

Mia did, and then followed Beth down the hall. Jack and Angie were still outside, but Mia accepted the offer of a glass of wine. When the others ventured back inside, Beth and Mia were sipping Merlot, and snacking on cheese and crackers at the table.

Once all four were nestling their wineglasses, Angie glanced over at Mia. Her eyes were the color of copper.

"So, how long have you and Jack been together? It's not often he brings anyone to see us."

Mia looked quickly at Jack. Had he not told them what was going on? She had assumed he would, especially with Beth having been a ranger.

All eyes were on her now. Was Jack grinning? What was she supposed to say?

"Just a few months," Jack announced. "So don't go buying wedding hats just yet."

Beth and Angie laughed.

"Honestly, Mia," said Angie. "Jack is the elusive bachelor. He's like Teflon when it comes to relationships—nothing sticks."

"Oh, thanks for that," Jack retorted. "Way to help my reputation, Angie."

"She's right." Beth's eyes met Mia's. "Jack's so secretive about women we thought he might be gay. The fact you're being introduced to us is tantamount to getting a dating Emmy." There was more laughter. Mia felt herself blushing. What was Jack up to? If these were his friends, why the masquerade?

* * *

Jack saw Mia's face getting anxious. He had, of course, neglected to tell her he was not divulging the true nature of his visit, under orders from Ed. Jack was supposed to be low-key, and draw no attention to them.

So far, so good. He'd declined Angie's invitation to take them out for dinner, claiming they were tired from the drive and needed an early start, which was the truth. He did not elaborate.

Another bottle of wine was opened. They ordered take-out from a nearby pizza place the women loved. Mia, relaxed after two glasses of wine, became bolder by the minute. She exclaimed she would eat nothing with wiggly legs on top of her pizza.

Hoots of laughter ensued from Angie. "What are you talking about?" she asked once she'd stopped laughing.

"Those creepy-crawly things you eat here."

"She means crawdads," Jack stated.

"On pizza?" exclaimed Angie. "No, honey, you can't put them on Italian sauce. You gotta eat them with new potatoes and plenty of Cajun spices."

Mia looked relieved.

The pizzas duly arrived, much to everyone's pleasure, and no one was disappointed by the toppings. They were outstanding.

Jack had finished one glass of wine and stopped there. Though he acted relaxed and genuinely was enjoying seeing his friends again, he was unsettled, and would be until they reached Miami.

His glaze flickered over the scene before him. A table laden with pizza boxes, plates and wineglasses. Three women who were each so different from one another yet bonded for the present. Even Mia was finally chilling out. It was good to see her laughing at something Angie had said.

Though he'd withheld their true situation, Jack couldn't help but enjoy the facade of pretending they were a couple. It was strange to think this scenario, and the one with his parents, could have been a natural outcome if he and Mia had stayed together.

Yet how had that been possible? They were separated by different goals and the damned Atlantic Ocean.

"What's your preference, Jack?" Angie asked.

Jack blinked. "Huh?"

"About Mia's hair, goofball?" chimed in Beth. "We're having a discussion about coloring hair. Do you like hers bleached?"

He was on the spot, and he knew it. Careful with the answer, he told himself. "Love it both ways," he said. "She looks like a tomboy with it short, and a siren when it's long."

"My God," gasped Angie. "Did Jack just say *siren*? Do you think he knows that's not just a noise his truck makes when he's in pursuit?"

All three women laughed.

Jack got up. "While you three harpies mock me, mind if I take a quick shower and turn in? I'm pretty wiped."

"Go ahead," said Beth. "You know where the spare room is. Get some rest, and we'll be up early enough to see you off."

Jack thanked Beth. He had seen Mia stiffen when Beth mentioned the room. She hadn't realized this was a tiny house, with only one spare room. Oh, well. She'd get over it when she saw he was going to camp out on the floor. Right now, he was so tired he didn't care where he slept.

Stepping out of the shower, Jack heard the echo of conversation and periodic bursts of laughter emanating from the kitchen. He'd debated about whether to stay here rather than a hotel, and this had definitely been the right choice.

Both he and Mia needed to be somewhere with atmosphere, in a home, not a sterile hotel. Lord knew they were getting ready to do that the next day. This evening was all about them being themselves, before the call of duty kicked in.

Jack snuck down the hallway with a towel wrapped around his waist. His mom had packed a few things for him that he kept at her place, so he at least had something fresh to change into.

In the blue bedroom, it was fairly dark. Beth had left a small light on next to the bed but turned the main light off, leaving a fan humming softly.

He picked up his sports bag and rummaged inside, looking for deodorant, when the door clicked open and Mia stepped into the room. She automatically flicked on the light switch and was greeted by the sight of a man naked but for a bath towel. Her face froze in surprise.

"Oh," she gasped.

Jack backed away, not sure what to do next. Then he collected himself. Good grief, he wasn't naked. Only his chest was bare.

"Sorry if I interrupted," Mia's voice wobbled. "But I needed to talk to you." Her eyes took in their surroundings. "Are we sharing this room tonight?"

"Yes," he said. Then added quickly, "But not the bed. I'm sleeping on the floor. I was instructed not to talk to Beth and Angie about what's going on. It was easier for them to surmise what they wanted. I know I should have cleared it with you, and I'm sorry. But I'm a bit punch-drunk and short on sleep."

"Yes. I figured you have to be. I've had plenty of rest, but you've been awake since yesterday."

"So you're okay with this for tonight?"

Mia smiled, and Jack's heart melted a little. She looked so pretty with her tousled hair. Her face was soft from the wine, and her lips…

"I'm going to tell our hosts good-night, and then get ready for bed. Okay?"

"Yup," he said, anxious to get out of the towel and into his boxers.

He was half-asleep when Mia came back into the bedroom. There was a lovely scent she brought into the room with her, but he wasn't sure what it was. It smelled like the outdoors, fresh and clean.

Jack kept his eyes closed and tried to forget how uncomfortable he was. Hardwood floors did not a mattress make, but he was so exhausted he could sleep standing up. He heard the bed protest slightly as Mia climbed into it. Heard the rustle of sheets, the plumping of pillows. The sound of the lamp as it was clicked off.

Then nothing. He sighed.

"Jack?"

"Hmm?"

"You awake?"

"Yup."

There was a shuffling sound, and then he was being prodded in the back. Reluctantly, Jack sat up. He could see Mia's outline, but that was about it. "What do you need?" he asked. Sleep tugged at the back of his eyelids. His body felt like it weighed a ton.

"You should get in the bed and sleep. I don't want you sleeping down there."

That woke him up. "Huh?"

"Get in here with me and sleep. You need rest, and you won't get any lying on the floor. You're the one who has done all the work. It should be me down there, not you."

"I don't think that's a good idea."

"Don't be silly. We're only going to sleep. We've been together the past thirty-six hours, and we've been okay. Come on. We can put pillows between us if that makes you feel better. But please, get up off the floor. I won't sleep a wink otherwise. I'll be worrying about you."

Jack's better judgment screamed at him to stay where he was. But the lure of a soft bed, and the presence of a beautiful woman near his side, was overwhelming. He got up from the floor and climbed onto the bed in the space she'd vacated.

He lay down on his back, and felt each muscle and bone thank him for the comfort. He couldn't help but sigh with pleasure.

"Doesn't that feel better?" Mia said from what seemed to him like inches away.

"It's heaven," he said quietly.

"I like your friends," said Mia. "They are really a lot of fun, and nothing like I thought they would be."

"Because they're lesbians?"

"No, don't be daft. They look the opposite of what I

expected. I would have pegged Angie as the ex-ranger and Beth as the hairdresser."

He chuckled. "Appearances can be deceiving." Jack rolled from his back to his side so that he faced Mia. She was staring at him.

"I mean," he continued. "Look at you. You changed your appearance and had me completely fooled." He looked into her eyes. It was dark in the room, but a swath of moonlight filtered through the blinds and Jack could see her well enough, but no detail.

"I wonder if you'd have figured it out eventually. I bet if you had come into the diner every day, at some point I would have messed up." She smiled.

"If we were still in Jasper, I think you could guarantee I wouldn't want to eat anywhere else but where you were." Jack stopped. Had he really said that out loud? He took a breath and hoped he hadn't crossed the line.

"I missed you, Jack. I mean, after you left England. It was never the same." Mia raised her hand and touched his cheek, tracing a line down to his lips. She brushed against them with her fingertip.

Instinctively, he kissed her finger, and heard her sudden intake of breath. Jack took hold of her hand, and with his eyes still riveted to hers, he opened her palm and kissed the soft skin, his lips moving gently, slowly to her wrist.

Her breathing had become faster, as had his own. Jack raised himself up on his elbow. He leaned forward. Mia's face came nearer. They were so close that the tips of their noses touched.

Still they gazed into each other's eyes. Jack released

her hand and moved his to cup Mia's face. Then he tilted his head, bent it lower and pressed his mouth against her soft lips.

She opened her mouth to his, and her mind exploded with pleasure. All the years fell away, all the sorrow forgotten in that moment of utter bliss. Mia felt the roughness of Jack's whiskers scratching her skin, while his lips, pliant and gentle, teased her own.

How could this feel so right? How did this man elicit so much with just one touch? Mia rested her free hand on Jack's shoulder. The solid muscle of him made her ache to be wrapped up in his arms.

His fingers found her hair and threaded through the tangled mess, pulling her closer still. And then just as quickly as it had begun, Jack suddenly pulled away.

"What?" Mia surfaced from what seemed like a dream. The empty space between them felt cold, hollow. "What's wrong?"

He didn't answer.

"Jack, please. What happened? Why did you stop?"

Jack rolled onto his back. "This isn't right," he mumbled. "It can't be like this. Not with what's going on right now."

Mia sat up. She couldn't decide which she felt more, fury or embarrassment.

He wasn't finished. "It's the wrong time for us to complicate this situation. We are in the middle of a crazy mess, and you're in no state to deal with a relationship. It's my job to protect you. Not just your life, but your well-being. I'd be a total hypocrite to take advantage of you at a time like this."

Mia was angry. "How unlike you to be so noble, Jack." She wanted to hurt him. "When did you suddenly become so chivalrous?" *And when did I become so enamored of you?*

He turned to her. She could feel his irritation. "That's unfair. I'm happy to take blame where it is due. But in this case you're the one who asked me to get in bed. I tried to say no, but you insisted."

"I was being nice," she said angrily. "You've hardly had any sleep since I showed up at your office. I know how exhausted you are. It didn't seem fair you should sleep on the floor. I had no ulterior motive, Jack. So don't flatter yourself."

"Mia," he sounded wiped out, and for a moment, she felt guilty for being so cross. "Mia," he said again. "Please don't be mad. I don't have the energy to argue with you. Let's forget this just happened, can we? It's late, we're both tired, and we have an early start in the morning. Regardless of everything, we're still friends, aren't we? Can we just stop fighting and go to sleep? We'll have all day tomorrow to rehash this scenario. Please?"

Mia hesitated. But he was right. He needed rest more than a discussion about a kiss.

"Sure," she said. "Let's both get some sleep. Good night, Jack." Mia turned over so that her back faced him.

He didn't move, and it seemed only a moment passed before she heard his slow, rhythmic breathing. Jack was out for the count.

She lay awake thinking. The effects of the Merlot had worn off. But the aftereffect of Jack's kiss had not. Where had that come from? *What a ridiculous question. She knew where.* It was the result of spending time with a man she'd been in love with. It wasn't her fault. If you took any vulnerable person and put them in a life-threatening situation, threw in an ex-lover as the hero, something was bound to happen. She'd learned that from *The Princess Bride*.

Mia closed her eyes. She touched her bottom lip with the tip of her tongue. His mouth had just been there. She allowed herself to think about the kiss, not just think, but relive it. It had been excruciatingly lovely. Jack's kiss felt right. Mia was no maiden. She had dated extensively and knew her way around a kiss.

She couldn't put it in words, even in her head. She and Jack Brannan matched. They were like two pieces of a jigsaw puzzle, two spoons nesting in each other, or, to be corny, mac and cheese, bacon and eggs. Mia giggled at her nonsensical thoughts. Perhaps she was feeling the effects of her wine. Now Jack was even calling her Mia. For some reason it pleased her.

Then she remembered why they were here, in this room, in Louisiana. Suddenly nothing seemed funny anymore. She closed her eyes. Tomorrow would be here very soon.

When she woke, Mia knew immediately she was alone. That did not surprise her. Jack was on a mission, and he would have been up with the birds, preparing to leave.

Mia got up and dressed, then went to brush her teeth and get ready. She packed her bag, then stripped the bed, folding everything up neatly before heading to the kitchen in search of the others.

She smelled the coffee all the way down the hall. Everyone was up. Jack sat at the table eating something, while Beth stood at the stove cooking. Angie paused in the act of pouring a drink and looked over her shoulder.

"Morning, Mia," she said cheerily. "I hope you managed to get some rest."

"I did. Thanks. It was very comfortable. I appreciate you letting us stay."

"Want some scrambled eggs?" asked Beth. "There's toast and bacon on the table. Grab a plate and bring it over."

Beth put a spoonful of eggs on the plate, and Mia took it and sat at the table, not facing Jack, but off to one side. He was staring at his phone while eating breakfast and, other than glancing up with a brief smile, ignored her.

Angie brought her a mug of coffee. "I wish you guys could stay a little longer, but I understand you have to be somewhere tonight. Maybe when you head back, you could let us know and stay with us again? Right, Beth?"

Beth brought her own plate and sat down. "Absolutely. We'd love to have you back."

Mia thanked them, feeling guilty for not being able to be honest about what was really going on. It was unlikely she'd ever see these two women again. When they had asked her questions the night before about her being from England, Mia had told a lie and said she'd moved here with her job. Then promptly changed the subject.

A discussion about the weather forecast ensued, and Mia stayed out of it and ate her breakfast.

At eight o'clock, Jack pulled into the parking lot at the FBI office in downtown Lafayette. Before getting out of the vehicle, he made a call to let them know they had arrived. Within a couple of minutes, a suited man came out of the building and walked over to the SUV.

Jack got out and shook his hand, then gestured for Mia to get out of the car.

The man did not introduce himself to Mia, but quickly ushered her inside the building. Only then did he turn and look at her.

"Hi, Mia. My name is Agent Wessels. I've been appointed to accompany you for the remainder of your journey today."

Agent Wessels looked to be in his mid to late thirties. He had thick brown hair cut very short, and his hazel eyes were kind.

"It's nice to meet you." She gave a wan smile.

Jack knew Mia was uptight, which was to be expected. He hadn't helped the situation by his behavior the night before either. What an idiot he'd been. Taking advantage of Mia's vulnerability was unforgivable, but he'd also been dishonest. The reason he'd ended the kiss had nothing to do with it being inappropriate, and everything to do with the past.

Agent Wessels took them through the reception area. He used his ID card to gain access through a heavy steel door, then led them down a hallway and into a small conference room with a long table and many chairs. On one wall hung a massive screen and on another, a huge white board.

Everyone sat down.

"Okay," began Agent Wessels. "Let me bring you up to date. Jack, Ed Mills is en route to Miami as we speak, and he'll meet you this evening for a briefing. There's been another change of plans since. After much consideration, the decision was made to take you both by plane and get you off the interstate. You're not flying commercially but on a chartered flight, and I'll be accompanying you both. Once we arrive in Miami, we'll go to a safe house that is ready for you." He looked at Mia. "I'll take a statement from you this afternoon once we get settled. It won't be anything you need to worry about, it's just procedure. Once that's finished, I'll meet with my peers, and we will apprise you of our next steps tomorrow morning."

Mia frowned. "At some point in time, can I please speak with my friend Kelly? I'd like to make sure she's all right. Obviously, I won't disclose anything that's going on here."

"I'm sure we can work something out," Agent Wessels said. "But let's do that once we get you situated and know we're on secure phone lines. The last thing I want to happen is for anyone to discover your location or your friend's."

"She is safe, though, isn't she?"

"One hundred percent," he said reassuringly.

"What time do we fly out?" Jack asked.

The agent looked at his watch. "In about forty-five minutes. So, shall we get going?"

Chapter 9

Miami, Florida

The flight to Miami was uneventful and saved thirteen hours of driving. It was just the three of them on the flight and the crew. Jack was troubled by the fact Mia barely spoke a word, but he understood. They were taking a big step into the world of law enforcement and legalities. Daunting to anyone, never mind a civilian mixed up in a murder case.

The FBI agent had made a favorable impression on him. Wessels seemed a straight-up guy, not too friendly but approachable. If Jack were honest, he was glad to have another person along for the ride. It felt more secure having a G-man around.

They left the airport in a government vehicle. Jack figured it was probably bulletproof. By the time they arrived at a small hotel deep in the heart of the city, it was almost two in the afternoon.

The SUV pulled up at the back of the hotel. The agent got out first, looked around and then told Jack and Mia to get out of the vehicle. They went straight in through a back door, and boarded a freight elevator.

Jack held on to Mia's arm the entire time. She made

no protest but just went along willingly. She still had not said much.

They got off on the top floor of the hotel. Jack was pleased to see a guard posted by the elevator. Only one door on this floor, so he assumed it was the penthouse.

The hotel was not terribly swanky, but it wasn't a cheap motel either. It made sense to get the top floor isolated for a safe house, because no one would come up to this floor unless they were associated with the FBI. It was always easier to control a smaller area.

Jack half expected they'd be kept somewhere outside of the city, a place more remote and away from the evil eye. However, without knowing the reach Carlos and the Marinos had, it was a case of keeping your friends close and your enemies closer still.

Being in the city offered all the resources available. Here they had the police department minus the crooked cops, the county, the DEA, CIA and the FBI. Along with fire and ambulance services, this was the wiser move. The advantages definitely outweighed the risks.

The penthouse was a huge suite of rooms engulfing the entire top floor and housed an open-plan dining, living room and kitchen, with a biggish bathroom off to one side. A short hallway led to three bedrooms with en suite bathrooms.

One wall of the living room had large glass doors leading out to a spacious balcony. It was here Jack went immediately to canvass the area. He stepped out into the afternoon sun and gave himself a moment to enjoy the breeze. It was much warmer here than in Arkansas.

He looked around. They were on the twelfth floor of this building. Consequently, there were several taller skyscrapers in the immediate vicinity. This did not impress him. He went back inside.

"Agent Wessels, I don't know that I like being surrounded by other buildings that have a direct view of this room."

The agent walked over to the window. He smiled. "I can understand your concerns, but why don't you step back out there, close the doors and look in."

Jack went back out onto the balcony and followed his instructions. He could not see through the glass at all. He stepped back inside. "That's pretty clever," he said. "Next thing, you'll be telling me it's bulletproof glass as well."

Agent Wessels nodded. "Got it in one."

Jack was both relieved and amazed.

Mia sat down on the sectional couch watching them. Agent Wessels took a seat at the opposite end.

"Right. How about I get some room service up here and we can eat a late lunch? You guys can settle in and then I'll take your statement, Mia. Sound okay?"

Mia had never felt so far away from home as she did right now. She washed her hands using the hotel's fancy soap and looked around the beautiful bathroom. All chrome and white, everything glistening and clean. She dried off and walked into the bedroom.

This room had no windows, which was fine with her. Mia felt safer being closed in. The bed was king-size and large enough to sleep an entire family of eight. Everything really was bigger in the USA.

But her nerves were getting the better of her. With Jack, the easiness between them helped dull the seriousness of her predicament. Now, back in the city she had run away from, Mia had never felt so vulnerable. How would it feel if Jack was taken away, and she was alone with Agent Wessels and his cohorts?

They had ordered lunch, which seemed ridiculous considering their situation. It was like dining with friends at a nice restaurant, only after dessert they planned to discuss a violent murder.

There came a knock at her bedroom door.

"Come in."

"It's just me," said Jack. "Lunch has arrived." He didn't leave but stood and stared at her for a moment. Then he came in and closed the door behind him.

"You getting overwhelmed?"

"Is it that obvious?" said Mia.

He approached, and she did not protest as he hugged her. There was no romantic intent; this was purely support. She knew Jack understood how daunting it was for her when a few months ago she'd lived quite an ordinary life.

"You can handle this, Mia. Try to make it more abstract in your mind, like standing in front of a classroom full of kids. You separate the emotional part of your brain and focus on the database part instead. That's who they need to hear from. How you felt about everything isn't important at this stage, it's all about facts. Because facts are what they need to utilize the law in the way it was meant to be enforced."

He let go.

"Thanks, Jack. That helps. I'll just feel better once we get this over with."

He followed her out of the room into the dining area, where Agent Wessels waited.

* * *

After lunch, Jack left the penthouse and went down to another floor to find Ed Mills. Ed had texted his location, and as Jack did not want to interfere with Agent Wessels speaking to Mia, he thought it a good time to make himself scarce.

He felt guilty abandoning Mia, but if she'd been taken in for questioning, he wouldn't have been allowed to stay anyway. He explained it to her before he left, assuring her he was only a couple of floors down in the same building.

Ed opened the door.

"Jesus, you look like hell."

"I love you too." Jack brushed past him into the room. He made for the armchair over by a window. Ed sat on the edge of his bed.

"Well, how's it going up there?"

Jack shrugged. "I feel like a heel for leaving her on her own with the FBI. But Wessels seems to be a decent guy. I don't think he'll be too hard on her."

"Good," said Ed. His brown eyes showed real concern. "Now then, how about you and me have a little chat regarding this young lady of yours. Kind of a coincidence that you wanted me to do a check on her, and the next thing I know she's on the run with you and involved in a nasty business in Miami. Care to explain that to me, Jack?"

"Not really." Jack had known Ed would bring it up straight away.

"Like me to rephrase my question a bit more sternly?"

Jack looked over at his mentor. Ed was the wrong side of sixty. His physique advertised his preference for riding in a golf cart and eating too many cookies, instead of going to the gym and living on salads. His white hair was thinning, but his moustache and beard made up for it.

"I'll talk," said Jack.

Jack spent the next twenty minutes explaining the relationship he'd had in the past with Emilia Jones. He stayed with the facts, and then described his surprise seeing a waitress who looked just like her in Jasper.

"That is pretty crazy," said Ed. "Hell, you should have gone out and bought a lottery ticket that day. What are the odds?"

"Tell me about it." Jack repeated everything that had happened since, even though he had told Ed quite a bit already.

"Do you trust your gut feeling about her?"

"Yes."

"You sure about that, son? It would be pretty tough turning on her, all things considered."

Jack leaned back in the chair, feeling deflated. "You know, a lot can change in ten years, but I don't think the core of who someone is changes. Mia is a good person. She recently lost her parents in a terrible accident and has been depressed for a while. This trip was a big deal for her. It's just unfortunate she met the wrong people. She hasn't got that kind of evil in her. I also don't think she has the capacity to tell lies."

Even as he spoke the words, Jack remembered Mia had moved on so quickly when he'd come back to the States. Did he really believe she was incapable of lying? She'd told him she loved him. But if that had been true, she and Dan wouldn't have hooked up as soon as Jack's plane left Heathrow Airport.

"Well, as you're aware, this is the FBI's case going forward. But I know you've promised to stick around. Because of our ongoing partnership with the DEA and this Marino investigation, it's given me some wiggle room so they'll let you stay. Now, understand you don't have any say in anything, and you have to do what those nice federal boys tell you to do. But you can stick around and look out for your girlfriend."

"She's not my girlfriend, Ed."

"Tell that to someone who doesn't know you. I reckon you have unfinished business there, so you're in it up to your neck. Better off keeping you in the picture. That way I got eyes on the game."

"Got it."

"Now then." Ed got up and wandered over to the little refrigerator by the door. "What can I get you to drink, Jack? All this talking's got me thirsty."

"You did a great job, Ms. Jones." Agent Wessels closed his laptop. "I know that was extremely unpleasant. It's the worst part of my job sometimes. Bad enough people have to go through something frightening and traumatic. I hate being the guy who makes them relive it all over again. But I promise you, it really is for a good cause. To punish the evil people in this world for their actions."

"Call me Mia, Agent Wessels. I do understand this part of your job is necessary. All of this seems surreal. Even now it's hard wrapping my head around the fact I inadvertently got mixed up with Carlos. After what I saw him do, I hope he rots in hell. I'm just terribly worried about what happened to Jeannie. She's a nice person who didn't have to be my friend. She was so excited about her new job at the clinic. It was going to change her future. And I guess it has."

Mia wiped her eyes. She'd been determined not to get upset and cry. And although she'd steeled herself not to become emotional, it was impossible to talk about unspeakable acts and not be moved to tears.

The agent had informed Mia they didn't have any leads on Jeannie at this time. But part of that reason was because they needed to establish a crime had been committed in order for them to get a full-scale investigation going. Now she had given her statement, Agent Wessels assured Mia this would prove vital to achieve that end.

Mia got up and walked around the living room. Although the penthouse was massive, it was already beginning to feel small because she knew she couldn't leave. Going out on the balcony was impossible under the circumstances.

Agent Wessels went into the kitchen and started yet another pot of coffee to brew. He glanced over at Mia.

"You're pacing the room like a wild animal does at the zoo. Not that I blame you. It's kind of a mental psychout, being kept in one place. We can put the TV on, rent some movies, and I can get some books and magazines brought in, if you like."

"How long do you think I'll be here?"

"That depends. If this turns into a long investigation, you'll have to be kept safe until you testify. You wouldn't be kept here, but asked to stay in a secure facility where you'd have a little more freedom."

"I'd have all that and more if they'd let me go back to England."

Agent Wessels laughed. "Well said. You're probably

right. But in situations like this, your safety is our top priority, and we wouldn't have the resources to protect you that far away. Obviously, if you were the president that would be an exception." He had the grace to grin.

"President? I've never even been anyone's princess," Mia retorted. "Not that I'd want to be on a pedestal." She joined him in the kitchen. It was weird, not knowing the man, yet after she'd related such dreadful things a while earlier, it had broken the ice.

"Agent Wessels?"

"Yep?"

"Do I have to be so formal when I speak to you? I don't like calling you Agent Wessels all the time. Does it breach FBI etiquette if a witness called you by your first name?"

"Absolutely not. My name is Jeremy, feel free to call me that."

A knock sounded on the door, and she heard Jack's voice ask if he could enter. Jeremy peered through the spy hole, unlocked the door and let him in.

Jack looked worn out. "Did you guys get everything taken care of?" he asked, taking a seat on the sectional.

"Sure did. Mia handled everything like a pro."

"I wouldn't doubt it for a moment," Jack commented. His eyes slid over to where Mia stood looking inside a well-stocked fridge.

"You two are speaking like I'm not even in the room. It sounds like you're at a parent-teacher conference."

"I can see you're feeling better, Mia. You've got your sharp tongue back," Jack said.

She shut the fridge door. "Sorry. I feel like I'm in someone else's bad dream. My moods are swinging so quickly I'm getting dizzy."

Jack laughed at that. "Do we have a bar in here, Agent Wessels?"

"We're calling him Jeremy, now," said Mia. "We're all living together so we might as well be less formal."

"Kind of like the show, *Three's Company*," added Jack. He briefly explained the premise of the show to Mia.

"They stole that idea from England," she said. "Ours was called *Robin's Nest*."

"You guys have completely lost me," Jeremy muttered. "Aha, we do have a stocked bar here. I'm not allowed to drink, but there is nothing stopping you guys. At least this evening. We took care of our business, so the night is yours."

Jack fixed himself a whiskey on the rocks and a vodka tonic for Mia. He handed her the glass and turned to Jeremy.

"Would it be okay if my boss stopped in this evening? If you wouldn't mind double-checking with your HQ, I'd like him to meet Mia."

"Let me call it in. He's staying at this hotel, correct?"

"Yes, on the ninth floor."

"Once I get the approval, he'll get escorted up here. I'm gonna head back to my room and make a couple of calls."

"You don't mind meeting Ed, do you?" Jack asked when the agent left them alone.

"Not at all. Did you have a good meeting?"

"It was okay. He needed to tell me my role going forward."

"Which is?" Mia thought it sounded ominous.

"Nothing different, in my capacity watching over you. It's mainly jurisdictional stuff. The FBI trump me when it comes to this case. But I already knew that. Our department is involved in this purely because of the DEA. That's actually turned out lucky for me, because it allows our guys a hand in the game."

Mia did not appreciate her future being referred to as a game, but she decided to keep that to herself. She really did want to meet Ed Mills. He was obviously an important person in Jack's life. Although she and Jack were not a couple, Mia found she wanted to know more about the man who had stolen her heart all those years ago.

Mia took a sip of her drink. It was delicious and just what she needed after the afternoon's ordeal.

"I asked Jeremy what we would do up here while we're locked in. There's not a lot to occupy my mind, so he offered to get some books, or rent a couple of movies. Any other time I would give my right arm to lie around and do nothing but read. Why is it that when you have an opportunity to do things, your mind isn't prepared to go along with it?"

Jack grinned. "I know exactly what you mean. I remember when I was a teenager I had my appendix out. I couldn't wait to stay in bed playing video games while all my buddies had to go to school. I imagined reaching all the high levels of the games, that my mom would bring me my favorite junk food, and I'd be in heaven."

"And?"

"My insides hurt so bad I could only eat Jell-O. After one day of gaming, I was so bored I wanted to scream. All my friends kept calling to tell me they were going out to play football, or go fishing, all the things I couldn't do. Life is like that, isn't it?"

"You don't adhere to the 'If life gives you lemons make lemonade' saying?" Mia asked.

"Hardly. I'd make a lemon drop martini."

Mia thought that sounded rather good. She sighed. "I feel really weird, Jack. This room feels like I'm in a *Doctor Who* episode, and there's no sense of time. I think it wouldn't be so bad if I was in the UK, because everything would be more familiar. The food, the TV, the scenery."

"But instead, you're locked in a fancy American hotel, in Miami, no less. You're supposed to eat baloney sandwiches and watch reruns of *Frasier*."

"That's about the gist of it. I can't imagine staying here for very long. I'd probably end up jumping off the balcony."

"Don't say things like that, Mia." He said it so vehemently she was slightly taken aback.

"I was only joking. I'm just feeling a bit panicky at the prospect of being locked in here. I didn't mean anything bad." Mia looked at Jack. His expression had changed into a frown. Why had her comment upset him so much?

"Your boss got the all clear," Jeremy said as he rejoined them. "They've gone down to get him now."

"Great," said Jack.

For dinner, they had thrown together things from the refrigerator. No one was really hungry after such a late lunch. Ed Mills joined them, and it had been a pleasant time.

Now, Ed was on his second cocktail and did not seem to mind being the only one imbibing. But he explained that he was leaving in the morning, and so technically was now off-duty. Jeremy did not have that luxury, and Jack and Mia had stopped after one cocktail.

Ed regaled them with a story about the day he met

Bill Clinton. Jeremy and Jack had laughed along with her when Ed recalled the moment he had tripped over Bill's foot, and dropped a plate of food he was carrying at a fundraising dinner. He had a way with words and Mia decided he was a natural storyteller.

Ed looked more like someone's grandfather than a guy high up in a government job in DC. But then, that would perhaps work to his advantage, Mia thought. It would always be easier to trust a man who looked more like Santa than Putin.

"So, what's it like living in England?" Ed asked. "I've only been to London once. All the other trips I made were back when I was in the military, and I never got to leave the base."

"I didn't know you were in the military. Which branch?" asked Jack.

"The mind-your-damn-business branch," said Ed with a chuckle. "Some of us like to keep our pasts confidential, son."

Mia saw something flicker across Jack's face. Had his boss touched a nerve? If so, what?

"Not everyone has an interesting past to keep secret, Ed," Jack said. "For example, I don't tell just anyone I was a Boy Scout."

Ed burst out laughing. "I doubt I'd share that either." Ed looked at Mia. "Seriously, though, what is it like over there in the UK?"

She considered the question. "There are many parallels between our two countries. But I'd have to say the largest difference is in all our history. America is so young, at least since the time Europeans came here. At home, everywhere you go you see the past. You touch it, you hear it… There's nowhere in the country you can go without being aware how long it's been populated, even where there aren't towns and cities. Whenever I go for walks in the countryside, it always crosses my mind that some-one had their foot in the exact same spot at some point in history, because it has been occupied for so very long. It is a beautiful place. And you can't beat the British sense of humor."

"Or their soccer teams," piped in Jeremy. "I've never been over there. But it's on my list of places to go."

"The food's not great," added Jack.

Mia groaned. "Typical American. Just because we don't saturate everything in spices, seasoning and sauce, or think cinnamon is a food group, doesn't make our food bad." She glared at him. "Don't even think about bring-ing up kidneys."

Jack laughed and held his hands up in surrender. "Okay. I'll admit that fish and chips are outstanding. The Brits have the best chocolate, their breads and pastries are delicious, and the beer is great if you don't mind drink-ing it warm."

"You lost me on the beer," said Ed grimacing. "It's got to be cold, or it's gonna be whiskey. What about family, Mia. Do you have a big family back home?"

"No, no one actually. I lost my parents a couple of years ago and I don't have any siblings. Mum was adopted, and my dad was an only child in a very tiny family. So nope, there's just me. I wish I did. What about you, Ed, and you, Jeremy?"

"I'm not allowed to share any personal information with our clients." Jeremy looked almost embarrassed. "If I could, I would."

"Same goes for me, I'm afraid," said Ed. "But I can tell you that my wife wears the pants in our house, and we have a very badly behaved poodle."

"Riveting," drawled Jack.

"Are you under a secrecy clause with your job, Brannon?" Jeremy asked.

"No. I'm not as important as you and Ed. I've got my parents, aunts and uncles, a few cousins, and my grandfather is still alive. Mom's a full-blood Cherokee, and we are proud members of our tribe. I'm really into Native American history, especially since we can trace some of my ancestors back to the Trail of Tears."

"Wow. That's awesome," Jeremy said. "I remember learning about it in school. A tragic time in American history when that happened."

The sound of a phone ringing interrupted. It was Ed's. He pulled it out of his breast pocket and frowned.

"Mills here. Let me call you right back." He hung up. "Well, folks, I guess I'd better call it a night. I appreciate you spending time with me. It will definitely have reduced my bar bill downstairs."

After Ed was gone the room seemed to deflate a little. Jeremy said he was going to double-check the roster for the guards posted outside in the hallway overnight.

Jack and Mia took their dirty glasses into the kitchen.

"I liked your boss. He's quite a character. Have you worked for him a long time?"

"Since I started working for the National Parks. Actually, I first met Ed when I was a Junior Ranger. He was kind of a pen pal of sorts. We kept in touch the entire time I went through school, and he ultimately became my mentor. By the time I was qualified, he was destined for bigger things, and ended up in DC."

"It's great having someone to work with like that. You are very fortunate, Jack." Mia stifled a yawn. "I think it's time to turn in. I'll see you in the morning." Without looking at him, she set off down the hallway. At least they were in separate rooms this time.

As Mia settled down for the night, she played over the evening in her head. The conversation about family had stayed with her. Jack still had not mentioned a brother. So, who was the other boy in the picture? And why was she so interested?

Chapter 10

Mia woke up screaming. Her bedroom door burst open, and both Jack and Jeremy rushed in. Jack reached her first.

He sat down on the bed and pulled her into his arms. "It's okay. Everything's all right, Mia. You're having a bad dream, you're safe. Don't be scared." He held her trembling shoulders in his arms. It must be dreadful to have the nightmares she was having.

"I'll leave you to it," Jeremy said softly and walked toward the door.

When Mia stopped shaking, Jack loosened his hold. He sat back and looked at her. Her face was damp with tears.

"Better?"

She nodded. "I'm sick of dreaming about Carlos. Bad enough he's messed up my life, why does he have to screw with my sleep as well?"

"I guess it's just the way our brains process stuff. This will get sorted, and once it does, I bet you anything the nightmares will go away." He only wished it were true. He still dreamed about Neil and the night of the crash.

"I hope so. I'm sorry I woke everybody up."

"Don't worry about it."

She looked at the digital clock next to the bed. "Is it really only two fifteen?"

Jack nodded. "Think you can go back to sleep?"

"I'm not sure. Maybe I'll put on the TV with no volume, so it lights up the room a bit. You go on back to bed. I'll see you in the morning."

Jack stood up, but his feet didn't want to move. He sat back down on the side of her bed. "Seeing as I'm already in here, why don't I hang out with you for a little bit. Maybe if you wake up properly and then go back to sleep again, you'll have shaken it off completely." The look on her face showed relief. He'd called it right.

"Are you sure? It's my fault you've been wiped out the last couple of days as it is. You'll be glad to see the back of me so you can finally get a good night's sleep." She tapped the bed. "Here. I'll move over, and you can stretch out better and get more comfortable. This bed is the size of a cruise ship."

Jack moved over, propped up some pillows and leaned back against the headboard. The space he left between them was broad. He was not going to get tempted again.

Mia clicked on the remote, and an infomercial appeared.

Jack groaned. "Jeez. I'd rather have a bad dream than watch one of these shows." He had spoken without thinking and he cringed. That had been in poor taste. He glanced over at Mia. She was smiling, thank goodness.

"I agree." She clicked on the remote again, and kept clicking, until they landed on a movie channel. The movie playing was *The Proposal*, with Sandra Bullock and Ryan Reynolds.

"Remember this movie?" Mia asked. "You probably don't, but we saw it together."

"We did?" Jack wasn't about to tell her he hadn't forgotten. That would make him sound like a complete sap.

"Yes. Initially you didn't want to go because you thought it was a stupid romantic comedy. But you caved, because Ryan Reynolds was in it, and you liked him. It's a cute movie. Predictable, but the acting is good, and so is the location. I think it's somewhere in Canada."

It was strange watching the show with no volume, but they sat quietly for the next twenty minutes and watched the end of the movie. When the credits started to roll, Mia looked at Jack.

"Are you ever going to tell me about who you met since England? Surely there's been someone important in your life. You can't have done any worse than me."

"If that wasn't so true, it would be funny. But I respectfully refuse to laugh as you have had rotten luck." He looked at her sheepishly. "You seriously want to hear about other relationships I've had?"

"Sure, why not? I mean you were a free agent. It's not like you betrayed me or anything. You're only human. I wouldn't expect you to be celibate."

"I'm not going to talk about those kinds of details," he said quickly. Jack didn't want to talk about any of it. He was just humoring her to take her mind off her bad dreams so she could go back to sleep.

"I didn't date much until I finished my Ranger course and graduated. They moved me to Arizona, and I met a yoga instructor, Aspen. She was from LA."

Mia sighed. "Now you're going to tell me she looked like Barbie."

He chuckled. "Yoga Barbie, actually. Aspen was a health guru who'd never eaten a potato chip in her life. She was a good person, and we were together quite a while. I think we both needed the companionship and that worked, but it was never going to be anything more."

"When did you break up?"

"A couple of months before I moved to Arkansas. We were already cooling off. I was thinking about other places I might want to work. It coincided with me catching her in bed with one of her yoga students, and that made the decision much easier." Jack took a quick look at Mia. He expected a sympathetic expression on her face, but she was giggling.

"What are you laughing about? That's pretty tactless of you, Mia."

But instead of her looking guilty, she laughed even harder.

"What on earth is so funny?"

Mia hiccupped a couple of times and then managed to stop long enough to say, "When you said you caught them in bed together, I was imagining what yoga position they were in." She burst into giggles again, and this time it was contagious. Before long they were both laughing, more hysterically than her joke deserved.

Eventually, it subsided. They'd both needed something lighthearted after the past forty-eight hours they'd been through.

"What about you, Mia? Did you meet anyone after I left?" he asked, though he already knew the answer to that, thanks to Dan.

She gave a derisive laugh. "Seriously? I'm no glutton

for punishment, Jack. The last thing I wanted was a relationship. But Dan, remember him?"

Jack nodded. Oh boy, did he remember Dan. The jerk.

"He asked me out the day after you left. I told him no, of course. I wasn't ever interested in him that way. But he hounded me all through university until I moved away on my first job. Eventually I did date, but it was difficult, because I traveled so much with my work. Besides, I didn't want to get tied down."

Jack had stopped listening. He was busy picturing his hands around Dan's neck. That damned lying son of a gun.

"After this is over with, will you go back to Arkansas? Jack?" Mia had already moved on.

He roused himself quickly. The subject of Dan could wait for another time. "Yes, of course. Remember I told you about my grandfather. That was the real reason I moved there in the first place." That part of his life was very far away right now. "What about you? Where will you go?"

Mia shrugged her shoulders. "I'm not sure. I'll need to find a job. I think I've had enough of being an au pair. Maybe I'll check out the Lake District, or even go up north to Scotland. Both places are lovely." She yawned again.

"I think we should call it a night. You're yawning, and we're running out of things to talk about. So, I'm off to bed. If you have trouble getting to sleep, just put your infomercial back on, you'll be out in seconds." Jack made for the door. He was ready to be by himself and think.

"Hey, Jack. Thanks for being a buddy tonight."

Jack made a mock bow. "The pleasure was all mine."

* * *

Back in his room, Jack lay in bed wide-awake. Mia's nonchalant comment about her so-called friend Dan had been a tiny bomb exploding in his head. He'd made a huge decision, years ago, based on the information given to him by a damned liar.

Jack remembered his last conversation with Mia, the night before he left to fly back to the States. They'd had an awful fight. By the time he got home, he'd been determined to get her out of his mind.

In the beginning, it was hard, but little by little, as days turned into weeks, weeks into months, he'd finally gotten a grip. Until Neil's birthday rolled around.

It was a day Jack always struggled with. One he never shared with a living soul, even Mia. But on this particular day, after a really tough exam, Jack had drunk one beer too many, and tried to call her.

Her number was no longer in service. Panicked, he searched for any other British number he had in his phone and ended up calling Dan Finney. Dan had been a tagalong with Mia, Kelly and the others. Jack liked him okay, but the guy had never been overly friendly.

It had been a mistake. By the time Jack hung up the phone, he felt worse. According to Dan, Mia and he were dating, and they'd been serious for a while. Dan said she seemed happy and settled. He said he would take good care of her.

That was all Jack had needed to hear. He hung up, deleted all the British numbers he had in his phone, then drunk more beer until he passed out.

Jack rolled onto his stomach with a groan. Ten years ago he'd broken up with Mia because of the conflict in his mind whenever he thought about his brother. And then, in the only moment he'd had a change of heart, he'd bitten off the lie Dan had told him, hook, line and sinker. He'd given up on the woman he'd fallen for, without even trying. Dan's lie had essentially changed the course of his life.

Until now.

When Mia awoke it took her a few seconds to get her bearings. Once she had, she wished she hadn't. The last place she wanted to be was in a hotel in the heart of Miami.

Glancing at the clock, she was surprised to see it was already well past nine in the morning. After Jack had left her in the middle of the night, she had obviously fallen into a deep sleep.

Unsure what the coming day would bring, Mia traipsed into the bathroom and took a long, hot shower. Feeling human again, she picked through the small assortment of clothing provided, and settled for a pair of jeans and a loose, navy blue T-shirt.

She had no makeup to put on, and her hair was still spiky, but Mia couldn't bring herself to be bothered about how she looked. It wasn't as though anyone would see her but an FBI agent and an ex-boyfriend. That sounded like the start of a bad joke, she thought.

Jeremy was at the breakfast bar with his laptop open and a large mug of coffee within his reach. He glanced up as Mia came into the kitchen.

"You finally got to sleep, then?"

"Yes. I'm sorry I woke you guys up last night. I hope you got more rest?"

"Oh, yeah. I never have trouble falling back asleep.

There have been tiny babies in my life. That will train your sleeping habits to sleep anytime, anywhere."

"I shall immediately forget you have told me that, Jeremy," said Mia. "You are still an unknown entity to me."

"I knew I was going to like you," he said. He pointed over to the cabinets. "There's cereal in there, and croissants, bagels and doughnuts in the yellow cardboard box next to the sink."

"Wow. You FBI people don't mess about. You take your unhealthy food seriously."

"You betcha."

She went over to check them out. "Have you seen Jack?"

"He left about seven. He had to meet Ed for breakfast before he flew back to DC. They were meeting downstairs in the hotel restaurant."

"Do you think it's safe for him to be so visible?"

"That's a good question. Personally, if it was me, I'd lie pretty low. But we have plenty of our people throughout the building, and I think Jack knows that. He probably just wanted another opportunity to talk to Ed."

Mia opened the yellow box and selected a fat, fluffy croissant. The buttery surface stuck to her fingers. She pulled off a piece of paper towel and leaned against the breakfast bar.

"Had you ever met Ed before last night?"

"No. I've seen his name on a recent case we've been looking at, but it was my first time meeting the guy. I liked him. He's obviously made a big impression on your friend Jack." Jeremy raised one eyebrow. "Speaking of Jack, there's some story behind the two of you, am I right?"

Mia raised an eyebrow as well. "Are you asking in your official capacity as an FBI person, or as Jeremy?"

"Jeremy, of course. I just noticed you seem very comfortable around each other, and he certainly has your best interests at heart. I thought he was here because of the investigation. I didn't realize until we were in your room last night that he was your friend."

"We met a long time ago. But we lived in different countries, and lost touch. Ironically, I wound up in the same place that he recently moved to. When the Marinos' thugs showed up at the diner where I worked, I went to Jack for help. Luckily for me, he was willing to do that. Without him, I'd probably be lying dead in an old RV by the Buffalo River."

"I'd call that a damn good friend. I'm glad he could help you, Mia. I know how tough this whole mess is on you, but what you're doing is really important. If more people stepped up in times like this, we'd be able to clean a lot of dirt off the streets."

"I'm not having a good time, that's for sure. But what about you? You do this every day. You've seen a lot worse than I have," Mia said.

"Enough to lose faith in humanity sometimes. The most difficult and gut-wrenching part is dealing with situations involving children. Closely followed by the scourge of human trafficking that goes on every day. It's modern-day slavery. It's despicable. And as far as I'm concerned the people who perpetuate it should be shot."

Mia had not meant to bring up such a sensitive subject. "I'm sorry, Jeremy. I shouldn't have said anything about what your job entails."

"Don't apologize," he said. "It's a fact of life. That's

why what you're doing means so much to me. I am only too happy to be a part of this investigation. I have a great deal of respect for you, Mia."

"I hope I can live up to that." She took a bite of her croissant. "Let me change that statement. I just hope I can live."

Jeremy looked stunned and unsure how to react.

Mia grinned. "All part of the new plan. I'm so sick and tired of being frightened, I've decided to look at it through a humorous slant."

"Good, because I have to tell you something you aren't going to like."

"What's that?"

"I'm taking you to the courthouse at four o'clock today. The judge wants to talk to you."

Mia put down her croissant. Her appetite had disappeared. "Why do I have to do that? I already told you everything I saw."

"I know you did. You were required to answer my questions. But they need an actual deposition, and that has to be done with an attorney present, for you, and for the people we are pressing charges against. It is the usual way things go. The only difference is this one is moving fast because of what it entails."

"Will I be accused of anything because I ran away?"

"No. This only concerns your testimony of what you saw. Once you have been deposed, the bench warrant will go out and everything gets going properly."

Jeremy's words had sucked all Mia's desire to be funny. She shrank back into herself as fear and anxiety began to claw away her insides.

Jeremy's phone buzzed. He read the text. "Jack's coming down the hall," he announced, heading to the door where he peered through the spyhole before unlocking it.

Jack strode in, his face hard and concerned. "We need to talk," he said brusquely to Jeremy. He flicked a glance at Mia. "Can you give us a moment, please?"

She frowned. What was going on? One look at Jack's face told her to do as he asked.

"What?" Jeremy looked shocked.

"Ed got the word right when he was leaving. I don't know who sent it, but under the circumstances, we must take it as a direct threat."

Jeremy grabbed his phone and made a call. He paced back and forth with agitation. Jack pointed down the hall and Jeremy nodded. He went directly to his room, took out his 9mm SIG Sauer semiautomatic from the bedside drawer and put it into his shoulder holster.

Adrenaline pumped through his veins, but he tried to keep his mind clear and focus. The threat was real. Someone deep within either the Feds or the police had leaked information and identified where certain agents were being kept in position. If anyone connected Jeremy Wessels to the Marino case, their location was now vulnerable.

They would have to move Mia, and fast.

Both Jack and the FBI agent knew the layout of the penthouse in detail. In the bedroom where Jack slept, an emergency exit was concealed inside the large walk-in closet. It did not connect to the stairwell of the hotel, but a separate staircase that descended three floors before joining the public stairwell.

He hoped they didn't need it.

Jack stopped outside Mia's room and rapped on the door. She opened it and looked at him, white-faced.

"What's happened?"

He wasn't about to lie. "Security breach. Our location may be compromised. There's a chance we'll have to get out of here in a hurry. Grab anything important and stuff it into your jacket. No bags, okay?"

She nodded and quickly did what he said, then followed him back into the living room.

Jeremy had just put his phone away. "Backup's on the way. They should only be…"

A loud succession of popping noises came from the hallway and outside the door. Jeremy reached inside his jacket and pulled his weapon. He looked at Jack, his eyes bright.

"Get her out of here," he ordered. Then he ran to the wall and hit the fire alarm. It began shrieking.

Jack grabbed Mia's hand and pulled her out of the room. She opened her mouth to speak, her eyes terrified as she looked back to where Jeremy had squatted down behind the sectional, his gun trained on the door.

"Come on," Jack said through gritted teeth. "No time. Run!"

They raced down the hall into Jack's room. He slammed the door and turned the lock, then pulled Mia behind him into the closet. He pushed open the fire door and stepped onto the dimly lit landing, closing the door behind them. Then he grabbed Mia's hand and took off down the stairs.

When they reached the main artery of the stairwell, the alarm was deafening. Jack thought he heard gunshots still being fired from above. People were evacuating from the floors below. They hurried down one flight and then burst through the fire door, onto what Jack thought would be the eighth floor.

Without speaking, he linked his arm through Mia's and walked briskly toward the back of the hotel and the freight elevator. He hit the button, and then stepped to one side next to a pillar and pushed Mia back against the wall behind him.

As soon as the elevator arrived, Jack pulled Mia inside and hit the button to shut the doors, then selected the fourth floor. Only then did he look her in the face.

She was ashen and absolutely terrified. There was no time to console her, nor would it do any good. They both needed to be scared, it would help them get away.

"We're going to the fourth level and into the parking garage," he said. "There's a vehicle waiting and we're going to get in it and drive like crazy until they lose our scent. Got it?"

She nodded obediently and he grabbed her hand again and squeezed it tightly to stop her trembling.

"We've outrun danger before," he reminded her. "You know the drill. Stay calm and follow my lead." He winked.

The elevator seemed to take forever, but Jack still thought they'd got a good start. By now, the FBI would be all over the hotel, but he didn't know whom he could trust, so they were better off getting away from them all.

The elevator stopped with a shudder. The doors opened and Jack again broke into a run, pulling Mia along with him through a set of double metal swing doors and out into the adjoining indoor hotel parking lot.

Jack knew exactly where to go. He had already looked

at the car before meeting with Ed the previous day. He found it within a minute, they both got in and he started the engine.

No one followed them out of the parking lot. They'd been lucky, Jack thought. Still, just to be safe, he had Mia stay down low on the back seat and out of sight.

Jack cleared the downtown area and randomly picked a highway, anything to get them into the suburbs. Once he merged onto one, he called Ed.

"Thank God you made it out. And Mia?"

"Yes. What have you heard?"

"Wessels has been shot. But I'm not sure of his condition."

"Damn."

"One of the guards is in a bad way, and there are two others with minor gunshot wounds. Three perps down, but in no condition to talk and maybe others as yet unidentified."

"Any word on where the leak came from?"

"Not yet. But with this many officers down, this will blow the lid off whoever's responsible. Where are you guys, Jack?"

"Hell if I know. Let's see," Jack muttered, looking around for another sign. "I'm on Highway 836, wherever that is."

"Hang on. Okay, here we go. You need to stay on it until you can get onto 41 West. You got that? 41 West. That will get you to Naples in just under two hours. I want you out of Miami. I've just cleared security at the airport in Miami. Get to Naples, find a hole-in-the-wall and call me again. I'll come to you."

"Got it." Jack hung up. He glanced back over one shoulder. "You okay back there, Mia?"

"I've had better days."

Jack smiled. Thank God she wasn't hysterical. She had every right to be.

"What was Ed saying about Jeremy?"

"I'm not going to lie to you, Mia. He was shot. But I don't know his condition."

"No!"

He could hear the pain in her voice. "Jeremy's an experienced agent, and he was wearing a bulletproof vest. Chances are he's going to be fine, so we mustn't get worked up about it. The guy was protecting me and you, Mia. That's his job, and he knew what could be at stake. As soon as we get stopped somewhere, we'll get more information about him. Ed's going to meet us in Naples. We've got about an hour and a half of driving. Then I'm stopping at a friend's until Ed lets me know where he is."

Their eyes met in the rearview mirror. Mia said. "Do you know people in *every* city in America, Jack?"

Mia's neck ached. She'd wrenched it jumping into the car and then lying down for so long. She was completely out of sorts. Her life had become insane. Everything was spinning out of control, and she was lost, helpless in the vortex.

The episode at the hotel in Miami was like shows she'd watched on TV. How had she ended up in this ugly mess? And what about Jeremy? Her heart ached at the thought of that nice man lying wounded in the hotel room. What if he died? What about the children she knew he had?

Mia would never forgive herself if anything happened

to Agent Wessels. So many people had placed their lives in danger because of one bad family. It was maddening. Why couldn't she go rogue, like they did in the movies, where a woman would exact retribution on all those who had hurt her.

Reality was dismaying. She was a pathetic, unarmed woman, hiding in the back seat of a compact car, on the run like a coward, yet again. Mia didn't think she could keep this up. The utter fear and panic she had felt when the gunshots were fired outside their room would never leave her, like the night when Jeannie had been stabbed.

How she wished she was a braver person. Why couldn't she be more like Jack?

He hadn't said much since talking to Ed. Mia understood he needed time to think and get his head clear. He was the brains of their escape, after all.

She looked out the window and felt the tug of home. She was beginning to think she might never get there. Judging by what she'd seen so far, how were they going to get through this alive? The thought was disturbing, frightening, and she struggled with it. Feeling so scared, stuck in a situation completely out of her control, Mia could understand why some people gave up and just walked toward the bullets. She'd only been on the run for a few weeks. What was it like to do that your entire life?

"Do you need me to stop? We're getting close to a gas station," asked Jack.

Their eyes met in the rearview mirror once again. "I'm okay, thank you."

"Great. I'm just going to push through, we're only twenty-five minutes out from Jan's. She's who we're going to see. Jan lived in Tulsa back when I was a kid, and we went to the same schools growing up. She moved to Naples after she graduated college. I reconnected with her at our ten-year high school reunion, and we've stayed in touch since. I don't really want to drag her into this, but if we go anywhere else, we'll have to use my ID, or some form of payment, and I don't want the exposure. We'll go to her house, wait for Ed to call, and go from there."

"How do you know Jan will be there? Maybe she's out or at work."

"Jan works from home. It's possible she's out running errands, but I'd rather chance it and see what happens. If she's not home, we'll hide out in a restaurant or something to kill time."

Their conversation ended and Mia returned to getting lost in her morbid thoughts.

Jan's housing division reminded Mia of the *Golden Girls* set from the TV show. The neighborhood was lovely. Spotless sidewalks, manicured lawns, flower beds teeming with exotic plants that looked as though they came from another planet. Mia loved the abundance of palm trees, and the houses were gorgeous.

"Wow. This place is beautiful. It's so clean and tidy, you could eat off the pavement."

Jack shrugged. "It's much different than Miami. There's a lot of neighborhoods just like this in Florida. They all look the same to me. A little too crowded for my tastes. And no fun in hurricane season either."

"I could put up with that if I lived somewhere this pretty and so close to the sea. They get much nicer weather as well, overall."

"You say that because you're a Brit. You guys like the

sun and heat. Trust me, living in a place that doesn't have definitive seasons gets boring."

"Sounds like a really tough existence," Mia said with sarcasm.

Jack turned the car into the driveway of a beige bungalow with a dark red roof. There was no grass in the front yard, just decorative gravel surrounding large beds full of big-leafed, green plants.

"I'll wait here while you see if she's home," suggested Mia before Jack could say anything.

He left the engine running and went to the front door.

The large oak door swung open and revealed a tall, slender woman dressed in white linen who gasped in surprise when she saw Jack standing on her doorstep. Mia couldn't hear what was said, but the woman pulled Jack into a hug and Mia felt a twinge of jealousy. Was this a school sweetheart from yesteryear?

Jack said something else and pointed over to the car. The woman nodded.

He came back to the car and turned off the engine. "Come and meet Jan. You're going to like her."

Chapter 11

Naples, Florida

The inside of Jan's house was stunning. It reminded Mia of a Spanish villa in Valencia she'd stayed in while being an au pair, with its red-tiled floors and whitewashed walls. The furniture in Jan's house was some of the loveliest furniture she had ever seen. Each piece looked authentically Spanish and extremely expensive. Heavy, carved chests, a sideboard that easily had to be a century or two old, wrought iron sconces on the wall and beautiful pictures painted to look like icons.

They stepped down into a sunken den consisting of two dark brown leather sectionals facing each other and a square wooden coffee table in the center.

"Have a seat," said Jan. "Jack, you need to introduce me to your friend."

"Jan Stanley, this is Mia Jones. Mia's a friend visiting from the UK. I've just picked her up in Miami and we're meeting up with my boss shortly. He hasn't arrived yet, and I'm waiting for his call, so I thought I'd stop by on the chance you were home and say hello."

"I'm so glad you did," said Jan. She turned her attention to Mia, who thought Jan a very striking woman.

She had straight, chin-length hair, a lovely shade of mahogany. Jan would never be called pretty, but her features were terribly striking. With pale blue eyes, an aquiline nose and a generous mouth, she definitely caught your attention.

"It's nice to meet you, Jan. Thank you for making us so welcome."

"Please, it's my pleasure. Such a delightful surprise to see Jack at my door." She threw a glance at him. "Though I am annoyed he didn't tell me he was coming to Florida. We could have made some plans, you could have stayed a while. But I'm glad you guys at least had time to stop by. Why don't I get us something cold to drink. Is lemonade all right with you both?"

Mia's mouth watered. "That sounds wonderful, thank you."

The tall woman stepped out of the den into the dining and kitchen area.

"So," said Jack. "What have you been up to since we last talked?"

Over the chink of ice falling into glass, Jan responded, "I've just released a new book, and I'm taking a couple of weeks off before I get busy again."

Jack had not mentioned his friend was an author. Mia was intrigued. She watched as Jan's willowy figure carried a small tray back into the den. She set it down on the table and poured three glasses of lemonade and handed one to each of her guests.

Mia took a sip and exclaimed, "This is absolutely delicious. It tastes like these lemons just got picked from the tree."

Jan smiled, obviously pleased by the compliment.

"Well, actually, they were—just yesterday. I have an amazing lemon tree in my yard. It's been very prolific this year."

Mia couldn't imagine having a lemon tree growing in your garden. The most exotic thing they'd ever had growing in her childhood back garden was a plum tree. Lemons didn't stand a chance growing in a climate like the UK's.

She looked at the attractive woman in the white linen outfit. Jan wore bulky jewelry, all solid silver in a rustic design. Fat silver hoops hung from her earlobes, many of her fingers sported chunky rings, and every time she moved her arm several silver bracelets jangled. She *looked* like a writer. The word *bohemian* came to mind.

"Where do you live in the UK?" she asked, leaning back against the cushioned back of the sofa.

"I'm from a place called Kingston-Upon-Thames. It's in Surrey."

"That's just down the river from Richmond, isn't it? I have been in the area many times." She looked at Jack. "Didn't you go over there right after college?"

"I did." He sounded surprised that she remembered. "That's where I met Mia."

"And now Mia is visiting you? How come Florida? I thought you said you were moving to Arkansas?"

"I did. I live there now. But I had business here, which coincided with Mia's visit, and I brought her along for the ride."

Mia watched their exchange and wondered why Jack wasn't telling his friend the truth. He'd shared some of their story with his friends in Louisiana. Perhaps that was because Beth had once been a ranger, and he trusted her and knew she would not let anything slip. It was different with someone who led a life outside of law enforcement, she supposed. He probably decided the less Jan knew, the better.

"And where is the meeting you mentioned? Anywhere close?"

Jack didn't bat an eyelid. "My boss is arriving this afternoon, so I'm waiting for him to let me know the venue. It will be where he's staying, I imagine."

Mia thought she'd help steer the conversation in a different direction. "Jan, what kind of books do you write? I'm an avid reader."

Jan smiled warmly. She had very white teeth. "I'm a ghost writer," she said.

"Wow." Mia was genuinely impressed. "That has to be really hard to do."

Jan shrugged thin shoulders. "To be perfectly honest, all writing is much harder than people realize. There is just so much to think about. When you write for another person, it gets more complicated because you have to climb inside their head and pick out the important stuff to say. Sometimes, my clients disagree with my suggestions and think they know better than I do. So it can be stressful. However, I don't have to come up with a storyline, because they have already lived it. I just have to make sure my perception of their story is theirs and not mine."

"I would be terrible at that," chimed in Jack. "I can't even keep a shopping list straight." They all laughed.

"How's Sid doing? Has he started treatment yet?"

Mia guessed they were talking about Jack's grandfather. She hadn't known his name.

"In another week. He's got a great attitude, though, and I think they've caught it early enough to get him in remission. He's a tough old guy, and he's in a good place mentally to fight this."

"Have you met Sid, Mia?"

Mia shook her head.

Jan continued, "He's a grumpy old man who doesn't tolerate fools and speaks his mind without hesitation. I've been a target once or twice, and I still bear the scars."

Jack looked at Mia. "She's exaggerating. Jan just got pissed one evening because my grandfather told her she looked like a hooker."

"Which I did," Jan admitted.

A clock chimed somewhere. It was almost three o'clock. Jack stood up. "Jan, would you mind if I stepped out back and made a quick call?"

"Be my guest," she said, refilling Mia's glass.

When Jack had gone out of the back door, she turned her gaze to look directly at Mia, who was taking a sip of the delectable drink.

"Are you in love with him?"

Mia almost choked. She coughed, and then set down her lemonade. She met the other woman's eyes. "Why would you ask that?"

"Because it's written all over your face. Are you two a couple?"

"No," Mia said quickly. "We were for five minutes many years ago. Now he's just my friend." A thought occurred to her. "How about you and Jack? Were you an item back in school?"

Jan threw back her head and laughed. "Good God, no! I thought he was horrible most of the time. He was always more interested in insects and nature than girls. Although he was terribly good-looking." Jan grinned, and Mia found herself starting to like the somewhat aloof woman.

"I dated Neil. He was much more my type. Tall, handsome and so intelligent."

"Who's Neil?" asked Mia.

Jan's dark brows drew together, and she looked puzzled. "Neil? Jack's brother, of course."

The door opened and Jack came back inside. Mia was still registering what Jan had said. So, she had been right the whole time. Jack did have a brother and that was who she'd seen in all the pictures at his mom's house. Then why had Jack never mentioned Neil?

"I talked to Ed, and he's ready for us to meet him as soon as we can get there." He didn't sit back down.

Taking his cue, both women got to their feet, and Jan led them back down the hall to the front door.

Jan gave Mia a brief hug but hung on to Jack for a while. "I miss you, Jack," she said. "Don't be a stranger, okay?" She let him go, and Mia couldn't help but notice the striking woman had tears in her eyes.

As soon as the car reversed down the driveway and was back on the road, Mia asked, "Where are we going?"

"To the Naples Beach Resort, it's only a few miles from here and it's where we're meeting Ed."

Mia remained quiet. She longed to ask Jack about his brother. The one he had never mentioned. She was beginning to think something must have happened to Neil, because no one ever talked about him. But now was not the right time. It could wait. For the immediate future they needed to focus on staying alive.

* * *

When they turned off the main road toward the hotel, Mia thought she had died and gone to Hollywood. The driveway itself seemed a mile long. They made a final turn and pulled up next to a massive fountain in front of the building.

They'd passed flamingos on the grounds and seen a golf course in the distance. The place screamed extravagance. Mia had never seen anything this fancy.

She let out a whistle. "Your department must have a huge budget if this is where they put their employees up."

Jack laughed. "You must be joking. Ed has probably played golf here a time or two, depending on who he had to kiss up to. There's no way he's actually staying here. But it is a very secure place with such an elite clientele. It'll be because he thinks it's a safe venue, big enough where we can talk privately, undetected."

Jack stopped the car outside the main reception, and a young man appeared like a genie, holding out his hand for the keys. Jack handed them to the valet, collected a ticket and led Mia inside the building.

This was certainly how the other half got to live. Everywhere Mia turned her head she saw opulent elegance. The outside of the building resembled a French château, and this was continued into the interior.

The decor was not her personal taste, but one had to appreciate how beautiful the pieces were. From the antique furniture to ornate mirrors and crystal chandeliers that dropped like tears from the ceilings, the hotel boasted wealth.

Jack made inquiries at the front desk, and they were led into a large, formal dining room. The tables were currently vacant, but they were escorted past them and into a private room at the back.

Ed Mills sat looking out the window, the wineglass in front of him almost empty. He did not get up but smiled at Mia as she and Jack joined him at the table.

"You two are a sight for sore eyes. I'm glad you got here in one piece. Mia, I am so sorry you were in danger on the FBI's watch. That was never meant to happen. Obviously, it's all imploded and they're doing everything they can to flush out whoever did this. The question is what do we do in the meantime? Technically, you're their witness, but for the time being I would feel uncomfortable about you being anywhere but in Jack's capable hands."

"What are you saying Ed," asked Jack. "You want me to keep her out of the way, from everyone?"

The older man nodded, his brows knotted in a frown. "Just for a couple of days. Look, son, if we were in DC, I'd have all kinds of ideas and options. But you know as well as I do that can't happen, because this whole thing is about Miami and not my jurisdiction. Let's get a recorded statement from Mia, with a legitimate time stamp. Then you two need to disappear for a bit. There's plenty of places along the coastline where you can be invisible. If you steer clear of anywhere with big hotels, find somewhere old and not trendy, I reckon you'd be hard to find. Until we have a better idea who's in the frame and responsible for the breach in security, no one needs to know where you are, and that includes me." Ed reached down to his briefcase and pulled out a thick, yellow envelope.

"In here there's cash, a burner phone and a couple of fake IDs for you both. Shut off your own phone so they can't ping you, and stay off the internet. The only number on the cell phone is mine. Call me tomorrow at six in the evening your time. Then I should be able to advise you what has transpired."

"Wait," Mia interrupted. Both men looked at her as though just remembering she was there. "If Jack hides out with me will that compromise his job? It's all very well my running away from the bad guys, but I don't want him in trouble or getting prosecuted for running from the FBI."

"That's a damn good question," Ed said. "In normal circumstances, you're right, that might bring a charge with it. But in this situation there is reasonable motive to run, when your life has been threatened. Because your hotel room was attacked and had to be defended by government agents, there's no questioning the events necessitating flight."

Mia nodded, then asked. "How is Jeremy, I mean Agent Wessels?"

Ed's face grew serious. "That's one brave sonofagun. He took three bullets, and thank goodness, they all hit bone. I'm sure he wouldn't agree he was lucky, the man's in a lot of pain. But he's alive and he'll heal in time."

Mia felt tears pricking her eyes. She blinked quickly. No more crying.

"Here." Ed handed Jack the envelope. Then, a set of keys.

"Another vehicle?" Jack said. "After the economy one we just drove, are we going up in style?"

Ed looked affronted. Then he grinned. "This one's a pickup."

Jack had always considered himself a Ford guy, but the Dodge was pretty nice. The truck was a couple of years old, and not flashy; they didn't need to draw attention to themselves after all, and he liked that the windows were tinted.

They parted ways with Ed, who was trying, yet again, to fly back to the capital. Before leaving the hotel, Ed recorded Mia giving a verbal statement about what she had seen the night of Jeannie's murder. Now there was nothing else to do but lie low for the next forty-eight hours.

"So, we're just going to show up without any reservation at a random hotel? Have I got that right?" Mia asked Jack when they were back on the road once again.

"That's the plan. I haven't had time to canvass this part of Florida and see what our options are. Maybe a last-minute thing is best. If *we* don't even know where we're staying, then the bad guys don't have a hope in hell, right?"

"You've got a point." Mia looked out the window for a few seconds and then looked back at him again. "I have a request. Considering we are currently knocking on death's door, can we stay somewhere close to the ocean? It doesn't have to be anything fancy. I don't care if I sleep in an RV. I've been living in one for the last few weeks, remember?"

"You know what, that's actually not a bad idea."

"What? I was only kidding about the RV."

"Maybe so. But think about it. When you check into a hotel, you become part of everything public. I know we have fake IDs, but even those get put on the hotel's database, a restaurant you eat in, maybe even where we park this truck. If we went to a campground or something like that, it's much more private. There, all they care about is you're paying for the site, and you are on the designated spot you're given. If you pay up and don't leave a mess, it's like we were never there."

"As much as I hate to say this, Jack, you make several good points."

"Okay. So, let's discuss your level of comfort, Miss…"

Mia quickly pulled out her new ID from her jeans pocket. "Baker. Toni Baker." She groaned. "That's not a very interesting name, although Toni's not bad. What's your new name?"

"Zachary Dean. And we should probably start using those first names at least."

"All right, Zach. As far as sleeping arrangements, I could do a tent if I had to, but I'd rather not. A camper would be fine, an RV or maybe they've even got cabins like they do in Jasper."

"I think when it's located near the sea, they're called cottages. They won't be made of logs, but white clap-board, complete with picket fence."

"Maybe we can find something like that? Want me to look at the map?"

He nodded. "I'm pretty useless without my phone any-more. That's a good lesson in reminding me to go back to basics after all this is over with. How good are you at reading maps?"

Mia had the roadmap of Florida spread out on her lap. "There're a lot of blue roads on here."

"Great. Those are rivers and streams, Mia."

"I'm kidding," she said. "I may not have been a studly Junior Ranger, but I was a very intelligent Girl Guide. I too can build a fire, and I can also boil water for tea on an open flame."

"Perhaps you should be signed up for *Survivor*," Jack said and grinned.

"I thought I already was."

"Touché, Toni Baker. Now then, check out the coastline."

Chapter 12

The final destination was Haven. Just slightly off the tourist track, Haven was a small town with an even smaller beach. Mia thought it quite picturesque, as the architecture looked old-fashioned and dated, like a throwback to the sixties.

Along the way they passed one campsite with a sign that said Closed for the Season. After passing two more that were also closed, they weighed their options. When they arrived in Haven and came upon a small motel, Jack made a quick decision. It looked like the kind of place most people would drive past. An L-shaped building with an office, and several adjoining rooms in one long row, all with their own outside door and parking place. Haven wasn't a top destination for tourists in Mia's opinion.

They checked in using Jack's fake ID and the false license plates on the truck. The lady at the front desk looked as though she'd rather be doing anything other than working there. She showed little interest in the new guests.

Their room was second to the end, and the number on the door was 18. Jack had requested a room with two full-size beds, and Mia was relieved to see that was in fact the case. She was less thrilled with the decor of the interior.

"Whoever decorated this room bought everything off a clearance rack at a thrift store." She wiped her hand across the surface of the dressing table and looked at the dust on her fingertips.

"My, my, Toni. Aren't you becoming the motel snob?" He grinned and Mia could not help doing the same. She laid her jacket on the bed.

"Don't you think there's something wrong with us? I mean, here we are on the run from not only gangsters, but law enforcement as well. And we're cutting up jokes in the tackiest motel room I think I've ever been in. We've lost the plot, *Zach*."

Jack was busy opening all the drawers and examining the room and the adjoining bathroom. "I think they call that survival mode in psychology. It's our brain's way of coping with an overwhelming situation."

Mia groaned. "I much preferred my theory. I'd rather I was going mad than just coping. At least if I was losing my mind, I'd forget about what's really happening."

Jack came out of the bathroom. "Everything looks okay. How about we walk into town and pick up some supplies." He stared at her for a moment. "What do you think about putting a different color in your hair?"

She feigned a pout and touched her head. "What, you don't like me as a blonde now? I thought all gentlemen preferred blondes?"

"The keyword being *gentlemen*. And no, personally I do not. I just thought it might be a good idea in case they know what you look like now. Or we can get something to cover it. Actually, both of us wearing hats and sunglasses wouldn't be a bad thing. I saw a few stores as we came through town, so why don't we do that real quick?"

Mia enjoyed the short walk to the shops. It was nice being outside after the past few days. Without a regular highway coming through the area, everything seemed close together and she did not feel as vulnerable. The scent of the ocean was everywhere, and the air salty when it hit your tongue.

They went inside the first tourist shop they came to. Jack spent some time picking out baseball caps with the name of the town emboldened on them, some cheap sunglasses and a couple of T-shirts for them both.

A few doors down was a sizable surf shop, although Jack wondered why. What he had seen of the water so far didn't necessitate any kind of board. But this shop had a variety of clothing that was reasonably priced. He told Mia to pick out a bathing suit and a pair of shorts and T-shirt. He did the same, since they had not had time to bring anything with them.

On the way back to the motel, they stopped at a small convenience store and picked up a few toiletries before finally heading back to their room.

Though the beach in Haven was small, its proximity to town was extremely convenient. Behind the motel's building, a path led straight down to the ocean. On this side of the gulf, the sand was fine and pale. Mia loved the feel of the warm grains filling the gaps between her toes. It was so different to the pebbled beaches of home.

When they reached the beach it was almost dinnertime. Consequently, there was no one in the immediate vicinity, just a few people scattered here and there further away. Jack spread out the towels they'd brought from their room. He looked over at Mia, who like him had put on a bathing suit with a T-shirt and shorts on top.

Jack looked up at the sky. "The day is coming to a close, so I guess if we're going to swim we should do it now. Afterward, we'll go back to the motel, and I'll call us in some dinner. Sound good?"

"Whatever you say, Zach." Mia couldn't help herself.

Jack rolled his eyes. Then he reached up and tugged off his T-shirt.

Mia's eyes were immediately riveted on his naked chest. Jack's skin was the color of caramel. There was not a strand of hair on his torso, and the contours of his body were smooth, lean and beautiful. He didn't appear to notice her scrutiny, but just grinned, then turned and ran into the water.

Mia didn't hesitate. She pulled off her shorts and T-shirt, and before giving herself time to feel self-conscious, ran in after him.

"I keep forgetting how warm the water is in Florida," she said, wading in until she was chest-deep. Mia dipped her head backward to wet it. "Whenever I'd go swimming in England, I used to watch my hands turn blue with cold."

"I remember it being like that in Cornwall when you and I met. I got the shock of my life when I first got in the sea. I thought I was going to lose my toes to frostbite. And it was even a hot day. No wonder you Brits are made of such stern stuff. Ice-cold oceans, too much rain *and* bad food. That'll make a person tough."

Mia held out her hand and pushed the water toward him, splashing him in the face. "Ungrateful colonial. That sterner stuff is what got you lot over here in the first place. It's interesting how quickly you forget the people responsible for your success. The fact my nation has forgiven you for talking so strangely and making bad tea, shows the depth of character it takes to be British."

Jack laughed out loud. "I've missed your sense of humor," he said. "Even though I was often the target of your stinging wit and razor-sharp words, you always did make me laugh."

"It just shows you have good taste," said Mia. She turned and began to swim parallel to the beach.

The warm water engulfed her skin and felt marvelous. What was it about the briny ocean that made you feel it washed away your troubles? Swimming through the waves and tasting salt on her tongue, Mia felt like a mermaid with nothing but the sea before her to disappear into.

Something tickled underneath her stomach. She tried to yell but swallowed water instead. Immediately she stopped swimming and trod water, looking around for a fish or a large piece of seaweed, but it was Jack.

He grinned like an idiot, and she punched him, missing his chest and hitting his shoulder.

"That wasn't funny, Brannon. I thought you were a fish."

He jiggled his eyebrows.

"You look daft."

He narrowed his eyes. "Perhaps I'm a stingray."

"More like Nemo."

They both laughed. Then Mia sighed. She looked up at the sky and watched a couple of seagulls at play. The sun had dropped and looked huge. Soon the ombré color would darken to red. How she loved sunsets on the beach. But then everyone did.

Jack challenged her to a race, and they set off at a fast swim. He beat her, but Mia put up a good effort. While they bobbed in the water, catching their breath, they watched a handful of beachgoers packing up their belongings for the day.

"Ready to go back to the motel?" Jack asked.

"Not yet. Could we stay a little while longer and watch the sunset? We've been cooped up inside, or stuck in a car for the last two days. If you think it's safe enough, I'd like to sit out here for a bit."

"That should be okay. There's hardly anyone around and we're close to our room. I'm going to get out and dry off."

Mia stayed put, watching him wade into the shallows and up the beach to their towels. Strange how Jack had been out of her life all these years. And then out of the blue, fate, or circumstance, had thrown them back together.

Now she was older, more mature, Mia saw why they had been such a good fit, even ten years ago. Yet life never made it easy for some people. Everything had been perfect for them to meet and fall in love, only the time hadn't been right.

What about now? What was between them? Surely it was something because she felt it. Mia was in no position to call it by name, especially after the way he'd acted in Louisiana when they kissed.

Did she love Jack Brannon? If she were honest with herself, yes, she'd never really stopped. But how could she know for sure? Mia had felt a lot for Carlos too, at the start, and look what happened there. No, she remonstrated. That was unfair. Carlos was charming, handsome and determined to have her. Of course, she'd had feelings for him, or she would never have stayed with the man. But Mia had never called it love.

Deep down, she had known her future was never going to be in Miami, or even the US. But for once, she'd given herself permission to throw caution to the wind, lived in the moment, allowed herself that luxury after a year of hell.

Mia laughed.

Well, she was paying for it now.

Surprisingly, their down-market motel used big, soft towels. Both Mia and Jack lay on theirs, eyes closed, enjoying the warmth of the sinking sun as it dried their skin. They hadn't spoken much, each lost in their own thoughts. At one point, Mia heard Jack's breathing slow, and she suspected he'd fallen asleep.

She turned her head. In the distance, a small family packed up to leave, and one of the children burst into tears.

Jack sat upright so fast his sunglasses fell off.

"Cool it, soldier," Mia said in a fake American accent. "It's not the enemy, it's a toddler. Go back to sleep."

Jack picked up his glasses and pushed them onto the crown of his head. "I wasn't sleeping."

"Zachary…what have you been told about lying."

He grinned, and her heart melted a little bit. Part of the reason she found Jack so attractive was his apparent ignorance about the effect he had on women.

Mia pulled herself up to a sitting position. The sun

sank lower on the horizon, and the clouds looked like pink cotton candy sprinkled with fairy dust. The water glittered like liquid crystals and the tranquil beauty of the scene stole her breath away.

Jack got to his feet, picked up his towel and shook out the sand. He pulled on his shirt and shorts, folded his sunglasses and tucked them in his back pocket. "Want to take a stroll along the beach before we go to our room?"

"Yes. That would be nice." Mia got up, put her T-shirt and shorts on, shook out her towel and threw it over her shoulder as well. They went down to the shoreline to paddle as they walked.

An egret, a few steps in front of them, tiptoed in the shallows searching for a snack. The gentle sound of waves rolling in was soothing, and Mia inhaled the fresh, salty air, loving how clean it tasted.

What was it about being near the sea that made a person feel so in harmony with nature? She had always felt a connection to the ocean, as though she herself had emerged from it when she was born.

"It's been a nice break this evening," said Jack. He stopped to pick up a perfect, dusky rose shell and handed it to Mia. "Here you are. Now you can't say I never gave you a gift." He grinned playfully.

She took the shell from him and examined it in her palm. "It's so pretty. There's something so pure about the colors near the ocean."

"It's a far cry from what I'm used to. I grew up swimming in muddy lakes, where the red dirt stained your towel and the bottom of your feet."

She shuddered. "I'm not a lake person. There must be motion in water for me. The Buffalo River is like that, isn't it? Clear and always on the move. I think the flow of a current makes me feel like I'm going somewhere." She gestured to the horizon before them. "That's why I like being by the sea. You look out there and all you see is water, and you know there's a big world beyond where your eyes can see. For some reason that really speaks to me."

Suddenly a larger wave crested and rolled in with force. She shrieked with laughter and the two of them turned to run closer to shore. Mia stumbled, and Jack automatically grabbed her arms, pulling her up against him roughly so she wouldn't fall and get soaked.

Laughing, she was still in his arms when their eyes met. His thick black lashes were damp from where he'd been splashed, with little droplets hanging on the ends. His face was wet.

Mia licked her bottom lip and tasted salt. She saw him look at her mouth and she swallowed.

Jack bent his head closer, and Mia made a small gasp as his lips touched hers. His mouth was salty too. His lips were warm and full and hungry. He drew her closer still, and raised one hand to press against the back of her head to make the kiss deeper.

Mia couldn't get close enough. Their mouths danced together having been apart for far too long. The kiss was slow, passionate, and carried a message both could not ignore.

Jack pulled away, but his forehead still touched hers and he was breathing hard. "God help me, Mia. I don't want to stop."

She moved her head back and looked up into his eyes.

In the beautiful sunset, desire lit tiny flames in his dark irises.

She sighed. Her voice thick with need. "I don't want to stop either."

This time, it was she who leaned forward, and their mouths met once again. As the waves rolled in then trickled back out to sea, so the hot fire of passion between them became impossible to ignore. When the long kiss ended, Jack took her towel and put it with his on one shoulder. He held Mia's hand tightly and led her back up the beach toward the motel.

Neither spoke a word. It was as if ten years had fallen away and been carried out to sea. They were two people. A man and a woman. Walking along a sandy shore in the sunset. And though they were in Florida, in the United States of America, in their hearts, both were two young people on a beautiful beach in Cornwall once again.

Chapter 13

Haven, Florida

Jack had always been a light sleeper, a trait that came in handy in his line of work. He opened his eyes and stared up at the ceiling fan, which labored in slow circles. Lying on his back, he turned his head to look down at Mia, nestled snugly in the crook of his arm.

She slept deeply. He grinned. Hardly surprising because they'd been up most of the night. She seemed so young in slumber. Her eyes, beautiful when open, were still lovely closed as the sweep of her lashes formed a perfect semicircle against her skin. Her nose had freckles, just like he remembered all that time ago. Now they were more noticeable, no doubt because of the sunshine yesterday.

Her arm sprawled across his waist and unconsciously he took his fingers and traced the line of muscle stretching from her shoulder to her wrist. Under the cotton sheet, Jack felt the length of her body, velvet skin pressed against his own. His body reacted to the thought. He closed his eyes and savored the moment. He was at peace.

When he woke again, he heard the shower running in the adjacent bathroom. Jack blinked, then rubbed his eyes, surprised he'd fallen back asleep. He picked up his watch from the nightstand. Was it really nine thirty in the morning?

He pushed back the sheet, got out of bed and stretched. He was still tired, but more content than he'd been in a very long time. What he wouldn't give for them not to be on the run. In a normal life, this could have been the two of them on vacation at the beach. Other than staying in a crappy motel, everything else here was perfect. Jack could only imagine how wonderful a few days with Mia would be. But there was the small problem of someone wanting to kill her.

Mia stood under the spray of hot water, relishing the sensation as it woke up each pore of her body. As corny as it seemed, she felt half-asleep, in the midst of enjoying a delicious dream. Everything that happened after the kiss on the beach had only deepened her feelings for the man who'd stolen her heart a decade earlier.

Jack was a generous, passionate lover. A gentle and tender man who had not just taken her to bed but made love to her. With him she'd felt beautiful, oblivious of what she didn't like about her body. In his presence she'd felt like a goddess.

She did not hear him come into the bathroom but felt a sudden blast of cooler air. The door of the shower clicked open, and she turned.

Jack stepped in and closed it behind him. He held out his arms and she stepped into his embrace.

It was well past noon when they left the motel room in search of food. Neither wanted to leave the idyllic oasis of being alone, but hunger won the day.

Wednesday, in October, was not tourist season, therefore the streets in town were quiet. Due to the temperate weather, most of the shops had their doors wide-open to the street, and restaurants offered outside dining everywhere they looked.

They settled on a small, rustic-looking place with a billboard offering a variety of seafood fresh from the ocean. Jack refused to sit out on the street, claiming it was too unprotected, but they picked a table closest to an open window where they could at least enjoy some fresh air, and Jack had a good view of the street.

A waiter brought them the menu, and they ordered drinks. They perused the choices, both ravenous from lack of food and sleep. At first, Jack threatened to get oysters, but Mia told him she would travel on alone if he did. Reluctantly he relented and ordered gulf shrimp and cheese grits, while Mia picked grouper and scallops.

They chatted amiably, still unable to keep their eyes from each other, the heat of their lovemaking a tangible presence between them. Eventually their meals were brought out. Conversation ceased as both Jack and Mia tucked in. Their waiter brought a basket of sourdough bread and refilled their drinks.

"I had no idea I was this hungry," said Mia, buttering her second chunk of bread.

"Would you like me to explain why you've developed such a healthy appetite today?"

"No," she retorted quickly. "Nor do I want you to be flirtatious. It's creepy. You're not that type. I much prefer you when you're your natural self. I've come to depend on your bad manners and sarcasm."

"Ouch." He pretended to be offended. Jack took a sip of

his drink. "We have to get in touch with Ed at six o'clock this evening. But until then, we're free agents, although that sounds hypocritical under the circumstances. I don't know what happens next, but I'm guessing it will involve more time in a vehicle and being holed up somewhere not as nice as this. So, what would you like to do this afternoon while we're still invisible."

Mia dabbed at her mouth with a napkin. "I saw a hair salon down there." She pointed out the window down the street. "How about I go there next and have them color my hair. I really don't want to do it myself again—it's a hassle and it makes an awful mess."

"I don't know if you should. It might be dangerous staying out so long."

"That's silly. We're sitting here, aren't we? I don't think anyone's going to expect me to be in a small town salon getting my hair done when we're on the run for our lives."

"Fair point. How long will it take?"

She shrugged. "Once they get the stuff on my hair, about forty-five minutes."

"Okay. That works." He finished what was on his plate and pushed it away. Jack stared at her across the table. Her eyes were bright. They were blue rather than gray this morning, and her blond hair was sticking out in all the wrong directions. He thought she was beautiful.

Memories tumbled into his mind, no longer focused on their history, but of the recent past. The night they had spent together and even this morning in a warm steamy shower were images and feelings he would never forget. His body gave an instant response.

He loved her—had never stopped, even when he'd thought she'd moved on with her life without him. Jack understood some of the reasons why he'd tried to hide his true feelings. Yes, he had been conflicted about his education, his future, and it being the wrong time to start an international relationship. But it had always been more than that.

Neil.

Somehow, everything always came back to his brother. How could Jack be legitimately happy, excited about his future and loving every moment of life, when Neil did not have the same opportunity?

It didn't matter that it hadn't been Jack's fault. He hadn't been the one behind the wheel that night. Yet his guilt would never leave because he had been drunk. Sixteen years old, with a belly full of beer he wasn't supposed to be drinking. Neil had been drinking too. Even more than his little brother. Plenty more than he should before getting behind the wheel of a very fast car.

He'd put Jack in the back of the Mustang and buckled him in, always looking out for his kid brother, but hadn't looked out for himself.

Neil had died on impact. Not wearing his seat belt, he'd been ejected through the windshield like a stone from a catapult.

"Are you all right?" Mia's hand touched his forearm and startled Jack out of his somber thoughts.

He snapped out of it. "Yeah, I'm good. We ready to go?"

She nodded and Jack gestured for the waiter to bring their check. He left the money on the table, and they headed toward the hairdresser.

Mia told the stylist to leave her hair wet. It had felt great having the mess she'd made trimmed up by someone who knew what they were doing.

Jack had gone next door into a beach store and bought a couple of items. Then he'd loitered outside the hairdresser, uncomfortable getting too far away from Mia.

When she finally came out onto the street he did a double take. She looked stunning. Jack didn't know the first thing about women's hairstyles. They'd chopped quite a bit off Mia's hair and it put him in mind of Demi Moore, back in the day. Mia had looked great being a blonde, but now her hair was the color of chocolate. And it made her eyes dazzle.

"Does it look different?" she asked as soon as she reached him.

"Different enough that the bad guys won't recognize you? Yes. Different enough that I might wanna date you? Always."

Mia groaned. "Seriously, drop the flirting. That time I almost got nauseous."

Jack grinned and put his arm around her shoulders. "Come on," he said. "Let's go to the beach and enjoy our last few hours of freedom."

Mia threw back her head and laughed as Jack dived through a garish-pink inflatable ring, complete with flamingo head and showed her his "tricks."

"Don't call up Cirque du Soleil anytime soon," she said between fits of giggles. He looked so clumsy, and the daft expression he pulled at the completion of his act cracked her up more than anything.

After a while, they both tired of the silly game. Several kids in the water swam fairly close to them. Their parents must have come to the beach after school was out for the day.

Jack headed in their direction and pointed at the pink flamingo ring.

"Hey kids, go ask your parents if it's okay for you to play in this. If it is you can have it." A small cheer went up and four children rushed back to the shoreline. Jack grabbed Mia's hand and followed in their general direction.

They reached the beach and their towels. By the time they got comfortable, the kids were back, their beaming faces telling Jack the answer.

Once they had run off, flamingo in hand, Mia turned to look at Jack. "That was kind."

He shrugged. "I was unable to impress you with my acrobatics, so I thought I'd move on."

Mia grinned. "Oh, really? Any other ideas?"

"Now who's being a flirt?"

"You're right. But let's face it, I'm much better at it." Mia looked at Jack and felt such longing, such yearning for all that he was. Jack was a good man. He was generous, brave, and thank goodness, he was with her.

She rolled to one side and lifted up her sunglasses. She reached over and touched him on the chest. "Now that you've shown me all your tricks, how about we go back to the room, and I'll show you some of mine."

Six o'clock came all too soon. They sat on each bed facing one another, their hair still wet from the shower. Jack looked over at Mia, who stared at the phone in his hands.

"Before I call Ed, I want you to know that the time we've spent in Haven has been the most fun I've had since being in Cornwall, with you."

Mia reached out and grasped his free hand. She lifted it to her mouth and kissed his palm tenderly. "Ditto, Ranger Jack."

Jack looked at the cheap phone and turned it on. When the dim screen lit up, he hit the contact button and laughed.

"What is it?" asked Mia. "What's so funny?"

"Ed. Remember he said only his number was in here?"

"I remember."

"Check it out." Jack turned the screen to face her.

"That's cute. He gets a point for that." But she didn't even break a smile and Jack could tell her mood was already changing now reality had stepped back into their lives.

He hit the button and held the phone to his ear. Ed picked up after two rings.

"Is this Zach?"

"It is. I'm looking for a Mr. Buck Nekkid. Would that be you?"

Ed giggled on the end of the line. "I know that was childish of me, but I couldn't resist. Anyway, I thought you'd get a laugh. You sure as hell needed one."

"You were right. I've not been looking forward to this call. Any news? How's Wessels?"

"He's going to be okay, though he'll be in the hospital for a while yet. What about you guys? How are you holding up?"

"We're good. We found a quiet place and got some much-needed rest. I think both of us feel better for that."

"Good, that's good. Okay, are you ready for an update?"

"Shoot."

"Turns out the leak came from an IT guy with the police department in Miami. Of course he's denying it, giving a story that he only gave the information to a higher-up. But they feel pretty confident he worked alone. Now, as far as the perps in the hotel are concerned, the guy who shot Wessels died in surgery and his buddies are still in the hospital being questioned. They've identified two others who got away."

"Damn."

"I know. They're running checks on them, but it's doubtful they'll come up with anything. Meantime, the Feds want you guys to come back in ASAP."

"Figures. Where?"

"Still Miami, but a smaller place, a condo. I'll text you the address after we get off the phone. In other news, we had no results finding the woman's body from the night at the clinic. Unfortunately, Rodriguez is alive and well. This morning, a warrant for his arrest was issued before he could get out of the country, and as of an hour ago, he's staying in a one-star hotel, courtesy of the United States government. He'll be questioned in the morning, in the presence of his attorney. Apparently, the clinic has been closed since the night in question.

"Yesterday they obtained a search warrant and started going over the place with a fine-tooth comb. There's evidence it's been cleaned thoroughly, but because of Ms. Jones's statement, the techs have been able to focus on very specific areas. They feel confident they'll find DNA evidence. Fingers crossed."

"What about the Marinos?"

"It gets a little stickier there. The wives, kids and the youngest sons, Basilio and Diego, flew out by private jet the day of the hotel fiasco, before we got our warrants. The old man, Sandro Marino, was apprehended easily as he'd just come out from having a colonoscopy. Turns out the old guy has early-onset Alzheimer's and doesn't know what day of the week it is. Apparently, Juan, the oldest son and heir apparent, has been running operations for the past two years. We suspect he's the one who took Daddy's drug empire and expanded it into human trafficking.

"We don't think Juan's left the country yet. But he's gone underground. No sign of him, or his goons. The local police are cooperating with the help of an undercover division."

"I thought we didn't trust the local cops?"

"Don't have much of a choice at the moment. We need their resources and feet on the ground. Sandro's been charged with drug running and being held at a high-security prison hospital. The department's working hard to put together language on all the trafficking charges which we need for the son. The judge has been made aware of it all."

"One Marino on the loose is one too many," said Jack.

"I agree. Juan and his goons pose a very real threat to Mia's safety. The Feds have Carlos and now the old man. We know Mia's statement can put Rodriguez away for life. But if Rodriguez decides to turn, and cooperate with the Feds for a plea deal, he can incriminate the Marinos one hundred percent."

"The Feds need to keep pressure on him. Makes sense. But now that makes him a potential target as well."

"Bingo."

They wound up the conversation after that. Ed was back in DC. Consequently, Jack's situation was out of his hands completely and in those of the Federal Bureau of Investigation.

Jack disconnected the call. He looked at Mia, who had not moved the entire time he was talking.

"Could you hear what Ed was saying?"

"No. What did he say about Jeremy? Is he going to be all right?"

Jack recounted the gist of it.

Mia looked instantly relieved. "Thank God. I hope I get to see him again one day. I'd like to thank him for what he did."

Jack nodded. "They rooted out the leak in Miami, and now we have to report back to the FBI. They'll set us up in a condo." Jack placed his hand on her knee. "They've arrested Carlos."

"What?" Her eyes rounded and her face paled. "He's not dead, then?"

"Unfortunately, no." He quickly sought to reassure her. "He's locked up and been denied bail. So he can't get anywhere near you. They've also arrested the head of the Marino family, the old man. Two sons have already fled back to Cuba, and the oldest has gone underground in Miami."

Mia was still white as a sheet. "Where does that leave us, or rather, me?"

"From what Ed just told me, your testimony is what they need to put Carlos away indefinitely. Although you can testify against the Marinos, it's not substantial enough to get them behind bars. However, with Carlos in custody, facing a very serious charge which could even carry the death penalty, he's got plenty of motivation to plea-bargain with the prosecution."

"What do you mean?"

"If Carlos turns, his evidence would be enough to convict the Marino family one hundred percent. Of course, he'll risk becoming their next target if he does, but the Feds will say they'll protect him, even keep him segregated while he remains incarcerated. But if Carlos stays quiet and covers for the Marinos, he has a good chance of winding up on death row." Jack looked at her, hesitant to ask a question.

"What?" Mia said.

"I'm just speculating what he might do. What choice he'll make once the Feds start pressuring him. What kind of a guy is he? Besides being a murdering bastard?"

Mia's eyes turned to flint. Her jaw clenched. "He's a coward."

Ed's text arrived within the hour. He stated the FBI wanted them on the road that evening to get them settled into the new accommodations. Without saying anything to Mia, Jack responded in the negative. He asked Ed to pass on the message they would arrive by noon the next day. He turned off the phone before his boss could respond, knowing Ed would not be happy, put the phone inside the nightstand drawer and went outside.

He knew Mia wouldn't have strayed too far. She hadn't. He walked down the path leading to the sea and saw her sitting on the beach. She didn't turn around to look at him as he approached, and he quietly sat down next to her.

"You okay?"

She nodded, but he spotted a tear rolling down her cheek and could tell it wasn't the first. He put his arm around her and then pulled her to him so her head rested on his shoulders. They sat in silence, staring at the surf as the tide came in.

Jack waited for a few minutes to pass and felt Mia's breathing slow down as she relaxed against him. Without looking at her, he said. "I'm really sorry, Mia."

"For what?" Her voice was a mere whisper.

"That Carlos isn't dead. Men like him deserve to be treated the way they treat others. He's scum."

Her body tensed and he tightened his grip on her to reinforce that she was safe.

"You experienced something so traumatic that night, and all because of him. Bad enough you had to witness everything, but if he had been killed, it would have given you a sense of closure and helped your mind cope with what you saw. His being alive not only came as a huge shock, it keeps that experience open and raw." Jack pulled her tight against him. "You have been extremely brave, Mia. And though I know you feel really scared right now, things are going to get better. We'll get there. I promise."

Suddenly she jerked away. "Tell that to Agent Wessels."

Jack sighed. Anger always came after grief. "Jeremy Wessels put himself in the line of danger when he signed up for the job. He didn't die, Mia, and he will recover."

He watched her wipe her face with her hands to dry her cheeks. He could see the battle raging in her mind. She was terrified, vulnerable and feeling helpless. He knew that feeling only too well. Only for him, it had not been about an assassin, but a car crash and the loss of a brother.

Reaching again for her, Jack grasped her hands. "Mia, we've got to see this through, you and me. Look how far we've come already. When you think about being frightened, remember what you've already accomplished, and some of that all on your own. What happened was a fluke. Someone infiltrated the system, and we had a close call. But we made it, and we'll keep making it."

He stared at her as she looked into his face, her eyes almost blue in the evening light and still shining from her tears. Jack cupped her face, leaned forward and brushed his lips against her mouth. He felt her hesitate, and then she responded to the kiss. This was not the passion from earlier in the day. This kiss was a conversation. One that promised affection, care and, what else, love?

After a short while, they got to their feet and turned back to the motel.

"You know what we should do?" Jack said as they walked down the path.

"What's that?"

"We should go out on a date."

Mia gave a short laugh. "Not quite what I expected you to say. But Brannon, you constantly surprise me."

Jack, relieved her mood had lightened, decided to run with the idea. "I mean it, Mia. This is our last night in Haven. We know we'll be cooped up tomorrow. It's safe for us to go out here, so why not?" They reached the motel room, and he unlocked the door. "We could go out for dinner, find a place with some music, take a romantic walk on the beach. Come on, it'll be fun."

She finally agreed on the condition she could buy something other than shorts and a T-shirt to wear, along with a few other items. Jack agreed, and they made a trip into town. While Mia shopped, he waited outside the stores, surveying the area for anyone looking suspicious and also for destinations he could take Mia to that evening.

While she was inside a clothing store, he spotted a small restaurant that had the look of a pub. Outside, a chalkboard advertised music that evening. It was perfect.

"I'm all done." Mia appeared with one more bag in her hands. "Let's go back to the motel and I'll get changed."

In the bathroom at the motel, Mia looked at her reflection in the mirror. It was odd seeing her face with makeup on. She almost looked like somebody else. How quickly she'd forgotten what it was to wear mascara, eyeshadow and a hint of lip gloss.

In the scheme of things, she was being ridiculous. Who would give a damn about their appearance when they were on the run for their lives? She did.

Bad enough Carlos had stolen her liberty, her passport, her ability to sleep at night, he had taken her life, screwed it into a ball and tossed it into the trash.

Having Jack in her world had been completely unexpected, and the only good thing to come out of this nightmare. Since escaping Florida and holing up in Arkansas, Mia had been making do with anything at hand. She was fed up feeling scruffy, wearing other people's clothes, not looking like the person she had always been. Tonight, she wanted—no, needed—to be Mia Jones once more.

The dress made her feel almost pretty. The color of the sea, the shade of blue made her eyes look green. Mia had smudged gray eyeshadow on her eyes and lined them with kohl and added a few sweeps of mascara. She'd caught the sun, and her freckles were darker than normal, but she didn't care.

She ran a brush through her hair and was pleased to be a brunette again. Mia dabbed a little sandalwood oil on her neck and temples and took a deep breath. She wanted to forget everything just for one evening.

Hearing about Carlos had taken her so completely off-guard. She hadn't meant to get so upset, but everything had hit her all at once—fear, hatred, utter frustration at her predicament, all because of one evil man. And humiliation. That was the part she hated to admit, even to herself. That she had been duped, taken in, made a fool of.

Stop. She chided herself. *Don't think about it tonight.* Her thoughts went to the man waiting on the other side of the bathroom door. Immediately her heart filled with warmth. Though Jack had messed up their relationship years ago, he had more than atoned for his actions already. He had broken her heart. Now he had saved her life.

With one last look in the mirror, Mia opened the door.

Jack sat on the edge of the bed staring at the TV without even paying attention to what he was watching. He heard the bathroom door click open and glanced up.

The woman who walked toward him literally took his breath away. He blinked twice to be sure he was seeing right.

"You look beautiful," he said softly. His eyes devoured her. Her dress, a mix of blue and green, hugged the lithe body he knew so well. Her breasts pushed against the fabric, and as Jack's eyes lingered there he felt an instant physical reaction. Mia's neck and shoulders were bare, except for the wispy ribbon of a halter-neck strap, as thin as a shoelace.

But it was her face that always bowled him over. She

was lovely, with or without makeup, but whatever she had done this evening only served to enhance everything he already loved about the way she looked.

Those dove eyes were wickedly green tonight. Her complexion golden, dashed with dark freckles, and her mouth…staring at Mia's, plump, shiny, ready-to-be-kissed lips, Jack had to bite his own to slow down where his mind was leading.

"Jack?"

He swallowed. "Yeah, sorry. I was just a bit knocked out by how great you look." He glanced down at his outfit. A Haven Is Only One Letter Away from Heaven T-shirt, and khaki shorts. "I think I might be a little underdressed for this evening."

Mia came closer, and as she leaned to whisper in his ear, Jack inhaled the soft fragrance of sandalwood on her skin and shut his eyes. Her cheek brushed against his, and he held his breath.

"You have never looked better, Ranger Jack." The air stirred from her voice like a caress on his skin, making it tingle. Then it disappeared as she stepped back and smiled.

"Thanks for this, Jack."

He smiled at her, and in that moment, Jack Brannon wanted to give her the world.

Haven was not known for its nightlife. But as a coastal town, it still had a different ambience than most regular places Mia said she had been to. The main street was not long, but it had been illuminated with overhead strings of lights like you would see at Christmas, which gave the place an ethereal touch.

Jack led her to the pub he'd spotted earlier. They stepped inside and it took a moment for their eyes to adjust to the darkness. One side of the room was an open bar, with high tables and a large television hanging on the wall. The other was a restaurant area, decorated with all manner of objects typically found in the sea or on a beach. Starfish, pieces of fishing net and an assortment of shells.

They picked a table in the farthest corner and within a moment gave their drink order to a waitress. Tonight, they both chose large frozen margaritas.

Jack, ever watchful, had picked the seat facing the entire room and he quickly scanned the crowd. Nothing seemed out of place, and his gut instinct wasn't picking up on anything out of the ordinary. Good.

The drinks came, and tasted refreshing. They both ordered fish and chips off the menu.

"It won't be authentic," Mia commented as the waitress walked away. "But it will still be good. At least the fish should be fresh, right?"

Jack didn't respond. He was busy trying to sip his drink through a straw. "Why do you get a straw when the blasted drink is frozen? It's like sucking a football through a garden hose."

Mia laughed. "Don't ever write poetry, Jack."

He shrugged and used the straw to stir the drink. "English never was my strong point."

"You mean in school, or as a language?"

"Funny lady," he quipped, holding up his glass to toast her. "Here's to our date night in Haven."

Mia raised her glass to tap against his. "It's quite a bit different than Cornwall, wouldn't you say?"

Jack paused, his conscience suddenly saturated with

guilt. He didn't want the past to get in the way of the present right now. They already had enough to deal with as it was. "Yes, a lot different. That was another place, another country, and we were different people back then. A lot changes as you mature. In some ways I don't even feel like the same person as I was ten years ago." He realized he'd sounded morose. That was not the intention this evening. They both needed to feel good and pretend they were normal people in a normal life. He raised his glass again.

"Another toast?" asked Mia.

"Yes. But this one's to Haven, where we can pretend to be whoever we want."

"Great," said Mia. "I'll be Heidi Klum, and you can be Henry Cavill."

The fish and chips dinner certainly was nothing like Mia hoped it would be. It was as close to the British version as a hot dog was to a filet mignon. But it was tasty, and a nice change from fried chicken at the diner.

Jack insisted they share a warm fudge brownie slathered in vanilla ice cream. By the time he paid the check they were both full.

They left the table and headed over to the other part of the pub where Jack found them a spot near the door. The band had just set up, and several customers were still arriving, which made Mia think this band must have a following, so they might be quite good.

One of the bartenders moved tables and chairs away from the small stage area to create a mini dance floor. Jack went and got two more drinks, and they sipped these while watching what was going on.

They were a cover band as it turned out. Their repertoire consisted mainly of music that had been popular in the nineties. Although Jack and Mia had both been young in that era, they knew most of the songs as they were still played on the radio.

A few people were brave and got up to dance. It was up-tempo tunes, and Mia watched with interest as everyone had a different style of moving.

Jack leaned over to speak but had to yell over the band. "It's like watching people at the airport," he said. "The human race are a bunch of weirdos." He said this while watching one man in particular who was doing what he could only call a twerk. "It might work for Miley Cyrus, but it's not working for him."

"Sounds like someone's jealous of his moves. Have you got any, Ranger Jack?"

"None I'd show in public," he said this directly into her ear and ended the sentence with a kiss on her earlobe.

A shudder of warm pleasure rippled through her body. Mia loved being next to this man. The smell of his skin, the touch of his hands, the sound of his voice, were as delicious as the dessert she had just devoured. Thoughts of their time in bed earlier surfaced quickly, and she was certain, without any doubt, what they would do once they got back to their motel room. Her body pulsed with the beat of the music and anticipation for later.

The lead singer announced they would sing one more song before taking a break. He said it would be a slow song and encouraged any of the couples in the room to get up and dance. Mia had no intention of doing so until the band started to play.

It had been her parents' favorite love song. A song

called "At This Moment" by Billy Vera, from back in the eighties. She turned to look at Jack, who was staring at her. Somehow, he read her mind.

"Want to dance?"

She nodded. They set their drinks down on a nearby window ledge and stepped out onto the dance floor.

Jack wrapped his arms around her waist while Mia's snaked up to loop around his neck. Slowly he started to move, and she easily followed his lead. Their bodies swayed in unison to the slow beat of the song. They listened to the beautiful lyrics about what a man would give to have one more moment with the woman he loved, and their eyes locked and held.

It was not bright in the room, but it was light enough that they could see one another. Mia gazed up at Jack's face, lost in the moment, drinking in the words he spoke with his eyes. In his expression, she thought she could read everything that he couldn't say. And all that she read there was a complete reflection of what she knew radiated from her, to him.

With other couples dancing around them, even with music and other noises in the background, Mia was only aware of being in Jack's arms, and the beautiful words of the song. The intensity of their look grew stronger. Instinctively, they pressed closer together until their bodies met.

Mia's head bent to nestle in the crook of Jack's neck as his arms pulled her tighter against his chest. Her hands unclasped and her fingers ran through his thick hair. He bent his head and she lifted her face to look at him. The music played, the slow beat rhythmically moving their bodies as one. Jack's hand slid up her spine to cradle the back of her head. He lowered his face and pressed his mouth against hers.

His kiss said all she needed to know.

When the song ended, Mia did not want to leave the dance floor or the comfort of Jack's embrace. But the band was taking a break and everyone left the dance floor, so they had to do the same.

"How about we head back?" Jack suggested, reaching to take her by the hand.

Chapter 14

Haven, Florida

It was a clear night. The air carried a chill that came off the water. It would have been nice to walk along the beach, but it was late, and Jack definitely had other things on his mind.

Neither spoke as he led Mia down the quiet street; they were both lost in their own thoughts.

Jack locked the door as they stepped inside their room. He put the key on the dressing table and Mia went into the bathroom. After a couple of minutes, she came back out.

He was waiting for her. Standing at the foot of one of the beds, his arms open.

Without a word she leaned against him, relishing the sensation of his hard chest and thudding heart. Her hands grabbed his broad shoulders while Jack's moved down her back, lowering to slide across her bottom to pull her closer, leaving Mia in no doubt of the effect she was having on his body.

Jack let out a deep groan and hungrily sought out Mia's mouth. All tenderness gone, she felt the assault of his lips, the rough graze of the stubble on his face, and the hot hungry need of his passion.

Mia's body was a tinderbox and Jack's desire a flame. Her fingers raked through his hair, down his neck, across his shoulder blades. Her hands slid down his back as he plundered her mouth. She could feel his touch ignite every sense of her skin. She was on fire, and only he could help her.

Jack fell back on the bed, taking her with him, so she lay on top of him, head to toe. He still kissed her lips. Like starving animals, they explored each other's mouths, not wanting to stop, not wanting to breathe.

She had to get out of her clothes, needed to be naked and feel his skin against her own. Mia pulled away from Jack, then moved to stand up.

He raised himself up, leaning back on his elbows, his breath coming fast as he watched her.

Mia slowly lifted the dress over and above her head and dropped it to the ground. She reached behind her back and undid her bra, then shrugged off her panties. She looked at Jack and ran her tongue across her bottom lip.

Jack couldn't wait a moment longer. He reached out to grasp Mia's hand and pulled her down on the bed beside him. Half rolling over, he began to kiss her again, but it was tormenting. Each kiss made him need another, but a longer, deeper, wetter kiss.

And, dear God, she wanted him too. Jack could feel her desire match his own, and the sensation was as heady as whiskey. His hands explored her body, and although it had not been that long since they had lain together, knowing what the morning would bring only made their time now more important, more poignant, and necessary.

As she responded to his lovemaking, he grew more excited, ready, wanting, needing, yet behind all those emotions, all the passion, more than anything, Jack wanted to tell her the real truth of what this meant to him.

He loved her.

They checked out of the motel and got on the road. Mia could hardly believe that only the day before they'd been playing in the ocean. That last night had been a magical night, ending with her sleeping in his arms.

That chapter had come to an abrupt end. Real life demanded center stage again, and the enormity of the mess she was in, the imminent danger she faced against a group of maniacal criminals, took a firm and terrifying hold once more. It obliterated the joy in her heart.

That she'd even been able to lose herself in the last thirty-six hours seemed irresponsible and reckless. But it had happened. Her precious time with Jack had been important on so many levels. Mia truly believed it had stopped her from going out of her mind amid the vortex of insanity her life had become. But it had also left the door wide-open for her to be hurt once again.

It was incomprehensible returning into the den of the dragon. Back to a world of federal agents, police officers and legal jargon. If only they could have stayed on at the crappy Haven motel, their peaceful hideaway. A simple life seemed totally out of reach now.

Jack was quieter than normal. Mia realized he too must be lost in thought.

After the past days together, it was difficult speculating what would happen next between them. Yet history repeated itself, it seemed. They were still two people going in totally opposite directions. She was in the middle of a very serious federal investigation and a British national trying to get back home. While Jack, a law enforcement ranger, had been torn from his duties in Arkansas, taken away from his family and landed with keeping her safe.

Melancholy set in. She looked out the window and with dismay saw the downtown skyline of Miami.

Jack's hand enveloped hers. He gave it a reassuring squeeze.

"It's going to be okay, Mia. I know this totally sucks but have faith in the system. It's meant to protect you and not those scumbags who go around ruining peoples' lives. You're going to get through this, I know you are."

"Then what?" she said softly. But the ringing of his phone drowned out her question.

They arrived at their destination before five o'clock that evening. This time, the agent's name was Susan Gilmer. She asked them both to call her Sue and gave them a quick tour of the condo. It was situated in Fairbanks, a small suburb of Miami, and one of four condos in the block.

The ground level was fronted with a large garage and a front door set to one side. This, when opened, led directly to the stairs and up one flight to the condo itself. The place was surprisingly bigger than it looked from the outside. An open-plan living area on the first floor, with two bedrooms the next level up. It was a third of the size of the penthouse at the hotel. Would that make it easier to defend?

Mia couldn't bring herself to be very cheery. She hoped Sue would understand and not take it personally. In some ways, the past few days of happiness only emphasized the misery of her situation.

The agent showed Mia to her bedroom. "I'll leave you to get familiar with the room."

Mia looked around. There was no character in here whatsoever. It was genderless but clean. A contemporary bed and dresser, with one wall and closet. Only one picture on the wall—huge and very modern. Mia did not care for it at all.

She opened the closet and was pleasantly surprised to see a few items already hanging there. Leaving the door open, she wandered into the adjoining bathroom. The same in here. Someone had thoughtfully provided basic cosmetics and toiletries. Mia imagined that would have been Sue. She was grateful.

How long had it been since she'd had her own belongings? Two months had passed since she'd run away from Carlos, leaving everything behind. It only went to show that material possessions meant nothing. Survival was everything.

Now what? Was she supposed to stay in here or go and sit out in the living area and stare into space?

Mia perched on the end of her bed, all at once exhausted.

Everything was happening so quickly. How different would it have been if those two jerks had never shown up in Jasper? How much longer would it have taken to save up enough money for a passport and flight home? The all-too-familiar tug of being homesick nagged.

If she had made it back to England, could her life really be any different than it was now? Mia doubted it. Wouldn't she spend every day looking over a shoulder to see if someone from Florida was searching for her, still trying to hurt her?

She was between a rock and a hard place. Damned if she did, damned if she didn't. Overall, Mia understood what was happening now really was for the best. This situation needed to be resolved once and for all.

She just hoped she'd live to see it through.

"You're confident there won't be another breach?" Jack asked Agent Gilmer after she'd briefed him.

Sue leveled a contemplative stare. "Yes. The only people involved in this case have gone through extra vetting and have higher clearance. We've got four guards outside the perimeter of this building. Another set next door. And across the street there's twenty-four-hour surveillance. No one gets in and no one leaves without our knowing about it."

The agent's hazel eyes showed intelligence and confidence. Sue was all business. Short dark hair, khaki chinos and a black golf shirt, and a masculine vibe that Jack felt right at home with. In the Park Service, many of the women who served dispensed with frippery. Makeup, jewelry and other accessories only got in the way of them doing their job in the outdoors.

"Good," Jack said. "What's on the agenda for tomorrow?"

"We take her downtown."

"I think that's very unwise given the situation. Don't you?"

"It's not for me to say, Mr. Brannon. I just follow orders."

"Where downtown?"

"The federal courthouse. Judge Seton wants to interview Mia and ask her a few questions. The Rodriguez case will get a great deal of attention by the press and the constituents. The judicial system will come under direct scrutiny, and Seton wants to make sure all the i's are dotted and the t's crossed."

"Does it have to be Mia? She's just a witness."

"The only witness, Mr. Brannon. No one else will testify."

"What did you say?"

Jack and Sue turned at the same time when Mia spoke. She joined them in the living room and took a seat in an armchair. Jack worried that she looked so pale. Funny how a few hours of ugly reality could do that.

"I overheard you," Mia said. "You were talking about taking me to the courthouse tomorrow?"

"Correct. Don't worry, you'll be in an armored car and heavily guarded."

"You expect another attack, then?" Mia's voice wavered slightly, and Jack fought the impulse to go over and comfort her. Whenever her vulnerability surfaced, he automatically wanted to make her feel safe. But it would be inappropriate, and she would be annoyed if he broke protocol.

As far as anyone else was concerned, they were just friends, and it was imperative they maintained the illusion for both their sakes. One hint of a romantic relationship and Jack would be pulled away.

Sue took a seat on the couch and looked over at Mia. "Under normal circumstances we don't discuss our side of the patch with any witnesses. We want to downplay the seriousness of these complicated situations. I make an exception in your case because you successfully evaded capture without our help for several weeks, and you're completely aware how precarious things are. That said, the main players are out of the picture, which is good news for us. Our real concern is not knowing the location of Juan Marino. He's a viable threat and we're taking that very seriously, and not putting anything past him. Therefore, when you go to the courthouse in the morning, we'll be acting like there is a whole army waiting for you, which of course there is not."

"She'll need a bulletproof vest," Jack said and heard Mia's sudden intake of breath.

"Already sorted. You'll be wearing one too. I take it you plan to accompany us?"

"Just try and stop me."

"We'll go over the details of everything in the morning. The transport will be here at nine thirty, so we'll have breakfast at eight, and I'll explain what will transpire. Does that work for you both?" Sue asked casually, as though she was inviting them out for a shopping expedition to the mall.

"Yes," Jack replied, while Mia merely nodded her head in silence.

Sue got up and went into the kitchen, retrieved something. She passed Jack a small black device, the size of a cigarette pack.

"We would like for you both to carry one of these. They transmit directly to us and will keep us in constant communication. If there's any kind of problem, or you have questions, that gives you instant access to me and others on my team. Please keep it on you at all times. They're pretty easy to work, let me show you."

Jack said he was familiar with them. Sue handed a small transmitter that looked like a flip phone with an antenna. She described how it worked and said it was easy to operate.

"Right. I'm going next door to check in with my team. There's a list on the kitchen countertop of some local restaurants. Figure out what you guys would like for dinner, and I'll call it in. But we need to be quick as it's already getting late, and places will be about to close. We'll have it delivered across the street, then one of our guys will walk it over. I'll be back in about ten minutes. Use your radio if you need to speak to me. And obviously, don't go anywhere."

As Sue left the room, Jack figured she'd lock them in the condo anyway. There was no way the FBI was going to leave any exits for Mia, or anyone else for that matter. He glanced over at her, sitting somberly on the couch. Jack joined her.

"I'm worried about you, Mia. You've been a real trouper, gutsy from the word go. What's happened that's made you falter? Is it Miami? Something's different."

She shrugged. "I don't know. Maybe it's because the past few months have been so awful, and then the last couple of days was such a reprieve. Like getting good weather after weeks of snow and rain. You know what I mean?"

He nodded, understanding exactly.

She continued. "I hate being back in the middle of this mess. I'm not stupid. I knew everything hadn't gone away. But it was just wonderful thinking about the ocean, the salt in the air, and you. Now I'm living the nightmare again, and my survival instinct wants me to run. I get that I can't, Jack." She gave a long sigh. "I'll do better if you don't fuss over me. I know I have to get through the next 'who knows how long.' I'll be fine once it all starts up in the morning and I find the right headspace. I'm just coming off my high, I think."

He looked across at her and their eyes met, speaking words their lips could not say. Anger simmered in the pit of Jack's stomach at the injustice of what was happening to the woman he loved. "I totally get it. I wish we were still in Haven too." He wanted to say so much more, but it wasn't wise. As he'd told Mia on the drive in, the condo would be bugged. It was standard procedure.

He glanced at the paper in his hand. "I guess we'd better check out these menus Sue talked about. Maybe we can order oysters?"

For the first time since their arrival at the condo, Mia gave a small smile. And for Jack, it was like the sun had broken through the clouds.

The next morning was surreal. Kitted in her vest, Mia had been escorted to an armored car with Jack and whisked downtown to meet with Judge Seton in her chambers. Much to Mia's surprise, Seton was a female judge in her late fifties, who was incredibly personable and very grateful to Mia for being a witness for the state. She assured Mia their conversation was off the record, and she just wanted to go over a few formalities.

After an hour, Mia was back in the van and headed for the condo with Jack and Agent Gilmer at her side. Sue and Jack made polite conversation, and Mia remained silent.

When they arrived, Mia claimed to have a headache, and spent the remainder of the day in her room. Whenever Jack knocked on her bedroom door, she asked him to go away.

* * *

The second day in the condo felt like a week. When you were stuck inside a small building it was odd how your brain got easily bored, Mia thought, and she just couldn't settle. Books and magazines were impossible to read because her attention span was too short. Movies and television were just a lot of noise, and she wasn't even allowed to peek through the blinds covering the bulletproof glass windows.

Agent Gilmer spent quite a bit of time away. Mia supposed she was either next door or across the street. If she was going to be gone for longer than a few minutes, Sue would call another agent to stand guard at the foot of the stairs next to the front door.

Jack remained in the condo. He disappeared periodically into his assigned room to make phone calls on a secure line, presumably to Ed Mills. Was Jack on edge too? She hadn't helped by being distant. She just felt so out of sorts.

Jack was concerned. Ever since the trip to the courthouse, Mia had not been herself. She'd become quiet and introspective. He'd left her alone when she'd asked him to, closeted up in her room. He could respect the fact she needed a little time to collect herself now the situation had changed yet again. But this was only day two of what might be weeks, and he was beginning to get worried.

At lunchtime, Sue Gilmer left the condo to run next door while Mia sat on the couch pretending to watch whatever was on the television. Jack walked over to the coffee table, picked up the remote and turned off the set.

"What are you doing? I was watching that."

He looked at Mia and placed the remote back, then took a seat. "You weren't watching it at all. You've been staring into space all morning. What the hell is going on? You're just not acting right."

She glared at him. He saw her cheeks flush.

"Oh? And how am I supposed to act? I thought I was behaving quite well considering being here is no better than being in a bloody zoo. I'm a sitting duck just waiting for someone to come and kill me. And why? Just so your precious legal system can put Carlos in jail and then protect him from the same people he worked for? He doesn't deserve such good treatment. After what he did to Jeannie and to all those other poor women. It won't bring any of them back, will it? It all seems like a complete waste of time."

Jack was mortified. He'd never heard Mia speak like this or with such a defeatist tone. "You're not thinking straight, Mia. Nothing has changed since we first came to Florida. Why are you suddenly so angry?"

She wasn't going to answer. Her mouth was pursed together, and she stared at the blank TV screen.

"Mia, come on. This isn't you. What happened at the courthouse yesterday? Did the judge say something to upset you? Please, talk to me." He reached for her hand, and she snatched it away.

Jack tried again. This time she wasn't as quick. "Mia. Stop being weird. It's me talking to you, not the judge. What on earth is going on in your head?"

She turned to look at him, but not with teary eyes as he'd expected. She was furious.

"Trust me. You really don't want to know."

"Yes, I do."

She pulled her hand away from his and gestured to the room. "I'm fed up with all of this. I haven't done anything wrong, yet I'm the one imprisoned, even if it is in a swanky part of damn Miami. Not only is my life in danger, but I'm expected to sit here all day with nothing else to do than think about it. How would you feel if there was a psycho on the loose who wanted you dead?"

Jack nodded. He got it. She was so far out of her depth here that fear had taken over. All the weeks she'd been so brave, yet now it had never been so real. A visit with the judge had sealed it. The cold reality of what Mia was mixed up in was staring right at her.

"Look," he said. "You've every right to feel the way you do. And yeah, it all sucks and it's unfair as well. You are the one being punished at the moment, but that fault lies with Carlos. Whether you think his punishment fits the crime is neither here nor there, Mia. What matters the most is he pays. And if he's locked up and fed caviar for the next three decades, he's going to feel like he's in a zoo as well. And he'll be looking over his shoulder for the rest of his years, because it will only take one crooked guard to look the other way when the Marinos send someone to take him out."

Her eyes widened. "You think they'll do that?"

"One hundred percent. I think it's the death penalty either way for that sorry piece of crap. I know it still doesn't seem fair, but it's the hand you've been dealt, and you've got to play it. You think you're the only one scared of the bad guys? At least you've got a team of people trying to keep you safe. It could be worse. Those goons back in Jasper could have got to you first."

Jack knew he wasn't being gentle with her feelings, but

she didn't need cosseting, she needed a dose of reality to snap her out of her funk. He watched her face as she contemplated what he'd said. If he'd made her angry, so be it.

A moment past and Mia let out a long sigh. "I hate it when you're right, Ranger Jack."

That night they ate pizza, and the great pineapple debate raged, with Agent Gilmer and Jack teaming up against Mia, who said any fruit was acceptable on a pizza, making Sue groan with distaste.

"Fruit is sweet, and there's nothing sweet on a pizza," Sue insisted.

"You Americans always have to follow the pack. In Europe, we like to buck the system, try something new, be independent. Rules were meant to be broken." Mia smirked.

Jack shook his head. "Mia, you're saying that to two people who currently work in law enforcement. We arrest people who break the rules."

"And that's why you both like boring pizza."

"She wins." Sue got up from the table and gathered the empty boxes to take into the kitchen. "You guys need anything else?"

"I'm stuffed," Jack moaned. "I'm going to have to start a diet after all this lazing about."

"Maybe you could jog on the spot?" suggested Mia.

"There's a treadmill in the garage, Jack," said Sue. "Feel free to give it a spin whenever you want."

"Thanks. I might do that." He leaned back against his chair.

Mia got up from the table and wandered over to the bureau below which the TV hung on the wall. There were a couple of drawers and three cupboards. She opened one of the drawers and rummaged around. "Look. There's a deck of cards in here. Maybe we could play something later? I'll bet even Jack knows how to play Go Fish."

"Very funny," he drawled. "Just for being a smartass I'm going to beat you at Spades and we're going to bet real money."

"Good luck with that. The only money I have is back at the trailer park by the lake."

"I'm good with IOUs."

Mia looked over her shoulder and saw the lecherous grin on his face. Ignoring him, she opened one of the lower cupboards. Dropping to her knees, she poked about and eventually pulled a box from one of the shelves. She got to her feet. "Here's a jigsaw puzzle. Look, it's an old Norman Rockwell picture." She carried it back to the table. "It's been years since I've done one of these. I think I might have a crack at it. Anyone want to join me?"

"I have to go next door and check on a couple of things," Sue quickly responded.

Jack took one look at Sue's face and saw by her expression that she probably hated jigsaw puzzles as much as he did. He was about to make an excuse himself, but when he saw how eager Mia was to do something to occupy herself he didn't have the heart to turn her down.

"Sure. I'll help you with it, although I'm pretty bad. Maybe I could just sort out the edges and you can put them all together."

Mia sat back down at the table and together they started working the puzzle.

After a couple of hours, Mia had long given up, and Jack still sat at the table working on the puzzle.

Footsteps sounded on the stairs, and Sue Gilmer joined

Mia in the living room. She sank onto the couch next to Mia and glanced over at Jack, who was hunched over the puzzle, looking very focused. "You should take a photo of that," she said quietly. "Great evidence for blackmail later."

"You're right. He's like a little kid."

"He is a man, after all."

Mia nodded. She picked up the remote. "Fancy watching a movie?"

"Sure," said Sue. "We'll let the little ranger play with the puzzle by himself."

Chapter 15

Miami, Florida

"You can't go anywhere," Agent Gilmer said, staring at Jack sternly.

"I disagree," he replied, scribbling down his phone number and handing it to Mia. "Look, Sue. It's been four long days. It's late, we're hungry and we're all sick of pizza and sandwiches. I'm just going to run to this place and grab everyone something different. It's only four blocks away and they don't deliver. My truck's right outside, and you have an entire army here protecting Mia. Come on, give her a break. Let the woman have something special for a change. You've all got my number. And you can call if there's a problem."

Sue shook her head in annoyance, but eventually relented. The agent looked as tired as they all felt.

Jack headed down the stairs. He didn't like being told what he could or couldn't do. But it went with the territory for now.

The condo was beginning to feel about the size of a matchbox. Everyone's patience was wafer-thin. He did believe the security was tight, and that was the main concern. There'd been no sightings of Juan Marino since their return to Miami, but Jack wasn't too worried about being out on his own. They weren't looking for him anyway.

The newspaper advertisement that had caught Mia's eye earlier that day was a trending pub. The place bragged about having authentic British fish and chips, sausage rolls and sticky toffee pudding. Mia had looked so miserable today he'd noticed her face light up at the sight of English food. Why shouldn't she have something she liked for a change? She deserved a treat, after all. So he'd phoned in a large order, and hoped it would cheer Mia up.

When Jack pulled up to the building he was mildly disappointed. It might be advertised as a pub, but it looked like a small American place, just with a cool sign. The name of the pub was the Ace of Spades.

Jack went in to pick up his order.

Inside was a shotgun bar and a jukebox playing too loudly. A handful of people were there drinking, but it wasn't busy.

While he waited for the food to be rung up, Jack studied the posters hanging on the wall. Various scenes of London and other places in the UK. A couple of them looked familiar to him, and he wondered if he'd ever get to go back there again.

When his food was brought through, Jack paid the check and went outside, stashed two bags of steaming food on the back seat and then got into the truck. The smell of dinner was enticing, even if it was British-type fare, but he wouldn't tell Mia that. He loved teasing her about the blandness of the English diet.

His phone started ringing. He hoped Mia didn't want

to add anything to the order now he'd already left. He was almost halfway back. He answered.

"What did you forget…"

"Jack! They're here. Oh my God… Jack!" Mia screamed down the phone.

"Mia!" Jack floored the truck. He yelled. "Where are you? What's happening?"

But she must have dropped the phone, because all he could hear was gunfire, and people screaming and shouting in the background. No, no, no, no…this couldn't be happening! Not when he wasn't there to protect her!

Jack blazed down the streets, his heart pounding. Cars honked their horns as he recklessly dodged from lane to lane. He turned the corner to the condo, and saw men dotted around the building and on the street. Blue lights flashed, and several cars had their headlights on. Whatever had gone down was already over.

Where the hell was Mia?

Jack slid the truck into Park. He jumped out and raced toward the condo. The police were already getting in position securing the area. A cop in uniform spotted Jack and quickly approached.

"I'm sorry, sir, you can't go anywhere near the building."

"The hell I can't," he yelled. "That's where I'm staying. I need to get to Mia. Let me through!"

"Sir. Please, I need you to move back."

Jack gave the man a hard shove and sped past him. He heard him shout, "Stop!" and knew he would be chased. But he didn't care. He had to find Mia.

The door to the condo was wide-open, light spilling out onto the sidewalk. A group of people stood in a semicircle and Jack saw someone lying still on the ground. His heart hammered against his rib cage, his mouth went dry, and his legs didn't want to move.

He pushed his way into the group of agents surrounding the body of a woman. Her shirt had been ripped open. Close to the top of her bra there was a massive bruise. He strained to see her face, but someone was administering CPR.

"Mia?" His eyes filled. No, it couldn't be her. He would do anything, anything for it not to be his Mia. And then the woman coughed, and her chest began to move. The person who saved her moved back and Jack could see the woman's features.

Sue Gilmer.

Immediately, Jack yelled out. "Where's Mia? Has anyone seen her?" He tore into the condo, taking the stairs three at a time. He reached the top level and hurried through all the bedrooms, his fear mounting with every step.

She wasn't there.

Jack ran back down the stairs. An ambulance siren shut off as it pulled up as close to the condo as possible. As the doors opened and the paramedics ran to where Sue Gilmer lay, Jack turned to each of the agents and asked if anyone had seen Mia. Each one shook their head, quickly speaking into their radios, and Jack understood that in the confusion no one knew what the hell was going on.

He rushed over to where a patrol car was parked. A uniformed cop sat in the front seat.

"Officer…" Jack was having trouble speaking. The words did not want to come out of his mouth because then they would be true, and he didn't know how he would cope with the reality of what he needed to say.

"Officer. My name is Jack Brannon. I've been staying here under FBI guard with Emilia Jones. I have reason to believe she has been abducted by members of the Marino family and her life is in peril." And as he spoke, the rage began.

She knew there was blood on her face, and all down the front of her shirt, but Mia had not stopped to look and see if it was hers or someone else's. All she could think to do was to run. Her feet were bare, pieces of rock and trash stuck to the bottom of them, but she didn't care.

In her head she still heard gunshots ricocheting around her, the hysterical yelling of men as though they were in battle, and all the while Sue screaming at her, "Stay down, stay down!"

Mia didn't know how she'd gotten out of the condo. One moment she'd been talking to Sue, and in the next... everything was a blur.

Chaos ensued everywhere. Sue had led her down the stairs, opened the door, and then came the horrible sucking noise as a bullet hit Sue in the chest. Men appeared out from the bushes, while others came toward the condo with their guns firing... But who was FBI and who were the killers?

Run!

She hadn't stopped. Frantically, Mia fled, got away from the residential area, away from the guns and ran into the darkness. Now she hobbled down a road in a business district. Were they chasing her? Looking for her? What should she do? She needed to call for help.

Oh, dear God, she wanted Jack. She needed to call Jack.

That thought anchored her mind. Mia ducked into the dark doorway of a building and pressed herself into the corner.

Breathe...just...breathe.

It was late. Mia couldn't see anyone else out walking down the street. The only cars passing by drove at normal speeds. She must calm down and think clearly.

Mia bent over, put her hands on her knees and took several long, drawn-out breaths. After a minute, she felt it working. Slowly, rational thought took control once again.

A sudden thought had her thrusting her hands into her jeans pockets. There it was! The piece of paper with Jack's phone number. She could call him! He would be safe; he'd been gone when the insanity began.

Mia stepped out of the doorway and back onto the sidewalk. She had to find a place that was open, then she could make that call. Jack was the only person who could protect her.

Warm, yellow light spilled from a large restaurant window, and Mia ran toward it, a moth to a flame. She pushed the door open and almost fell inside.

At first, the maître d' attempted to ask her to leave. She obviously didn't look like a customer, with blood on her clothing and no shoes. But his repeated refusal made Mia's resolve crumble. She began to get hysterical, her voice raised and panicked. Several of the patrons stopped eating and stared.

A waitress came over to see what was amiss, and it was she who finally punched in the number for Mia on her phone.

"Is this Jack?" She handed the phone to the poor

woman with a bloody face and no shoes on. Mia put the phone to her ear and promptly burst into tears.

"Jesus," shouted Ed into the receiver, once Jack had told him a fast version of events. "Where are you now?"

"Headed to the restaurant to get Mia. What do I do next, Ed? I'm in way over my head here."

"Calm down, son." The reassuring voice of his mentor was keeping him steady. "Get to Mia as quickly as you can. I'll make a phone call, and you'll have backup there very soon."

"Who are you calling?"

"A buddy. Tom Sherrill. He's a major at the Miami Police Department and he'll get on this fast. Just hang on a little longer. I'll call you right back."

Jack parked the truck several cars down from the restaurant. When he reached the door of the building, it flew open, and Mia flung herself into his arms.

He stepped inside, hugging her fiercely as she buried her face in his neck, wrapped her arms around him and circled his waist with her legs. She clung to him as though she'd never let go.

Jack's heart swelled with relief. He drank in the fragrance of her hair, the feel of her body. She was on him like a second skin, and yet he wanted her closer still.

"Mia," he whispered in her ear. "I thought I'd lost you. Oh, God, I thought you were gone."

She pulled her head back and looked at him, her nose almost touching his. "The measures you will take to avoid eating English food are beyond ridiculous, Jack."

He laughed. He couldn't help himself. *How could he not be in love with a woman like this?*

Mia went into the bathroom and washed her face and hands while Jack thanked the waitress and maître d'. When Mia came out, he was waiting in the corridor, loath to let her out of his sight.

"You look better," Jack said.

"Did you find Sue?" Mia looked worried. "I think it's her blood that's on me. I know she got shot."

"She did," said Jack. "Luckily she was wearing her vest, which protected her heart and lungs. But she sustained a nasty wound to her head which likely explains the amount of blood. When I first got there, they were administering CPR, and it looked bad. Then she started breathing again and they took her off in an ambulance."

"This is crazy. No one else needs to die because of a mistake I made."

Jack put his arm around her shoulders. "Don't say that, Mia. Like I told you when Jeremy got shot, these people know the risks they're taking when they put on that badge. It's a calling, something they need to do. You can't control the actions of the bad people out there. They are the ones to blame—not you. Remember that."

His phone rang. It was Ed, letting him know their backup would be there within a minute.

"Come on," Jack said, lacing an arm across her shoulders. "Let's head out to the truck. The police are almost here."

They left the restaurant and started down the sidewalk toward the pickup. The sound of an approaching car broke the quiet and a black sedan drove slowly down the street.

"Here comes the cavalry," Jack said with relief.

As they neared the truck, the car slowed almost to a halt. The back window of the car opened.

Instinct kicked in. "Get down!" Jack yelled, pushing Mia to the ground behind the truck just as shots rang out.

Jack threw himself after Mia, lay down on his stomach, and drew out his 9mm SIG.

Mia lay huddled on the ground next to him. Jack listened to the hum of the engine. He heard a door open, and shoes hit the ground. Quickly, he fired a shot underneath the pickup and heard the squelch of his bullet entering flesh and a sharp cry of pain.

He rolled to his right, cleared the tire and shot twice, this time aiming for the chest. He hit his mark. The man's gun went off and pierced Jack's tire as he fell to the ground.

Jack rolled back. That left the driver and possibly one more. He had thirteen bullets remaining. Suddenly, the engine revved, and the car peeled away.

The door to the restaurant opened. The maître d' peeked out.

"Get back in and call the cops!" Jack yelled. "Now! And don't let anyone out here. These guys will shoot to kill!"

The door slammed shut. Jack reached out to Mia.

"You okay? Come on, let's get up. We've got to move. The truck's out of commission." Jack didn't want to take their fight into a crowded restaurant. He grabbed Mia by the arm and walked in the opposite direction. Keeping close to the buildings and in the shadows, he looked for somewhere to hide out.

"Give me your phone and I'll call the police," Mia said. Jack pulled out his phone, just as the screech of tires squealed around the corner.

"Down!" he screamed at the top of his lungs. Mia

dropped like a stone in the nearest doorway. Jack ran back toward his truck to draw their fire.

He leaped behind the bed of the truck as the car got close. He raised up, shot at a front tire and heard it pop. Then in rapid succession fired twice through the windshield at the driver. The car lost control, zigzagged for several yards and then crashed into the side of Jack's truck.

The Dodge jerked violently from the impact, knocking Jack so hard his feet left the ground. His body hit a concrete post, and he collapsed into a heap.

Mia watched in horror as the truck made an almighty noise and she saw Jack thrown into the air, hitting his head on a huge concrete pillar as he came down. He was hurt!

She pushed herself to her knees, desperate to reach him, and managed to get to her feet, though her legs wobbled and were weak with fear.

Before she could make another move, Mia heard the crunch of footsteps on shattered glass and her eyes grew wide with alarm as Juan Marino stepped around the carnage of his car to stand between her and where Jack lay. His gun was leveled squarely at her chest as he came closer.

She knew that face. He'd been in Carlos's home on many occasions. But then she had not understood what terrible deeds he had done. He was the epitome of evil. Mia stared at him in utter horror. Dear God, was this it? Was she going to die? She looked both ways for a place to run, but there was nowhere to go anymore. Her luck had just run out.

Juan Marino's black eyes, burning with hatred, locked on her face, while his mouth spread into an evil leer. *"Putain de pute,"* he spat on the ground.

Mia's chin lifted and she did not look away. She stared at him with every ounce of hate she could muster. And then time suddenly slowed, like the frames of a movie.

Mia blinked and heard the shot.

Nothing.

She opened her eyes as a bullet hit the back of Juan Marino's head, and it imploded like a hammer hitting a ripe melon. The gun fell to the pavement and the Cuban crumpled to the ground.

Behind him stood Jack. His arms extended, the gun still in his outstretched hands.

Chapter 16

"This was worth almost getting killed over," said Jack, sipping on a frozen margarita, poolside at a five-star hotel.

"Yep," agreed Ed, frowning at the pink umbrella in his drink. "Not too many rangers get these perks."

Ed had flown in the evening before to help Jack navigate his way through the legal mire of paperwork after killing Juan Marino. There was to be an investigation, although the FBI and police department were more than happy to see the Cuban go down.

Mia was a guest of the FBI and would be for the next few days. The state of Florida was preparing her as their prime witness for the preliminary hearing taking place as soon as they could clear the docket. Then, a trial date would be set, and she would learn when going back to England would become a reality.

Mia and Jack were unable to see each other but Mia was given a loaner phone so they could talk and message whenever they wanted. Jack hoped to see her sometime over the coming few days.

Jack finished his drink and studied his old mentor.

Ed looked awful in baggy shorts and an obnoxious Hawaiian shirt.

"Are you going to give me the skinny on why you're really back in Miami, Ed? While I appreciate all the concern for my legal wrangle, the department's lawyers are doing an admirable job."

Ed grinned. "Brannon, you're a smart kid." He took another sip of his drink and poked himself in the cheek with the umbrella. Ed glowered at it furiously, then unceremoniously pulled it out and tossed it on the table. "You don't reckon I was angling for a free vacation, then?"

Jack shook his head. "Nope. I know for a fact this isn't your idea of fun. You'd rather be on a pontoon at the lake, fishing for crappie."

Ed chuckled. "You got that right." He set down his drink. "Okay, here it is. On the night all hell let loose, you called me for help. Do you remember what I said?"

"Sure. You told me to get to Mia and stay put. You were going to make a call and get me some backup."

"That's right. And that's what I did. But someone else got to you first, before the cops, didn't they?"

Jack leaned forward and frowned. "What are you saying, Ed?"

"I'll let you know in a couple of hours, after I get done with my meeting."

Mia was getting used to having an escort whenever she left her hotel. Today, she had gone to visit Agent Jeremy Wessels, who, though healing slowly, was recuperating well, and she'd met his wife, Holly. The petite brunette had been really sweet to Mia, even though it was protecting Mia that had gotten her husband shot.

After that, she'd been escorted to a different hospital to visit Agent Sue Gilmer. Sue had sustained a nasty wound to her head where a bullet had grazed her. Though they had stitched her up, she was being kept under supervision for a few days. Sue's vest had protected her, but the force of a close-range bullet had put immense pressure on her lungs, and she'd lost the ability to breathe on impact. The quick-minded agent who administered CPR had saved her life.

They'd had a long chat. Mia promised to bring her pizza on the next visit, and swore there'd be no pineapple in sight.

After visiting the hospitals Mia ate a quick lunch in the hotel snack bar before coming upstairs. It was almost two o'clock in the afternoon, and she buzzed with excitement at the prearranged video call she was going to receive.

Her room was no penthouse, but spacious, with a balcony and a nice view of the pool. She sat down at the small table outside and propped up her phone against a small plant pot, relishing that she didn't have to hide behind drawn curtains any longer.

As soon as the first ring sounded, she hit the accept button. Her heart swelled with joy as the face of a stunning redhead with lovely green eyes filled the screen.

"Kelly!" she burst out in delight. "You have no idea how good it is to finally see you." Seeing her closest friend after all that had transpired, her eyes welled with tears. "Oh, Kelly, I'm so sorry I got you roped into this damn mess. You must hate me as I know it's upended your life. You've missed work and had to leave your house and the school's probably mad you've been gone. You won't lose your job, will you?"

Kelly shook her head and smiled reassuringly. "Don't be silly, you crazy Brit. Of course I won't lose my job. If anything, I've become quite the celebrity. I'll admit it's been pretty weird hiding out like I'm some sort of spy. But these federal guys have got me in a swanky hotel, and I've been able to watch all the streaming networks I can't afford to have at home. I've stayed so busy. Finally finished two books I was dying to read, watched a ton of movies, and made enough lesson plans to get through the semester. It's been quite a break not having to cook, do housework and run errands. I could get used to being waited on like this."

Mia chuckled. Typical Kelly. She was always so calm and cool about everything. Never any drama with her. It wasn't as if every day you were taken to an FBI safe house. Only Kelly Murphy could play it down.

Kelly pointed a finger at the screen. "Mia. The main thing is you're okay, right? I talked to some guy named Ed. He said you'd been through an absolute nightmare, but that everything was going to be okay now. He wasn't lying to me, was he?"

"No. I am doing all right. Only I'm not allowed to talk about the case for obvious reasons, but yes, I think it will all turn out for the best." Her mind immediately went to Jack Brannon. She was tempted to tell Kelly what had happened, but knew their entire conversation was likely being recorded.

"So, are you back home?" Mia couldn't see the background on the video, it was too blurry.

"No. Another day or so, according to the rather dashing agent in charge of my well-being. You?"

"Again, not at liberty to say, more's the pity. I don't

know how much longer they'll need me, but at least I got my passport back, so you won't have to do any more covert stuff on my behalf."

Kelly let out a relieved sigh. "Thank goodness for that. Although it was all a bit exciting in a way, wasn't it? Like we were on some crime show on TV."

"Kelly, there are many things I'd call what we were trying to do, but none of them would be exciting. Dangerous comes to mind. Foolish, irresponsible…"

Green eyes narrowed. "You always were a little more cautious than me, Mia. It's the English in you. Now in other news, according to my keeper here, they picked up the two goons who you saw in Jasper. They don't believe I'm in any danger as my part in this sordid tale is done. I think they are having the local police keep an eye on me for a while, just to be on the safe side. So I'll return home and get back into the normal routine of my humdrum life. Once you know what your plans are, be sure to tell me. I'd like to at least hug on you before you go back to the UK. Even if it means coming to wherever you are."

Mia agreed to do just that. They chatted a while longer and then she disconnected the call.

Weariness washed over her, and she went and got onto the large bed. She lay down with the phone in her hand. Mia glanced at it and thought about calling Jack, but yawned, and decided to wait until later on that evening. She could tell him about Sue and Jeremy, and her call to Kelly.

Last night Jack had mentioned Ed was in Florida once again, which surprised her. But she was glad Jack wasn't by himself now. His plans were to return to Arkansas in the next few days as the case he was involved in would be lengthy due to the shooting. He couldn't miss too much work but would be flown into Miami as required.

Jack's involvement in the Carlos Rodriguez case was minimal. They had already questioned him regarding conversations he'd had with Mia.

She stared at the ceiling and wondered how everything would finally play out. Court cases were notoriously slow. The prosecuting attorney for the state of Florida had already spoken with her about the possibility of returning to England before they went to trial. It was still up in the air, but she was hopeful she would get to go.

The search of Carlos's home had unearthed her passport stashed in one of his safes, along with a great deal of money, weapons and drugs.

It was amazing how much better she felt having her passport again. It was liberating. Even though she couldn't leave the country and would be flagged by any immigration officer, it was still good knowing she could travel at some point in time. Not to mention less paperwork to fill out. Mia was sick and tired of forms and statements already.

Tomorrow was Wednesday, and her last day to give statements. Mia planned to meet with Jack and ask if she could stay at his hotel, at least until he went back to Arkansas. She really missed him, and just thinking about the guy made her feel comforted. Everything Jack had done to help her this past week was beyond measure. He'd put his life on the line for her countless times. And at the end of it all, saved her from certain death. She wished the same could be said for poor Jeannie. Even now, the police were still trying to discover what had happened to her friend, though they were searching for her remains.

Knowing Juan Marino was dead gave Mia no pleasure at the loss of human life, but she couldn't help feeling utterly relieved. He signified the head of the beast,
the leader of the group responsible for human trafficking, but Carlos was just as bad. He'd given their wicked
deeds life as the main perpetrator.

Mia yawned. She had been sleeping well, but weariness still nagged behind her eyes every day. Of course it
was the emotional toll of everything that had happened.
Eventually things would get back to normal.

She made herself more comfortable on the bed and
flipped on the television. Randomly channel surfing, Mia
felt her eyes grow heavy.

A familiar voice penetrated her slumber. At first, Mia
thought she was dreaming and then realized someone
was talking on the television. She opened her eyes and
looked up at the screen. It was blurry. Mia blinked and
cleared her vision.

A man was being interviewed in front of the restaurant
where she and Jack had almost died. A good-looking man
in his early fifties, premature white hair, tanned skin, and
very striking blue eyes. The kind of man you never forgot, especially when he'd once been standing in the house
you'd lived in, chatting to your boyfriend about patients
attending a women's clinic.

Mia reached for the phone and called Jack's number.

When she saw Jack, he was in profile, staring out of
the hotel window. Mia stopped momentarily and allowed
herself the sheer luxury of watching him unnoticed. He

was beautiful. The regal bearing of his ancestry translated into such a noble, sculpted human.

Jack must have realized she was there, because suddenly he was looking at her, with such intensity she almost burned from the effect.

They walked toward each other, then stopped, unsure how to behave. The night at Haven had only been a few days earlier, but with all that had transpired, it could easily have been months.

They settled for a platonic hug.

"Let's go to the bar and talk," Jack suggested.

The cocktail bar was situated just off from reception and at the front of the hotel. Jack picked out a table, and as soon as they were seated, a waitress appeared to take their drink order.

Mia had abstained from alcohol, but decided her news warranted something stronger than a Coke. Jack ordered a beer, and the waitress left to get their drinks.

"What's happened?" Jack asked as soon as they were alone. "You were so evasive on the phone, why?"

"I suppose I'm paranoid after everything. It's been like a strange game of who trusts who? I wanted to tell you in person so you could relay this to whoever you deemed fit. Actually, I think you should talk to Ed and get guidance, because this is really going to upset the apple cart."

Mia knew the person she'd seen on television was high-ranking. But she didn't understand the hierarchy in all the different law enforcement departments within the United States. Jack would know how to handle the situation better.

The waitress returned with their drinks. Mia quickly took a large gulp of her vodka. "I was watching TV in my room a little while ago. The news came on and they were showing the restaurant where the shooting occurred."

"Yeah," said Jack. "I saw it too. I'm glad they didn't mention our names. My parents would be completely flipped out."

"The guy they interviewed. I think he was a cop?"

"Major Tom Sherrill. He's a good buddy of Ed's." Jack stared at her face. "What is it, Mia?"

"I've seen him before." She took another sip of her drink.

"He's on TV quite a bit lately."

"You don't understand, I'm not talking about seeing him on the television. I've seen him in Carlos's house."

Jack leaned forward. "What?"

Mia nodded. "We've never met in person, so he doesn't know me. But he was at Carlos's one evening when I came home. When I first moved in, Carlos told me I was always to stay out of the way when he had company over on business. He conducted all his meetings in his office, and I always steered clear. But this particular evening I'd been out doing something, and forgotten Carlos had someone coming over. I went down the hall and stopped myself just in time from walking in on them. But I saw the guy because he was looking at one of Carlos's paintings sipping a cocktail."

"Did you get a sense of what he was doing there? I mean, the guy's a policeman. Did it sound like he was there on official business?"

"I don't think so. I stood there for a moment and eavesdropped, but I couldn't hear all the conversation. The parts I did hear referenced how many clients Carlos was seeing at the clinic at that time. It seemed more like a social call because they were drinking. After he left I asked Carlos who his visitor was. Carlos would never give me specifics on anyone, and of course I understand why now. But I do remember him saying he was one of the investors in the clinic."

"Are you sure about that? It's important, Mia."

"Sometimes, Jack, I think you take me for a complete idiot. I would not have contacted you had I not been one hundred percent certain. The man I saw on TV is connected to Carlos."

Jack picked up his beer and drained the bottle. "Come on." He got to his feet and threw money on the table to pay for their drinks. "We need to find Ed Mills, right now!"

At the front desk, Jack phoned Ed's room. He answered on the seventh ring.

"Ed, it's Jack. I need to see you ASAP."

"Okay. I just got out of the shower. Is it important? I'm headed downstairs for dinner. Want to join me?"

"Trust me, you're going to want to hear this. Listen, I've got Mia here with me. See you in the dining room."

They were already seated at a table when Ed Mills joined them. His forehead was sunburned.

"I see your meetings must have been on the golf course today, Ed? Hard to get a tan inside, right?"

"Hello, Mia," Ed said, deliberately ignoring Jack.

Mia gave him a grin.

Ed turned to look at his protégé. "For your information, Ranger Brannon, it is the duty of a senior member of our department to put himself in harm's way for the cause. You of all people know that. Didn't you recently almost get shot?"

"I did. Although that's probably far less painful than the red beacon glowing above your eyebrows."

They ordered drinks and dinner from the menu. Ed's face became serious. "All kidding aside, Jack. What's going on, what do you have to tell me?"

Jack looked at Mia. "It's really for Mia to say, not me. Go ahead, Mia."

Mia repeated the conversation she'd had with Jack earlier. As she spoke, Ed's entire face turned the color of his bright red forehead.

"What is it, Ed?" Jack had expected him to be shocked, but the older man was enraged.

"That's what my meeting was about earlier. I was voicing my suspicions about who the leak could have been, but we still weren't sure. So it's been Tom all along." His voice was heavy. He shook his head. "Tom and I have known each other thirty years. We met when we were both fresh out of training, and although his path was with the police, and mine with the parks, we stayed in touch. When the Marino case started and the Feds reached out to our department, the only plus for me was getting to interact with Tom professionally. He's been my go-to guy throughout this whole caper."

He paused as their food arrived and was set in front of them.

Ed continued. "The suspected leak the other day was a guy in IT, who claimed he hadn't done anything wrong. He maintained someone in management contacted him and requested information regarding your location at the penthouse. He even gave us the name of the man who made the call. We checked it out and the name doesn't exist, no trace on the phone either. But something bugged me about the whole setup. I just met with Tom this morning and we talked about the case, specifically the IT guy, and Tom said the man was lying."

"Did you ever suspect it was Tom Sherrill?" Mia said.

Ed shrugged. "Something's been off since the other night. I've been trying to get my head around it, but it's just there, under the surface. I called Tom when you were attacked at the condo. He was the only person who knew where you were, besides me and Jack. Tom also knew the location of the hotel and the condo where you were being hidden. That would account for how Marino's men always knew where to find you. I never thought it would be him, maybe someone right beneath him."

Mia nodded thoughtfully. "I've gone over the night at the condo repeatedly," she said. "And I've wondered how I escaped so easily all things considered. I didn't realize it at the time, but maybe Marino's men mistook Sue for me. Otherwise, they'd have come after me. But I got away."

"Until I called Ed," said Jack. "And then he called Tom."

"That has to be what happened," Ed agreed. "Unwittingly, I played right into their hands by giving them your location outside that restaurant. They realized Mia had survived, and that's probably why Juan himself showed up. He obviously didn't trust anybody else to do his dirty work."

"What are you going to do?" asked Jack.

"Call the FBI."

On the drive back to Mia's hotel, they discussed how bummed Ed Mills had appeared when they'd said goodnight.

"That's got to be tough after such a long friendship. I wonder what makes successful men turn into greedy, despicable human beings?" She couldn't fathom how any person could do that to another. "It's not like these men don't have families of their own. The women they traffic are someone's daughter, mother, sister."

Jack agreed. "Something's missing in their genetic code that gives them no conscience. Their arrogance makes them think they're superior, and everyone else dispensable. You see it all the time with the treatment of animals. People who have pets and neglect or abuse them, don't think of them as creatures with emotions and feelings. They are a lesser thing, in their eyes. There are some damned evil people out there, Mia. Unfortunately, you had the misfortune to meet one."

"Hopefully, karma is coming to bite Carlos pretty hard. I hope they lock him up and throw away the key."

When they arrived at the hotel, Mia asked Jack to come up for a little while. She wasn't ready to say good-night. It had seemed normal spending time with him. When had that happened?

Up in her room, she offered Jack a drink from the mini bar, which he turned down as he still needed to drive back to where he was staying. Mia got them both a bottle of cold water and asked if he'd like to sit outside on the balcony.

It was close to ten o'clock, the sounds of the lit city fading as most of the population of Miami were at home. They each took a seat at the small wrought iron table. The temperature was perfect, and the breeze pleasantly warm.

"This is nice," said Jack, turning to look at her. "It's been good seeing you today, Mia. You know, I've gotten used to hanging around with you. It'll be weird going back to my regular world, and it will be a lot less exciting."

She smiled. "I'm happy with less exciting when it comes to drama, danger and exhaustion. These past weeks, and especially the past few days, are my quota of crazy for the rest of my life." She took a sip of water. "Did you find out how much longer you're staying in Miami?"

"Yeah, they let me know earlier today. I get shipped out Friday. I've given all my statements, and at this point it's all about whenever the courts schedule the upcoming trial on Rodriguez. I know you have to be here for the preliminary hearing, but they don't need me for that part, just the main hearing. Anyway, I need to go back to work and then check on my family."

Jack was automatically jumping right back in where he left off in Arkansas, thought Mia. Not once had he mentioned her in his upcoming plans. Ironic. History was getting ready to repeat itself. But what had she expected? They had been thrown together in a terrible situation. Yes, they had reconnected romantically, but could you really count the past forty-eight hours as a relationship?

"How about you? What's the word on your getting back to England?"

"The good news is they found my passport. That's saved a bunch of paperwork and a massive headache. The bad news is having to stick around for Carlos's preliminary hearing. But after that I'm not sure. Judging from what I've heard, it's going to take some time for both the prosecuting and defending attorneys to build their cases. Evidence on Carlos's case influences the trial being scheduled for the Marino family. I don't have to be present for that one, hopefully. They think I can participate virtually in a British court, under oath, while it's in progress. So, once I get this preliminary part done, I can go home."

"Have you figured out where you're going?"

"Not yet. I'll have to stay with a friend until I sort something out and find a job."

They fell quiet. Mia wondered if Jack was thinking along the same lines as her. What about them? Was there any future scenario where they would be together?

Jack finished his drink and set the bottle on the table. The chair scraped as he got up. "I'd better make a move," he said. "It's getting late."

Mia followed him back inside the hotel room. She felt as though several voices were arguing inside her head. *Ask him to stay! Don't let him leave! Take him to bed!*

She ignored them all. Something had already shifted between them, or he wouldn't want to leave, and Mia was not about to beg him to do anything. She'd done that once before and look how that had ended up. A nasty quarrel that had separated them for ten years.

Jack reached the door. "I'll call you in the morning, if that's okay. Maybe you can get finished early and have some time to play and not spend it with all those serious G-men. As it will be my last night here, we could go and have dinner?"

"Sure. I'll talk to you in the morning."

Jack stepped forward and took her in his arms for a long hug. Then he kissed her on the forehead and left her room.

Chapter 17

Miami, Florida

All the way down the elevator and out to the parking lot, Jack fought a battle in his mind.

More than anything, he wanted to go right back up to Mia's room, take her in his arms and make love to her. But what good would it do? Sure, there was no doubt they had real feelings for each other, but all those years ago they'd felt that way too. Look where that had ended. It was a repeat of the past—they were still on different trajectories.

He had a demanding career, and now the added concern of a seriously ill relative. How could he possibly embark on a full-blown relationship with someone who lived in another country?

Jack opened the door of his rental and got into the driver's seat. A voice whispered inside his head, *That's not what the problem is, you're still thinking about Neil. Well, so what? How can I be happy when he doesn't get to be anything but a pile of bones?*

Jack started the car and pulled out of the parking lot. Would nothing ever work out for him? The only way he could change things would be to go back into the past and stop Neil getting behind the wheel of the car that night.

One moment had changed his life forever. Stolen a future away from his big brother.

No. Surely it was better this way. Mia had been through enough, especially now. She probably couldn't wait to get out of the US. She deserved to go home and enjoy a normal life with a decent man, one who wasn't so screwed up, conflicted and miserable, like him.

Jack didn't think he'd ever find joy, because whenever something made him happy, the reality of the past snatched it out of his hands.

He got back inside his hotel room and stared at his phone. His fingers itched to call her, even though he'd spent the drive back promising himself he would do no such thing. Damn, he was such a weak person.

Disgusted, he threw his phone onto the bed, went into the bathroom and grabbed his bathing suit that was hanging up to dry. He slipped on his trunks and picked up a towel. Then he headed back out to the elevator. He needed to do something with his body and something with his mind. Maybe he could just swim laps until everything felt better? The sign by the pool indicated it closed at eight o'clock. Jack shrugged. Even a ranger got to break the rules sometimes.

Mia couldn't sleep. She wasn't thinking about the awful nightmares. She was having them while wide-awake. She lay in bed holding the little rose shell Jack had given her on the beach in Haven.

A thought crossed her mind. What if she tried having a frank conversation with Jack about their future? Not an argument, or anything that would become emotional. After everything they'd been through together, surely they could be honest with one another? If this was it, the end of their affair, Mia desperately needed to know.

There was no room in her life for a platonic friendship with the man she loved. She wasn't strong enough to maintain that kind of relationship when she wanted so very much more.

Yet knowing Jack, Mia realized her expectations were too high. Jack was deep, so deep even he couldn't climb out.

And what about his brother? Since the day at his friend's house in Naples, Mia had pushed that into the back of her mind. But why had Jack never spoken about him? Who didn't talk about a sibling?

Now she fervently wished she had pressed Jan for more information. Not that it changed anything. Having a brother or not didn't make you decide whether you wanted to be with someone.

No. They were never going to end up together. Perhaps that was why their short time in Haven was sweeter. Maybe they both understood on some level that those few hours were really all they were ever going to get before reality swooped back in and blew everything away.

Mia turned over and buried her face in the pillow. She knew tears were close, and she was so sick of feeling sad. Better to think about two people having fun on a beach, playing with an inflatable pink ring that looked like an ugly flamingo.

Wednesday morning at eight o'clock, Mia's phone rang and woke her up.

"Mia?" It was Ed Mills.

Immediately her heart picked up speed. "Ed? What's wrong? Has something happened to Jack?"

"No, Jack is fine. But he asked me to call you because it was too early for him to ring when he left this morning."

"Left? He's already gone? He said he was here until Friday."

Ed's voice was calm and reassuring. "He was supposed to stay, but he got a phone call from home to say his grandfather had been taken seriously ill and his family needed him there."

"Oh no. I am so sorry, that is terrible."

"Yes. He's pretty close to Sid. Anyway, Jack got an early flight to Tulsa this morning. In fact, he should be there by now. He didn't want to call and wake you, so I'm sure once he finds out what's going on he'll get in touch with you. I'm leaving later this morning for DC. All the mess with Sherrill has hit the fan. He's been arrested, and with his senior position, it's going to be a circus. Anyway, I won't get a chance to see you before I go, but I wanted to tell you how much I admire you, Mia. You've been so brave throughout this entire debacle. You're a feisty little lady. And if you ever need anything while you're in the good old USA, you can always reach out to me. I've enjoyed getting to know you a little bit, and I look forward to knowing you more. I don't think Jack's a big enough knucklehead to let you out of his grasp."

Mia was incredibly touched by his words. She liked Jack's boss. His good opinion meant a lot.

"Thanks, Ed. I've enjoyed getting to know you too. You're a big deal in Jack's world, and he's lucky to have you. If ever find yourself in England, look me up, and I'll give you a guided tour of any city you would like to see."

"Now, you've got a deal there," Ed replied. "I may

take you up on that one. Long as I don't have to eat any kidneys."

As soon as they were off the phone, Mia quickly wrote a text to Jack. She kept it brief but wanted him to know she was thinking of him. She sent her best wishes to his parents and said she hoped Sid was doing better. But deep down, she was disappointed.

He'd called Ed and not her.

By noon, Mia had finished giving all her statements and had a free afternoon. The rest of the day passed very slowly. Periodically, she checked her phone to see if Jack had responded. He hadn't. She hoped things hadn't gotten worse for Sid Brannon.

She was unsure what to think. Part of her desperately wanted to call, but what if there was a crisis going on? Jack didn't need anyone bothering him when he should focus on the problem at hand. She had an awful thought—what if Sid had died?

When her phone finally did ring, it wasn't Jack, but the liaison officer assigned to her on the Carlos Rodriguez case. They had pushed the preliminary hearing forward due to the health of Marino senior. As Carlos's and Sandro Marino's fates were intertwined, the hearing would be the first on the docket, Friday morning at eight o'clock.

Thursday morning, Mia broke down and phoned Jack's number.

"Hello." His voice was a whisper. He didn't sound like himself.

"Hi. I didn't want to bother you, but I hadn't heard from you and I've been worried. How is your grandfather?"

He gave a drawn-out sigh. "We don't know yet. He took a bad fall and has a suspected brain bleed. He's in a coma. They're trying to get the swelling down and see what's really going on before they make a full prognosis."

"Oh no, I'm so sorry."

"Yeah. It really sucks. Mom and Dad are here a lot of the time, but I'm camping out at the hospital and sleeping here, so mostly my phone's off. I'm sorry I didn't call, but I'm a bit preoccupied."

"I understand," said Mia. "Is there anything I can do? I won't bother you. I don't want to disturb you at the hospital. Maybe you can just let me know how things are going? I'll be thinking of you all."

"Thanks." There was a pause. "You holding up okay?"

Mia could tell it was him being polite. Jack wasn't even present on this call. His mind was completely elsewhere.

"I'm good, thanks. Look, get back to your family and just shoot me a text when you have a chance and let me know what's going on. Hang in there, okay?"

"Will do. Bye, Mia."

The line went dead.

The preliminary hearing on Friday was nothing like she expected. After all the work and preparation, the actual hearing was fast. It was, however, the first time Mia had set eyes on Carlos since the dreadful night at the clinic.

The large courtroom was crowded—this was big news.

Carlos sat in the dock wearing an ugly orange jumpsuit and handcuffs. When Mia was called to the stand, she felt his eyes boring into her face. After being sworn in, she lifted her chin, turned her head and looked straight at him.

She was shocked. In the space of a few weeks, Carlos had changed from looking like a magazine model to an old man. His swarthy black hair was streaked with gray and looked greasy. His ever-present tan had lightened to pale yellow. Being shot, then arrested, did not look good on him.

He stared at her boldly, his face contorted with anger, tight with rage, and Mia felt his hate radiate to where she sat in the witness stand. But having lived with fear for so long now, she'd finally had enough. she didn't flinch, nor did she look away. Instead, she thought about what he'd done to Jeannie, and his heinous role in trafficking all those poor women. Mia was standing in the courtroom not just for herself, but for them, representing those with no voice.

She tilted up her chin a little more with defiance and stared at Carlos Rodriguez with disgusted eyes. She wasn't frightened of that pathetic monster anymore. It was his turn to be scared of her.

After the hearing, Mia spent some time with a Detective McCarthy, giving a statement regarding what she knew about Tom Sherrill. Though the cop was not allowed to discuss the case in any detail, he was able to tell Mia that the investigation into Sherrill's relationship with the Marino family had turned up a hidden bank account registered in the Bahamas, and a string of dismissed cases where the crime family had managed to evade convictions. Though high-ranking, Sherrill had been on their payroll for years. There was no doubt in the detective's mind that the man had been responsible for leaking Mia's whereabouts.

* * *

Ed called that evening, to congratulate her on the results of the hearing. She thanked him, and told him she'd been interviewed about Sherrill.

"I still can't believe he's crooked." Ed sounded so disgusted. "What a waste of a good cop."

"On a brighter note, I'll finally get to go home, Ed." She was happy, but not having heard from Jack took the wind out of her sails.

"Have you talked to our boy?" asked Ed. "I've tried calling but he's not picking up. I guess that doesn't bode well for Sid."

"I'm surprised he hasn't been in touch with you, Ed. I talked to him briefly yesterday, but he really wasn't up for much conversation. He sounds depressed and wants his space to focus on his grandfather. He said Sid had a potential brain bleed, so it is extremely serious. But if I'm honest, I didn't expect him to be so radio silent."

"Oh," said Ed. "Now I get it."

"What do you mean?"

"It's Neil, all over again."

"You mean his brother?"

"Has Jack ever told you about Neil?"

Mia didn't want to lie. "No, he hasn't. I only know he exists because I saw photographs at his parents' place. I wanted to ask who he was, but the fact he's never mentioned him made me hesitant to say anything."

"That was a good call on your part, Mia. It's a tricky subject with Jack. Neil died in a car accident when he and Jack were teenagers. I knew Neil, he was a Junior Ranger along with his brother. I don't want to tell you the story because it's not mine to tell. What I will say is I didn't know if Jack was going to pull through at the time. Not because of any physical injuries he had, but because Neil's dying made Jack lose his head completely. If Sid is that ill, it's the closest Jack's been to losing someone he loves since his brother died. He's probably all over the map, reliving what happened again. Let him lie low, Mia. That's for the best. He's got family around him for now, and I'm sure they'll tighten the ranks at a time like this. I am sorry to hear it." In the background, someone called out Ed's name.

"Look, Mia. I'd better go. I'll be in touch before you fly home."

Saturday morning, Sid Brannon opened his eyes and stared at his grandson.

"Jack?"

Jack got up and went to the side of the bed. "Grandad. You're awake!" He reached for the old man's hand and held it tightly.

"Of course I'm awake," Sid said. "But whose bed am I sleeping in? It's damn uncomfortable."

Jack laughed at his grandfather's words, but he knew it was more from relief than anything.

"What did I do?" asked Sid. "Get in a bar fight over some hairy-legged old gal?"

"Yep." Jack played along. "Then you fell off her stepladder while you were changing her lightbulb."

"That's what I did?" Sid asked. "Fell off a ladder and broke my damned head?"

"Something like that. It knocked you out, and you've been asleep for two days. They were worried you'd damaged your brain."

"Nah," said Sid. "It was already broke."

They both laughed, and Sid winced as it seemed to hurt his head.

"Let me get Mom and Dad," said Jack. "I need to tell the nurse you've woken up."

He went out of the hospital room to the nurse's desk and shared the good news. Joe and Shirley were coming back from a trip to the coffee machine. They saw their son and rushed forward, their faces pinched with worry.

"Is it Dad?" said Joe. "What's happened?"

"He's back," Jack said, grinning from ear to ear.

When he finally managed to get away from the hospital, Jack drove back to the house, dying to take a hot shower. He stripped off in the guest room. His phone slipped out of his jeans pocket, and he picked it up and saw the battery was dead. That was what happened after three days in a hospital without a charger. He hadn't even noticed. Did he even have a charger with him?

The shower was soothing. Washing away the grime of wearing the same clothes too long, Jack felt as though the hot water removed all the anguish and fear he'd carried with him since the phone call.

He closed his eyes and rubbed shampoo in his hair, then leaned forward, pressing his hands against the wall of the shower while he rinsed off.

He grabbed a towel from the back of the bathroom door and dried off. It was like waking from a very long dream. He was awake, but his mind felt off-kilter, like it hadn't quite caught up with what his body was doing. It was exhaustion, and he knew it.

He returned to the guest room, peeled back the bed covers and got in.

Jack was asleep as soon as his head hit the pillow.

He awoke Sunday to a brand-new day.

It was cloudy outside and the wind rustled through the autumnal trees. Jack dressed, then wandered downstairs, only to find he was home alone. There was a note to say his parents had come and gone and were up at the hospital. They asked if Jack would pick up lunch and join them later.

Jack put on coffee, and then jogged back upstairs to retrieve his phone. There was always a charger in the kitchen, and Jack plugged it in. After a few moments, it beeped, came to life, and he saw there was a slew of missed calls and texts on there.

Scrolling, he saw several from Ed, but none from Mia, not since they'd spoken on whatever day that had been. Had he really expected her to send messages after he'd pretty much told her he didn't want to be disturbed?

Guiltily Jack tapped her number. It didn't even ring but went straight to a recorded message. *"We're sorry. You have reached a number no longer in service. Please hang up and try your call again."*

What? Jack scanned the breakfast bar. His mom's iPad was there. He punched in the code and then opened the browser. He typed in Mia's hotel name and found the number.

A receptionist answered.

"Hi. Can you please put me through to room 508?"

"One moment," said the polite lady. "I am sorry. That person has already checked out, sir."

Jack felt a thread of panic coiling inside. "When did she leave?"

"I'm sorry sir, but we are not at liberty to divulge any information."

He hung up.

Chapter 18

Jasper, Arkansas
November 1

Jack opened his eyes and immediately closed them again. His head throbbed like someone was hammering a nail into his skull. It was almost certainly something to do with the whiskey he had drunk with Tex Callahan the night before.

The other ranger had called not long after Jack pulled the Bronco up to the cabin after driving in from Tulsa the previous evening. Tex had offered to stop by, and although Jack hadn't been in the mood for company, he'd surprised himself by agreeing and telling him to come over.

They'd sat outside on the wraparound porch and watched the red sun sink low on the horizon, even spotted a lone deer off in the distance past the line of trees. It was chilly, but they'd both preferred the fresh air and brisk breeze over being inside.

Tex had caught Jack up on all the news in Jasper, which hadn't been much, and then asked a few questions about Jack's recent escapade. Jack had told him the gist of what had gone down…well, most of it.

He'd skipped the part about being in Haven with Mia.

Not mentioned how he'd felt when he thought she might have been killed. Said nothing about how gut-punched he'd been when he discovered she'd already left Miami. Tex hadn't pressed for details, just nodded here and there as Jack relayed the story.

Jack thought Tex was a good listener, but not much of a talker. He had that quiet way about him that other men either liked or found unsettling. Jack sensed the guy might have seen some action during his stint with the military. The kind of stuff men never wanted to even think about, much less talk about. There was something deep and brooding about the man, but Jack had a strong feeling they'd be friends.

Because he was driving, Tex had sipped on one glass of whiskey to Jack's three. When the ranger had headed for home, Jack knew his tolerance for the brew had diminished over the years. He seldom drank, and this night he'd over-imbibed.

He'd locked the cabin, wearily climbed up to the loft and fallen into bed, with the vague memory that Mia had been the last person who had slept between the sheets. With her face filling his thoughts, he'd fallen asleep.

He'd slept well, thanks to whiskey and exhaustion. But now he was paying for it. Jack opened the bathroom cabinet, grabbed a bottle and shook out a couple of aspirins. He swallowed them and chased them down with a gulp of water, then reached over and turned on the shower.

It was strange putting on his uniform again. But then it was weird coming back to Jasper as well. Being gone the past few weeks had changed Jack. He'd come to Arkansas with the bit firmly between his teeth, ready to make a new start and spend more time with his family. Yet in the blink of an eye, his strong foundation had wobbled, his direction pivoted, and Jack had become embroiled in what had turned out to be a very important criminal case.

That was already in the past. Other than the legalities of a trial coming at some point in the near future, Jack had returned to a sense of normalcy, which had quickly morphed in his mind as being mundane. Something tangible was missing, and he knew exactly what that something was.

Mia.

When had she become Mia in his mind, and not the Emilia he had known? Probably when she'd shown up with yellow hair sticking out all over the place and asked him what he wanted off the menu.

Where was Mia now? Already back in England, he'd guess. Would she ever get in touch with him again? Doubtful. He'd blown it once ten years ago, and you'd have thought he'd have learned from that, but he hadn't.

He'd been such an idiot leaving Miami the way he had without even telling her. But when he'd gotten the call from Tulsa about his grandfather, Jack hadn't thought or considered anyone but Sid. Just thrown his belongings into a bag and hightailed it home.

The trip to Tulsa had been torture. Jack had sat on the plane with his mind firmly planted in the past, fixated on his brother. They'd lost Neil. He couldn't bear the thought of Sid Brannon dying too. Death destroyed the people it left behind.

Being in the hospital, seeing the grief painted across his parents' faces, it had all been more than he could process. It didn't matter that he was a grown man. At the thought of his grandfather dying, Jack was a sixteen-year-old boy again.

When Sid had pulled out of his coma, it was as if Jack came out of one as well. Once he'd got caught up on some much-needed sleep, he'd quickly tried to rejoin the world again, but he'd been too late.

After getting nowhere trying to find Mia, Jack had turned to Ed for help, though he hadn't gotten very far. Ed told him the FBI had taken back Mia's loaner phone once she'd made plans to fly home. He added that they would not entertain any digging around about her whereabouts as she was still involved in an active case, and it had layers of red tape over it, which even Ed did not want to get tangled up in. He advised Jack to get back to work and let everything calm down.

Jack knew Ed was right. He didn't blame Mia for wanting to get as far away as possible, after all she'd been through. Until Mia contacted him, Jack had no way to reach her. The FBI would keep her personal information under wraps as long as they needed to.

But then, what would be the point of reaching out to her anyway? Mia would be happier back home in England, wouldn't she? She was always talking about her homeland when they were together.

The facts were straightforward. His life was here in the US and hers was not. The Atlantic Ocean was just too damn big for them to meet in the middle.

He had to stop thinking about them as a couple. But having spent the past weeks with her, how could he think any differently? Mia was constantly in his thoughts. Every time he closed his eyes he remembered the hours she had lain in his arms. The touch of her kiss, the scent of her skin. Dear God, he longed for her with a hunger he'd never had in his life.

But it was damned futile. It would never work. Being Mia's lover would mean turning his back on his family, and the sacred memory of his brother. And as much as Jack wanted her, he owed it to Neil to keep the rest of his family together.

His mood darkened. Jack put on his hat and went out to the Bronco. It was early, too early to go to work, but he was antsy and didn't want to stay in the cabin. Besides, his stomach needed something solid to settle it down, and everything in the cabin fridge looked like a science project.

Jack drove into Jasper. And as he neared Billy-Jo's his stomach let out a hungry growl. Though still out of sorts he chuckled. It was karma. With a resigned shrug, he turned on his indicator and pulled off the main road. Biscuits and gravy would ease his stomach; he just wished they could ease his heartache.

There were several cars in the parking lot, and an old bicycle propped up against the outside wall. Jack took off his hat, laid it on the car seat and got out of the Bronco.

He went inside and inhaled the wonderful aroma of coffee and bacon. Many of the tables already had customers, but Jack saw his previous booth was empty. He hesitated for a moment. Maybe this wasn't such a good idea, coming to the very place where he'd met up again with Mia. He turned to leave when a voice stopped him.

"Well, howdy, stranger!" The orange-haired waitress he remembered from before came over. "You in for breakfast, hon?"

Jack nodded. "I was, but…"

"Just sit yourself down." She pointed at the familiar booth.

He walked over and noticed a folded-over piece of cardboard on the table. The sign read RESERVED.

He frowned as he took a seat. "Isn't this booth reserved for someone?"

"Yes," said a soft voice from somewhere behind him. "It's reserved for you, Ranger Jack."

Jack spun around in the seat, his ears disbelieving. It couldn't be. "Mia?"

She moved toward him and came to stand by his booth. Mia grinned. "Yes, Jack. It's me. This time, I won't even try to deny it. Mind if I join you?"

He opened his mouth to speak, but nothing came out.

Mia slid into the seat across the table from Jack. The look on his face had been priceless. Nancy came over and put a cup of coffee in front of them both. She winked at Mia and disappeared back into the kitchen.

"It's good to see you, Jack," Mia said. She meant it. She'd missed having him by her side. It was like losing a limb.

"I thought you'd gone back to England." Jack sounded bewildered. "I tried calling you, but your phone was disconnected. The hotel wouldn't tell me anything, and even Ed said your information would be kept confidential because of the impending trial."

"Jack," she interrupted. "I think we owe each other an explanation," Mia said. "Why don't I go first?"

"You're going to have to. My brain is still in shock."

Mia took a sip of coffee and then a deep breath for courage. "Okay, here goes. When you left Miami, I knew it was an emergency, but I still didn't understand why you couldn't have called to say you were going, especially under such a terrible circumstance. We'd been through some scary stuff, you and I, and I thought we had an understanding, that we had each other's backs. But then I realized how much you had on your mind. Especially after all you've been through because of me.

"When I finally got a hold of you, you were so distant. Even though you were worried about your grandfather, I could tell it was more than that. It went deeper. You were already pulling away from me, just like you did all those years ago in England. I didn't know what to do. Then Carlos's preliminary hearing was brought forward, and once it was over I was told I could go home. I thought about buying my ticket, Lord knows I was ready to get out of Miami, but I desperately wanted to talk to you again before I put an ocean between us." Mia took another sip of coffee. This was going to be the hard part. "Jack, I know about your brother."

He visibly paled.

Mia reached across the table to grasp his hand. He did not pull it away, so she continued.

"I don't know details, nor do I need to. But I know what happened was tragic and has left an indelible mark on you. I started thinking about how such an awful experience would affect a teenager, and then stay with him as he grew up without that beloved brother.

"Things started making sense, the pieces fitting together. I think I finally began to understand why you are the way you are—especially when it comes to being with me and having a serious relationship. You have such a loving family, it's obvious how close you all are. And what happened to Neil has made you closer still because you recognize how precious you are to one another.

"With that in mind, when I think about a young guy on vacation in England who meets a girl and they fall in love, what does he do about his family thousands of miles away? They are the people he can't ever leave, because they've already lost one of their children. No wonder you panicked and ran away."

Mia let go of his hand. "Fast forward ten years, and when your grandfather is in dire straits, it's the same exact dilemma again for you. But this time, I'm old enough to accept my feelings for you are serious, and I don't think I could feel this way unless you did too. So, instead of getting a plane ticket and running away, I called Ed and had a long talk with him. I told him I was coming back to Jasper, and my old job, and I'd hang around for a few weeks to see if you showed back up again. I also swore him to secrecy. I promised myself I would not get on any damn airplane before we settled this once and for all. You saved my life, Jack. And I honestly think that by loving you, I can save yours."

Mia was shocked to see Jack's eyes fill with tears. He brushed them away with the back of a hand, and then took a drink of his coffee, which she presumed was to compose himself. He looked down at the table unable to meet her gaze.

"It's hard for me to talk about Neil. Really hard. We were only a year apart and I was the pain-in-the-butt kid brother who tagged along everywhere he went. When Neil wanted to join the Scouts, so did I. When he wanted to be a Junior Ranger, so did I. We did everything together and I loved it.

"It all changed on my sixteenth birthday. Neil took me out to celebrate, we got reckless, got our hands on some beer, and started drinking. God, we were so dumb— totally inexperienced with alcohol. He drank more than me, and I was more sober than him that night. I told him to let me drive, but he was the big brother, it was his car, and he refused. Neil pushed me into the back seat, buckled me up and took off."

He paused and took a deep breath. "It's the classic story. A kid who's been drinking, behind the wheel of a fast car.

"Neil took a corner too quickly, lost control of the vehicle and wrapped us around a tree. I walked away without a scratch as I'd had the seat belt on. The cops said because I'd passed out, my body was relaxed on impact, which apparently helped me as well. Neil had no seat belt on. He was ejected through the windshield and killed instantly."

Mia reached for his hand again. This time she held it in both of hers. "And you feel responsible for his death because you think you should have been the one driving as you were more sober. And you're blaming yourself because if it hadn't been your birthday, you would not have been out drinking that night. But Jack, you're equating what happened to Neil as your fault based on those two facts. Right?"

He didn't speak but met her eyes. Mia swallowed hard at the heartache shining from them.

"I get it," she said gently. "I've often felt guilty about what happened to my mum and dad. What if I'd been home the night of the fire, I could have saved them both. And then look at what's happened recently. First Jeannie died, then Jeremy Wessels and Sue Gilmer, both recovering from near-fatal wounds, all because of me. You don't think I feel guilty about that too?" She smiled. "You know, a good friend of mine explained why the recent carnage wasn't my fault." Mia looked into Jack's eyes. "That same friend should take his own advice. Because it's the truth. Jack, we can't live our lives carrying all this guilt. If anything, we owe it to the people who aren't here anymore to live our lives better, bigger, brighter." Mia squeezed his hand. "I want to be with you, Jack Brannon. Spend time with you and be happy, and I want you to do the same with me. Neil and my parents all forfeited their lives, but they were accidents. What I've learned from that is if I end up dying young, I'd rather go having lived a life first." Mia studied his face. What was he thinking? Had she gone too far? Pushed too hard?

Jack's eyes locked on hers, burning with emotion. "Don't go back to England, Mia. Stay and share your life with me instead. I promise I'll make it better, bigger and brighter, like you said. Look, I know it's a big ask. But Mia, I have an entire family here who'd like nothing more than to make you a part of it. You and me, we could make a wonderful home together. Hell, I'll even go back to England and visit whenever you want to go. But the truth is I can't bear not having you in my life. It's been a lonely place without you."

Mia ignored the tears running down her cheeks. Everything Jack said resonated inside her. Her heart, once a fallow field, suddenly bloomed with flowers. The emptiness and loneliness, her only companions since losing her parents, finally slid away.

She was loved.

* * *

They managed to get breakfast down, even though all they wanted to do was run out of the diner. Nancy insisted they needed to eat before either one of them made any life-changing decisions, and warned Mia not to go off gallivanting like she had the previous week.

As they ate, Jack recounted his failed attempt to reconnect with Mia years earlier. He told her about his phone call with Dan.

"Dan said we were what?" She almost choked on her coffee.

"That you were together. He said you guys were in a serious relationship."

Mia stared at him, aghast. "And apart from the fact he was a creep, you didn't think to confirm that with me?"

Jack had the grace to look ashamed. "I'd already deleted all your contact info. Anyway, why would I doubt him? You hadn't tried to contact me either."

"Fair point," Mia conceded. "I suppose it really wasn't supposed to be our time back then." She lifted her coffee cup in a toast. "Here's to leaving the past where it belongs."

Jack put an arm around Mia's waist as they crossed the parking lot in the direction of the Bronco. When they reached the passenger door, Jack turned Mia toward him and leaned her back against the vehicle. His hands settled either side of her, resting on the truck. He stepped closer, their faces almost touching. He looked down into her eyes.

"Ten years ago, I put an ocean between us. I was such a fool to do that, and I want you to know that not one day passed when I didn't think about you. I think I've always loved you, Mia Jones. Right from the very beginning. Thank you for never giving up on me. Thank you for loving me."

His hands dropped to gently cup her face, then he leaned forward, parted his lips and kissed her. His mouth was warm against hers. Soft, supple, then growing firmer with the promise and the need of so much more.

Mia closed her eyes and drowned in the sensation. Her arms wrapped tightly around him, and she pulled him close until the contours of his body aligned with her own. His kiss was like a drug, a taste of something so delicious, that she craved more and more still. The hunger she felt for this man was older than time.

The sound of a door banging closed and voices spilling into the air quickly ended the kiss.

Jack stepped back. His dark, smoldering eyes took in her appearance from toe to head. Then he grinned. "It's almost a certainty that I might have to call in sick on my first day back at work."

She giggled. "You do look peaky. Perhaps we should go back to your cabin and find some medicine to make you feel better?"

"What did you have in mind?" His mouth curled with anticipation.

"I don't know," she replied. "Steak and kidney pie, jellied eels, perhaps some haggis."

Jack burst out laughing. "I think I'd rather be ill."

He opened the truck door for Mia to climb in, then went around to the driver's side and got into the Bronco. Jack looked over at the woman sitting next to him and reached out to take her hand in his. He started the truck.

"Miss Emilia Mia Jones. Are you sure you're ready for whatever comes next between us?"

She grinned. "Are you kidding, Ranger Jack? I was a Girl Guide, and you were a Junior Ranger. Together, we can conquer the world!"

Epilogue

An American Christmas was vastly different than anything Mia had known growing up in England.

The celebration was basically the same. The customs were just different.

Although she had lived in the cabin now for over two months, Mia still found cooking in such a small space challenging. She'd insisted on keeping her job at the diner and managed to dodge making meals by bringing things home for Jack to eat. Cody was a much better cook than she would ever be.

Both she and Jack had flown back to Florida on two different occasions to testify for the state. Carlos had quickly thrown the Marinos under the proverbial bus, therefore eliminating any need for Mia to be a part of their impending trial. For that she was grateful.

But the worst experience had been when Jeannie's body had finally been found. The poor woman had not been disposed of in the ocean as they had suspected. Carlos had confessed the Marinos had buried her to ensure no one could find her. They didn't want to risk Jeannie being washed ashore anywhere. Her body had been placed in a shallow grave, alongside other unfortunate victims whose remains were discovered at the same time as her excavation.

That had been the hardest trip back. But Mia was determined to attend the funeral and meet Jeannie's family. She'd never forget her kindness.

Mia and Jack had managed to get through it all, just in time for Christmas. Mia was relieved. Perhaps now she and Jack could finally get on with their lives.

Today, Jack had invited a couple of his colleagues over to join them for an early Christmas dinner on Christmas Eve. Tomorrow, Jack and Mia would drive to Tulsa and spend the day with the Brannons. Mia particularly looked forward to seeing Sid. He was cantankerous and hard work, but a delight to spend time with and told the best stories, especially about his grandson.

It was four o'clock and Mia was running behind. Jack would be home soon, with Tex, and one of the rangers she had not yet met, Stella, who had recently come to the area. Apparently Tex had no family to speak of, and Stella was on duty over Christmas Day.

"Want some help?" Kelly strolled out of the bathroom looking like she'd stepped out of a scene from Lord of the Rings. She was dressed in a green velvet top, long, flowing, black skirt with a chain belt hugging her hips, and her hair hung down her back in a riot of red curls.

"Please. Can you peel the potatoes and pop them in the saucepan? I'm parboiling them for roasties."

"Yum," said Kelly. "I loved going to the pubs on Sundays for roast dinners when I was going to college. How can a potato taste so good? What else are you making?"

"I got the turkey from Cody as I wasn't about to attempt cooking one. Let's see. Roast potatoes, stuffing, peas, fresh carrots, some strange casserole with green beans and dried onions. Oh, and fresh rolls."

"Sounds delicious." Kelly began peeling the potatoes. She had spent the previous night at the cabin, sharing the bed in the loft with Mia, while Jack had taken the couch downstairs. "Who are these people coming home with Jack?"

"Tex is one of the rangers who started here about the same time Jack got to Jasper. I've only met him a few times. He's a nice guy, though he's pretty quiet. The other one is Stella. I don't know anything about her as she only got here last week. Jack doesn't even know her very well. But he said neither ranger had holiday plans, and he didn't want them to miss a Christmas dinner. Although by the time they've eaten my cooking they might wish they had."

"You have a point there, Mia. You were an awful cook even in England."

"Cheers for that." Mia feigned a wounded voice. "I can't be good at everything. Evading murderous criminals, living in the middle of nowhere, putting up with Americans, I feel I'm challenged enough as it is."

A piece of potato peel narrowly missed her face. "As an American, I should remind you you're slightly outnumbered." Kelly ducked as Mia threw the peel back at her. It landed on the floor.

"Even though you are rather rude," said Mia, "I'm glad you came over. It's been such a roller coaster, hasn't it?

It's nice to see you under normal circumstances and have something to celebrate."

"I wouldn't miss it. Wait, maybe the food, but not the company." Kelly grinned and her eyes twinkled mischievously. "It's wonderful that you and Jack found each other once again. It's good seeing you guys happy together. It's obviously meant to be."

"Speaking of things that are meant to be. You haven't said much about your latest guy."

Kelly paused from peeling and gave a shrug. "Not much to tell once I found out he was married."

"You're joking?"

"Wish I was. Another serial philanderer. They crawl out of the woodwork whenever I'm around. I've decided to take a breather from dating and romance. There are so many other things I could spend my time doing that are more worthwhile."

"You won't hear any argument from me," said Mia. "Let's face it, my track record's been bloody awful."

"I'll give you that. Murdering human trafficker trumps philandering husband every time." Kelly grimaced. "Was that too awful to say out loud?"

"Yes, but typical of you. That's why I love you, Kells." Mia went to the pantry and pulled out a bottle of Shiraz. She uncorked it and poured them both a glass.

"Here you go." She handed one to her friend and they clinked glasses.

"Cheers, and Happy Christmas," said Mia.

Jack could hear Christmas carols being played all the way down the driveway to the cabin. He saw smoke billowing out the chimney and knew a sense of pleasure arriving home. The change in his life was incredible. In just a few short months his world had gone from black-and-white to Technicolor and 3D.

Mia Jones was everything he could ask for in a partner. Funny, brave, gorgeous, hilarious, she was the full package, except for the terrible cooking. But that was a small price to pay in order to have her living in a tiny cabin in the woods.

Jack opened the door and walked inside, becoming engulfed in the wonderful aroma of something roasting in the oven that had not yet been burned. The large kitchen table was set for guests, and it looked rather jolly with a Christmas tablecloth and a vase filled with sprigs of holly. Kelly was at the stove, stirring a pan of gravy while Mia had her head practically inside the oven.

"What are you doing, trying to dry your hair?" Jack asked coming up behind her.

"Very funny, Ranger Jack." Mia shut the oven door. "I dropped one of the potatoes and was trying to rescue it."

He gave her a quick kiss on the mouth. "Roast potatoes? No mash?"

"I'd keep quiet if I was you." Kelly looked over her shoulder at Jack. "We've already had flying potato peel and that was one glass of wine ago."

"Message received." Jack hung up his hat. "I'm going up to get changed. By the way, Tex is on his way, but Stella can't make it. She's got a tummy bug and doesn't want to eat."

"She must have heard about Mia's expertise in the kitchen," Kelly said with a giggle.

Jack knew better than to respond.

* * *

Mia removed one of the place settings from the table.

"It's a shame Stella can't come. I was looking forward to meeting her. Oh, well, at least they'll be four of us. Although Tex is so quiet we might forget he's here."

"That's funny. Both times you've mentioned the guy you've commented on him being quiet. Does he come over very much?"

"I've only been around him a few times. He and Jack have become pretty good friends. I would describe him as the strong, silent type. There's a sense of mystery about him."

"You read too many books and watch too many movies. A strong, silent type means he's either got a low IQ or he's a serial killer."

"That's harsh."

"I'm bitter. What can I say?"

Jack rejoined them. He was dressed in jeans and his Haven Is Only One Letter Away from Heaven T-shirt. It made Mia smile at the memory.

"That is one ugly shirt," Kelly commented as she passed by him to refill her wineglass. She glanced out of the window. A black truck had just pulled up. A tall, dark-haired man got out and shut the door. "Hey, your buddy's here."

"I'll let him in." Jack went out the front door.

"Right, time for a quick check," said Mia. "The turkey's sliced, the veggies are cooked and the gravy's warming."

"What about the dressing?" Kelly translated. "The stuffing?"

"Damn," muttered Mia.

"You forgot to cook it, didn't you?"

"I did."

Kelly gave a howl of laughter, grabbed her friend's glass. "This calls for more wine."

The women were still laughing when Jack and Tex walked into the cabin. They stopped and stared at the lovely redhead and the pretty, freckle-faced woman.

"Is something burning?" asked Tex.

Besides the dressing, Mia forgot to cook rolls. The only thing burned was the casserole. The roast potatoes and turkey tasted wonderful, and the veggies passable. When Kelly announced that the gravy was good, if you didn't mind lumps, Tex surprised them all by laughing out loud.

After the meal, everyone cleared the table. The men volunteered to do the dishes, while the women retired to the couch, wineglasses in hand.

"Well done, Mia," said Kelly, making herself comfortable. "That was a lot of work pulling off such a big meal."

"Even with lumpy gravy?"

"*Especially* with lumpy gravy." Kelly grinned.

Mia took a sip of wine and noticed her friend's green eyes kept wandering over to the kitchen, where both men stood at the sink, chatting as they worked.

"What do you think of Tex?" Mia asked.

Kelly looked away from the men. "Seems nice enough, but quiet."

"He's good-looking," said Mia. Tex looked ex-military. You could tell by his physique that he worked out. He wore his dark hair short and neat, his chiseled face was clean-shaven, and his blue eyes were alert and intelligent.

"If you like that type," murmured Kelly.

with their chores, joined them. Tex took a seat while Jack added a few logs to the fireplace.

Kelly flashed a look to Mia, shaking her head quickly, not wanting her to tell anyone about her project.

"We were talking about her school plan for the kindergarteners," Mia replied.

"Where do you teach?" Tex asked, his blue eyes fastened on Kelly.

"Harrison."

"A noble profession. You must be a very patient person."

"Hardly," chuckled Mia. "She's the most impatient person I know, except she morphs into Mother Goose as soon as she walks into the school."

"True story," Kelly grinned. "Something about those rug rats is my kryptonite. Mean and hateful Kelly becomes Julie Andrews."

"Don't tell Julie Andrews that," laughed Jack.

"Never mind me," said Kelly. "What about you, Tex? What's your story? Are you from Texas?" she said sarcastically.

His eyes met hers. "Smart lady. What gave it away?"

"The drawl, and the boots. Seriously, whereabouts in Texas are you from?"

"Austin."

"That's a great place. I've only been a couple of times. Did you move here from there?" Kelly asked.

"Nope."

Everyone waited for him to continue, but apparently that was all Tex was prepared to say.

Tex stayed another hour and insisted he'd better get going. He thanked Jack and Mia for the evening. Mia watched as he shook hands with Kelly. There was friction there, but then Kelly had a knack of bringing that out in most people.

Jack walked his friend out of the door.

"You were right about Tex being a quiet guy," said Kelly. "He doesn't give much away, does he? I wonder why?"

"Merry Christmas," Jack said as Mia climbed into bed. She shivered with cold as there was no upstairs heater. Moonlight shone through the large skylight. The sky was clear and cold, but the stars were bright.

"Is it already past midnight?" asked Mia, snuggling into the crook of his arm and basking in the heat coming from his body.

"Yep."

"Then Merry Christmas to you too." She reached up and kissed him on the cheek.

Jack turned on his side to face her. "No, I'm afraid you're going to have to do better than that."

Their lips met in a gentle kiss, and Jack's hand rose to cup her chin. The intensity grew, the kiss deepened, and Mia gave a low moan. Jack pulled away.

"What is it?"

He laid his head on the pillow, turning to gaze at her in the soft light. "I just want to look at you for a moment," he said, tracing the line of her face, her cheek, her jaw with the tip of his thumb. "Sometimes it almost feels as if I'm dreaming. Here we are together, in a tiny cabin in Arkansas. Me and you, that gorgeous girl I met in Cornwall all those years ago. How crazy is that?"

"It's pretty wild," Mia agreed. "I'm sad we didn't stay

together back then, but in a way it's better this time. We're not kids anymore, and we know what we're getting into, right?"

Jack's thumb rubbed softly against her lips. "Right." Then he rolled onto his back and tucked his arms behind his head. "Is this okay, Mia? Me asking you to stay in my country instead of your own? Am I being too selfish? I mean, it is a lot to ask."

Mia frowned, wondering where this was coming from. She propped herself up to look at him. "Don't be daft," she said softly. "Although I'll miss being home, I can still remember how lonely I was there without you. Being somewhere with you is better than being anywhere without you, Jack." Mia leaned over him and softly kissed his lips. "I love you, Ranger Jack. And that's all that matters."

Jack moved his arms and pulled Mia on top of him. "I have a very special Christmas present for you," he grinned, and claimed her mouth in a passionate kiss.

Later, spent and tired, they lay on their sides facing each other. Jack watched as Mia's eyes grew heavy with sleep. He stared at her, marveling at his good fortune, that he had someone so good, so kind in his life.

Neil would have loved Mia. He would have got a kick from her sassy humor, her banter, but most of all, Neil would have loved her because she made Jack so happy. Of all the things that Neil had missed, this was the part that made Jack the saddest. He wished with all his heart Neil could have met Mia.

Jack rolled over onto his back and stared up at the skylight. Stars winked in the heavens, and he wondered if there really was such a place, and if Neil was up there right now looking down into the tiny cabin. He hoped so.

Jack gave a long sigh. He wasn't remotely tired now, even after such a busy day. Deep inside, he felt a burn of energy, of excitement, thrumming below his skin. Because tomorrow they would go to Tulsa and be with his family. And while there, in front of them all, Jack would get out the small velvet box hidden in his Bronco, and he would ask Mia Jones to be his wife.

* * * * *

Get up to 4 Free Books!

**We'll send you 2 free books from each series you try
PLUS a free Mystery Gift.**

Both the **Harlequin Intrigue®** and **Harlequin® Romantic Suspense** series
feature compelling novels filled with heart-racing action-packed romance
that will keep you on the edge of your seat.

YES! Please send me 2 FREE novels from the Harlequin Intrigue or Harlequin Romantic Suspense series and my FREE gift (gift is worth about $10 retail). After receiving them, if I don't wish to receive any more books, I can return the shipping statement marked "cancel." If I don't cancel, I will receive 6 brand-new Harlequin Intrigue Larger-Print books every month and be billed just $7.19 each in the U.S. or $7.99 each in Canada, or 4 brand-new Harlequin Romantic Suspense books every month and be billed just $6.39 each in the U.S. or $7.19 each in Canada, a savings of 20% off the cover price. It's quite a bargain! Shipping and handling is just 50¢ per book in the U.S. and $1.25 per book in Canada.* I understand that accepting the 2 free books and gift places me under no obligation to buy anything. I can always return a shipment and cancel at any time by calling the number below. The free books and gift are mine to keep no matter what I decide.

Choose one: ☐ **Harlequin Intrigue Larger-Print** (199/399 BPA G36Y)   ☐ **Harlequin Romantic Suspense** (240/340 BPA G36Y)   ☐ **Or Try Both!** (199/399 & 240/340 BPA G36Z)

Name (please print)

Address   Apt. #

City   State/Province   Zip/Postal Code

Email: Please check this box ☐ if you would like to receive newsletters and promotional emails from Harlequin Enterprises ULC and its affiliates. You can unsubscribe anytime.

> Mail to the **Harlequin Reader Service:**
> **IN U.S.A.:** P.O. Box 1341, Buffalo, NY 14240-8531
> **IN CANADA:** P.O. Box 603, Fort Erie, Ontario L2A 5X3

Want to explore our other series or interested in ebooks? Visit **www.ReaderService.com** or call 1-800-873-8635.

---

*Terms and prices subject to change without notice. Prices do not include sales taxes, which will be charged (if applicable) based on your state or country of residence. Canadian residents will be charged applicable taxes. Offer not valid in Quebec. This offer is limited to one order per household. Books received may not be as shown. Not valid for current subscribers to the Harlequin Intrigue or Harlequin Romantic Suspense series. All orders subject to approval. Credit or debit balances in a customer's account(s) may be offset by any other outstanding balance owed by or to the customer. Please allow 4 to 6 weeks for delivery. Offer available while quantities last.

Your Privacy—Your information is being collected by Harlequin Enterprises ULC, operating as Harlequin Reader Service. For a complete summary of the information we collect, how we use this information and to whom it is disclosed, please visit our privacy notice located at https://corporate.harlequin.com/privacy-notice. Notice to California Residents – Under California law, you have specific rights to control and access your data. For more information on these rights and how to exercise them, visit https://corporate.harlequin.com/california-privacy. For additional information for residents of other U.S. states that provide their residents with certain rights with respect to personal data, visit https://corporate.harlequin.com/other-state-residents-privacy-rights/.

HIHRS25

"Not bohemian enough for you?" Kelly had a history of dating artsy types. They were always attractive, yet were never a match for the forceful nature of Kelly Murphy. It was her indomitable strength that had got Mia to safety when her life had been in danger.

"Remember I told you I'm not interested in romance anymore? Seriously, Mia. I am fed up with it. Besides, I've got other ideas I'm working on."

Mia was intrigued. "Like what?"

Kelly set her glass down and fiddled with a long curl. "I'll tell you, but don't make fun of me."

"I won't. You're the one who does that, Miss Lumpy Gravy."

"Point taken. Well, I had an idea a few months ago to do a special project, something I've always wanted to do. I've never had enough time to get started. But when all the trouble began with you, and I was taken into hiding, I suddenly had time to do all kinds of things. So I got busy."

"With what?"

"I'm writing a children's book."

Mia was blown away. "Kelly, that's marvelous. If anyone could write for kids, it's you. What's it about?"

"A black bear called Kevin. He lives in the Ozarks and has friends he gets into scrapes with. Bobcats, squirrels and a plethora of critters. I'm only about halfway through, but it's been fun. I'm going to find an illustrator and see what happens."

"Wow," said Mia. "I'm truly impressed. You've always been so creative, Kells."

"Thanks. I hope you're right."

"Right about what?" asked Jack. He and Tex, finished